ZARINA

I want to laugh. I want to wave my hand and make the words Father said disappear, because they're absurd. And I would, if my parents weren't wearing their serious, stern faces that mean they expect me to do exactly as they ask. Whether that's apologizing to my cousin after taking her dolly at age seven, or grinning and bearing it when a Falcone son's hand brushes my ass at some gala.

The problem is, I usually do what they ask.

Because I probably shouldn't have taken my cousin's dolly out of her hands, even if she was being a jerk. Because some quote-accidental-unquote grab-ass is paltry in comparison to the deal they brokered with the Falcone Family at that gala. And because I understand cost versus profit and what is expected of the Gallo crime family's only daughter, the princess who will inherit not just money, but also the power to bend half of Louredo to kiss my toes if I so choose.

And right now, I would so fucking choose.

"Can you repeat that, please?" I stand behind a tufted leather chair in the library. Dark, cherrywood shelves with a rolling ladder for each section line the two-story walls, and deep-seated leather furniture takes up the middle of the room. A stately desk piled with neatly organized ledgers and reports sits at the top of the room, a wall of windows looking out over the inner courtyard behind it. And to my right, between the shelves, hangs a portrait of my late grandfather, the man who built this room. Built our entire estate. The man whose rich, brown eyes with veins of gold passed down to my mother—his daughter—and then to me.

I dig my nails into the chair back, holding on lest I either stagger under the weight of his gaze or throw something at both my parents' heads. Which is more likely is a complete toss-up.

"We've negotiated with the Accardis." My mother perches on the edge of the desk, dressed in an electric-blue power suit, jacket buttoned over a lace camisole and thumbs hooked in her pockets. She's tall, taller than my father when she wears her Louboutins, like she is at the moment. Her dark-brown eyes don't mirror Grandfather's painting right now. Their gold is muted, the richness dull and devoid of warmth. Like mud. "And they've agreed, along with their son, Marcus—"

"See, that's the problem." I grind my teeth. My orange silk dress, which usually hugs my thighs, my ass, and my chest exactly right to make me feel powerful in its embrace, is currently chafing against my skin. It's failing me for the first time. "*Son.*" I spit the word as if it's poison on my tongue. "Implying a penis-wearing *boy.*"

"Zarina," my father chastises from the window. He stands hunched, his black hair graying at his temples. That I inherited from him. Mother's eyes, Father's hair. For a brief, hysterical second, I wonder if I'll gray in the same pattern as him in thirty years. If my eyes will dull with the tempering of time.

I shake myself. This isn't a typical Thursday family meeting. We aren't discussing shipments or upcoming events. If we were, Father would look at me. If we were, Father would smile when he chastises me for "poor language."

RUBIES
and
REVENGE

A CARDINAL FAMILIES NOVEL

RUBIES AND REVENGE

A CARDINAL FAMILIES NOVEL

LEXIE A. LYNN

PAPER RIVER PUBLISHING

To my community near and far, old and new—
because of you, this book exists. Thank you.

Instead, he's looking at the unlit cigar held between his fingers. Like this is some impersonal business deal where we shake hands and go our separate ways, richer for the dealing.

But it's not.

Mother pushes off the desk to stand straight, adjusting her cuffs to lie just so. And then she continues as if neither of us have spoken. "They've agreed to clear our debts to them in exchange for a quarter of Gallo territory and you."

And you. As in marriage. To Marcus Accardi. A man.

It takes every ounce of strength in my hundred-sixty-some-thing-pound, five-foot-four body to keep my feet planted, my hands stayed, my voice a reasonable volume and tone. "You seem to be forgetting a very important conversation we had after you caught me kissing Isabella when I was fourteen."

Mother purses her red-painted lips. Father presses his fingers to his forehead.

"Allow me to remind you." I flick my hair off my shoulder, the blowout Mother "treated" me to this morning making a lot more sense now. "I am *gay.* I like pussy—"

"Zarina!" Father snaps.

I ignore him. "Men are disgusting, and the thought of marrying one, especially one with a reputation as notorious as Marcus Accardi's, makes me want to retch."

Mother presses her fingers to the pinching wrinkle between her brows. "Zarina, this is not up for discussion."

"It is absolutely up for discussion." I file away the fact she doesn't address Marcus's reputation. One where he is known for beating his capos, his lieutenants, his own family. The same fate waits for me if I become his wife. "It's my fucking life."

As usual, Mother ignores me. She ignores my wishes, ignores my pleas, ignores my free fucking will. She smooths out her jacket and rolls back her shoulders, pinning me with her wet-mud glare. "They'll be here for dinner within the hour. This deal is closing tonight."

I look to Father, like I always do when Mother hatches a scheme that asks too much of us. We've always reached for each other, tempered her maniacal greed together, but tonight, he won't meet my gaze. He stares at that stupid fucking cigar as if he can unroll the tobacco leaf paper and find the answers to all his problems written there. Something squeezes in my chest, but I can't name it, not right now.

I abandon him, like he has me, and return Mother's look tenfold, hoping my eyes are more blazing than empty. "Without me, there is no deal."

Mother strides toward me and cups her hand under my chin, her long, manicured fingernails stroking my jugular in subtle threat—how she does when I'm "throwing a tantrum" and embarrassing her. "You will do your duty to this family. We cannot afford to say no to the Accardis."

I fight back the urge to cry, because I know it will only feed her an excuse to ignore me. "My duty to this family does not require the violation of my body."

Mother's claws catch on the chain of the necklace she and Father gifted me when I turned eighteen. A blood-red ruby in the shape of a teardrop held by a noose—a play on the Gallo family name. And now the very thing tightening around my throat. "It is a woman's role."

"It was your role, Mother," I whisper, glancing at the man in the portrait hanging above us. The man who sold her hand in marriage to a small family with an ambitious son who would bring him more power and more wealth and run the family in his absence. A son so ambitious, he shed his family name to merge with ours. My father, Riccardo Toselli, now Gallo.

I wrap my hand around Mother's wrist and yank myself free of her grip. "I will not let your story be mine."

"Zarina Giovanna Gallo!" Father raises his voice from the window, finally deciding to join the conversation. "You will do this!"

"I'm not a child anymore." Fearful anger gathers in my throat. "You cannot compel me with a raised voice and my full name."

"Then stop acting childish," Mother snaps.

"Would you demand this of your capos?" I ask. "Would you demand this of a son?"

"We don't have a son." She waves her hand, dismissing the notion as easily as I wish I could dismiss this entire conversation.

I scrape my hands over my face, through my hair, grabbing it hard at the roots. "How did it get so bad? I've been asking to see the books for years. I could help find a better solution."

"There is no better solution." Father slips the cigar into his inner jacket pocket, probably saving it for a smoke with Alonso Accardi after Marcus "proposes" to me. I shudder at the thought.

I swallow past the acidic reply ready at the tip of my tongue and try for something with a bit more honey. "A new perspective might see something you can't."

"This is happening, Zarina." Mother pours herself two fingers of bourbon from the bar cart beside the mantle and turns with the tumbler in hand. "We expect you to be agreeable and pleasant to Marcus until the license is signed and the deal closed." She sips her drink and looks me up and down with a lazy shrug of her shoulder. "After that, behave as you wish."

"You mean as he allows." I narrow my eyes. "From what I hear, I'll be wearing long sleeves and high necks once he *owns* me."

Father squeezes his eyes shut as if they're his ears and he can stop from hearing me. "We have no other option."

I ask the question that terrifies me. "What could we lose?"

Mother drains the rest of her glass and stares up at her father's portrait, at our eyes reflected in his. "Everything."

I push down the fear stuck in my throat until all that's left is the rage. Fear is useless. But rage burns. "So you'll settle for a daughter and the Sallay neighborhood instead."

They stand there, the distance of a twenty-eight-year marriage between them, and look anywhere but at me, but at each other. Neither say a word to deny it or comfort me. It's not their way. Everything they do is for the Gallo name, for the legacy they either inherited or gave up everything to be a part of. And once a decision is made, it's made. There's no going back.

But not this time. Not for me.

I turn on my heel and stride to the door, throwing it open and letting it smack against the wall.

"Thirty minutes, Zarina," Mother calls. "Agreeable and pleasant."

I roll my shoulders back and shake out my hair, placing my armor piece by piece. Fuck agreeable and pleasant.

I'd rather riot.

TAMAYO

A rancid substance clings to the toe of my boot. I try to knock it off against one of the brick walls lining this decrepit alley, but it holds on like a blood-sucking leech. I glare down at the offensive glob and curse the Falcones. I wore my most expensive suit and my hand-stitched, supple, black Italian leather boots in an attempt to feel as powerful as I was hoping this deal would make me.

And then we found the address.

Some back alley stuffed between a Chinese restaurant and a dive bar. The smells of the two kitchens compete with the foul odor of their garbage piled in the dumpsters and the acrid stench of piss. For a second, I thought maybe there was a basement entrance to a club, a restaurant, anywhere that might show the respect due. But then Darius came back with a curt shake of his head. Nothing but garbage and feral cats.

"We should go." Darius stands a striking six-foot-three, his body built like a linebacker's—he might've been one, if he played football. The green and gold neon sign of the dive bar shines across his face, his Black skin lit like this is a photoshoot and not some back-alley mobster meetup. "We're too exposed out here."

I don't move. Antoni, our contact with the Falcones, offered to set up this meeting with his underboss. We spent weeks stroking the man's ego, wining and dining him, letting him win poker with shitty hands, to get to this point. My chest burns as I survey the alley again, my boot with the unknown substance stuck to its leather toe, all of it a clear signal of how much value Antoni and the Falcones place on the Tamayo Family.

The burn spreads through my body as anger, betrayal, and acidic guilt swirl together to become something just as rancid and insidious as the gloop on my boot.

"Chinese restaurant or American dive?" I stub my toe against the sidewalk, voice steady, hands loose.

Darius stares at me, dark-brown eyes calculating. I crane my neck and stare right back. My head comes up to his shoulder, my lean frame proportionately about one-third of his. Most often, people who don't know what's what look to him before me. I make sure they never make that mistake again.

Darius sticks his tongue between his teeth and considers the alley, the restaurants, the block. Antoni gave us this address for a reason, and we both understand what that is now. I want to stick around and meet the inevitable. Darius wants to leave before he's required to unbutton his suit jacket.

He sighs, shoulders slumping. "Chinese," he grumbles.

I grin, full-toothed and sly. "I love it when I win."

"Is it winning if there's no fight?" He holds open the door to the restaurant, eyes roaming over the tables, all empty, and then down the sidewalk, also empty.

I nod to the host when he greets us and hold up two fingers. "If I get my way, yes."

"I could forcibly carry you back to the car." Darius follows a step behind me.

"You could," I concede. Because, duh, of course he can. "But you won't."

"I won't." He shakes his head like I'm an annoying little sister he grew up putting into headlocks and giving nuggies to rather than his boss. Unfortunately for me, both are true. Except the sister part.

The host leads us past empty table after empty table draped in red cloth with fancily folded gold napkins. I snatch one as we pass, pausing to kneel and wipe my boot clean. Darius stops behind me without comment, while the host strides away as if he's being chased.

I don't rush, cleaning my thousand-dollar boots the best I can without the proper tools. Residue clings to the leather, but at least the goo is off. I rise to my feet and drop the napkin on a table at the same time four men round the corner.

"Why is it always the Chinese restaurant?" Darius grumbles. He unbuttons his jacket and shrugs out of it, hanging it off the back of the nearest chair with ginger hands. Two guns and a combat knife hang secure in his chest holster, but he doesn't reach for them, instead crossing his wrists behind his back and waiting.

I flip my black bangs out of my eyes, smoothing my hands down my jacket and stuffing them in my pockets. Antoni stands at the front of the pack with a slick grin and shiny skin, proud of himself for setting up this little meeting.

Or ambush, rather.

"Antoni." I keep my shoulders loose, my voice light, my face relaxed, hiding the heated anger building into a raging fire in my chest. "I'm surprised to find you here. I thought we agreed to meet at twelve-eleven Washington Street. Isn't this twelve-fifteen?"

"I could say the same thing, Tamayo." He stands with a hand on his hip and a condescending scowl on his face, as if *we* inconvenienced *him*. "I waited for you."

The flames inside lick up my throat, into my arms. "I'm sure you did."

"Imagine my confusion when my friend told me you were here."

"Ah, well," I say with a shrug, "we were hungry, and I had a craving."

"Craving for home?" he jabs, overly smug.

His soldiers chuckle, throwing each other sly eyes. They all look the exact same, with white skin and brown eyes and brown hair faded into styled coifs. Typical mobster fuckboys with typical white male superiority complexes.

I feign confusion. "Home?"

"Chinese food," he says like the connection is obvious.

"I don't quite follow," I lie. It'd be hard not to follow his meaning when it's the same bullshit I've heard my entire life. My mono-lidded eyes, my tan skin, my wide nose—all inherited from my Filipino father—are often generalized as Asian. And Asian in white America translates to Chinese, because people are too stupid to differentiate ethnicities from the most populated continent in the world.

I cock my head and frown at Antoni, a picture of bewilderment. "We're more known for tacos than noodles in Buckman Heights." Where I grew up in a third-floor walkup above a corner mart that always smelled like Swisher Sweets.

"No, because you're—you look like—you're Asian." Antoni's face visibly reddens as he's forced to explain his racist joke.

Darius snorts.

"You must not have grown up around here." I say the words flippantly, as if I'm not deeply insulting him. The Falcones don't accept foreigners as made men. None of the Families do. Another thing that sets me and mine apart from all of theirs. I wave my hand. "That's neither here nor there, though. Shall we?"

He doesn't answer—not with words, anyway.

Without a signal, Antoni snarls and charges forward. A small man with a smaller ego. The sudden move catches his men off guard, but then they're on their feet, three seconds behind their capo. It's enough.

Darius draws both guns in one swift motion as I duck and rush at Antoni. He tries to wrap his arms around me. Rookie fucking move. I sidestep out of reach and kick out at his knee, whirling around to slam my elbow into his back.

Two shots ring through the tight space. Two *thunks* follow.

I don't even consider that the third man will reach me, that he'll have time to fumble for his gun and aim it straight at me. I narrow my glare on Antoni and strike his Adam's apple full force. At the same moment, Darius steps over him and diverts the last soldier's hand to the ceiling before he fires. He wrenches his wrist backward until the gun drops and then slips his arm the size of my thigh around the man's neck, squeezing until he passes out.

Antoni writhes on the ground, clutching his throat. I kneel beside him and forcibly turn him on his back, digging into his pockets, waistband, and socks—disarming him. Three guns, a knife, and brass knuckles, all of which Darius takes for himself.

"Toni—may I call you Toni?" I smack his cheek as he tries to speak past the laryngeal fracture caused by my boot to his throat. He settles on glaring at me. "I've decided to give you one last chance, because I'm a reasonable person."

Darius disarms the dead and unconscious soldiers surrounding us. The front door of the restaurant chimes the arrival of someone, but he doesn't mind it, and nor do I. Tamayo soldiers—my soldiers—slip through the tables. One pair heads into the kitchen to take care of any security footage and record names and addresses of any straggling witnesses, while the other two unfold plastic tarps beside the dead.

I ignore it all, my eyes never straying from Antoni's livid face. "But my terms have changed, now. I don't take kindly to your betrayal of a friend. I honored the traditions, and you spat on me in return." I hold out my hand, and Darius drops the napkin with the glob of alley muck into it. I open it carefully in my palms, the goo and dirt clinging to the fabric, the rancid stench invading my nose. "That's not how we conduct business, Toni."

I take the napkin and wipe it from his forehead, over his eye, down his cheek to his chin. He tries to push me off, but Darius kneels on his chest and yanks his wrists to his sides. I make sure to rub the muck over his mouth before I finally pull away.

Antoni spits and sputters, one eye scrunched against the brown slime dripping over his lid and brow.

"Tell Jimmy Falcone the terms are no longer favorable and he has you to thank for that." I pat his cheek again—the clean one—smiling as if we're having a nice chat over dinner and drinks. The way this should have gone. I rise, my right knee twinging and shooting pain up my thigh after squatting for so long. I crack my neck, adjust the sleeves of my undershirt, and brush my jacket smooth, not showing a hint of pain. Darius stays on Antoni's chest as I prop his chin with my boot.

The fire burning inside me is barely banked. I wanted more of a fight. I wanted to feel the snap of his bones, to see bruises welt his skin, to leave my mark on him so he'd remember for the rest of his life how weak and stupid he was to betray me.

But the Council has very strict traditions and consequences to avoid sinking our city into war.

I stomp on his face. The impact echoes up my leg and sharpens the pain in my knee, but the satisfyingly wet crunch of his nose breaking is worth it. Blood flows from his nostrils, mixing with the muck on his lips and chin.

I breathe in deep and force the inferno inside me to retreat from my feet, from my hands, out of my limbs and into my chest. Without a look back at Antoni, I stride for the door and stop, hand on the handle, to call back, "I look forward to hearing from Jimmy within the week, Toni. Don't let me down!"

Darius shakes his head with that same fond annoyance, and I shoot him a wicked grin, tongue tracing the edges of my teeth. He grabs the door before it can fall shut and follows me onto the sidewalk. As soon as we're out of sight of the restaurant, he offers me his elbow. I take it, using it to deftly hide the shift of my weight off my right leg.

"Should I carry you?" he teases.

"Just get in the fucking car," I grumble.

ZARINA

*M*y room feels wrong when I enter it, like someone's rifled through my things and moved each object over half an inch. But everything is just as I left it. It's me who has shifted. I've lived here for all my life. I know it as intimately as the streets of Gallo territory, as my own body.

Which is no longer my own.

I flip the deadbolt locked and rest my forehead against the cold wood. The urge to cry and rage and destroy builds in my chest. The marigold silk draped over my four-poster canopy bed would go first. Then I'd grab the switchblade from my nightstand and rip into the teal chaise lounge. Then I'd fire the handgun that lives beside the knife at the bulletproof glass windows lining the entire south-facing wall. Would they hold at point-blank range? Would they ricochet and take me out and save me from this ludicrous deal?

Death before dishonor.

The Gallo Family words echo as I turn and my head falls back against my door with a soft thump. I grew up learning that hurting a fellow Gallo meant dishonoring the family, but if that were true, my parents wouldn't ask this of me. They'd let me *see* how badly we're fucked rather than sell me off to the debtor.

Thankfully, I don't need their permission.

I shove off the door and stride across the room, skipping the four steps to the lower level, where the chaise lounge sits in front of the working fireplace. I shove open the en suite bathroom door, ignoring the high-backed clawfoot tub and turning directly into the walk-in-closet. The chandelier and backlit shelves and racks brighten the moment I enter. Velvet, silk, denim, suede, leather, all neatly organized by occasion and then level of impression.

But I'm not here to change. I stand before the wall of shoes, perfectly spaced so as not to touch each other, and pull on a pair of garish, hot-pink heels with gaudy diamonds on the toe—a gift from an aunt with the same fashion taste as Paris Hilton circa 2003, *gag*. A latch clicks, and the wall swings open just enough for me to grab the edge and pull it wide.

Weapons hang from their hooks—another handgun, a pistol, a nightstick, a taser, brass knuckles in matte black, and even pepper spray. And in the middle, framed by the myriad of deadly tools, sits a safe tucked into the wall.

I twist the dial, around and back and around again, and with each number, my pulse thrums against my wrists. When it unlocks and I open the door, I stare at the three wads of petty cash, at the hardbound notebook, at the external hard drive, and chew my lip.

I snuck into the library a few months ago and plugged the hard drive into Mother's computer to copy the Gallo Family ledger. But I haven't had the guts to take it out of my personal safe since then, scared to learn what it said.

I knew something was wrong. I've known for months. It was in the small things. The way Mother would ask me to flirt at events more than usual. The way Father didn't come home before midnight most nights and skipped church on Sundays more often than he attended. The way a couple captains we'd always had, who had been part of the family my entire lifetime, no longer showed up to family dinner on Sundays.

I trace the drive's edges with my fingers. If I were to run to any of the other Cardinal Families, their rules would demand they return me to my parents, or worse—to Marcus. That can't happen. There's nowhere to go that I'll be truly hidden, no family to call on that will honor my autonomy. But I can't evade my parents or the Accardis without help.

And there's only one person who fits the bill.

One person with enough power to keep me safe and enough ambition to defy the Cardinal Families. One person who might sympathize with my situation.

I clear out the rest of the safe and elbow the door shut, twirling the dial to locked and kicking the wall of shoes closed behind me. I can't have more than fifteen minutes before dinner, before the Accardi family arrives with their son Marcus ready to bend one knee and perform a proposal scene. Nausea swirls in my stomach, and I clench my teeth against the acid rising up my throat.

My parents have gone too far.

I drop the hard drive and notebook on the gold ottoman in the middle of the room and yank a purse and a classic trench coat off their hangers. I have known I am as gay as a double fucking rainbow since I first felt attraction at the ripe age of eleven. My parents accepted that, accepted me, and have never asked me to do more than wield my feminine wiles as a weapon against misogynistic sons of rival families.

Until now.

But this is impossible.

I will not spread my legs and think of the Gallos. Not if there's any other option available to me. And the foggy idea that's been solidifying into a tangible and real solution at the back of my brain is far more palatable than a marriage to a man who is known for beating his own family.

A knock echoes through my bedroom and into the closet. "Zarina?"

It's Father.

I don't answer. I stuff the hard drive into the inside pocket of my purse and throw in the petty cash and notebook, too. I wish I had my laptop, but I left it in the solarium earlier, and I only have about ten minutes now. There's no time to waste.

I grab my most comfortable nude heels that go with anything and slip out of the closet.

Father knocks again. "Zarina, dear. I know this isn't what you want."

I pause, one hand carrying my heels, the other on the handle of the French door leading out to my private terrace.

"I am sorry about it," he says. "I feel as if...as if we failed you. Failed the family."

My throat thickens, and I squeeze my eyes shut. The Gallo ruby hanging at my neck shackles me to the spot.

"I wish we could do better for you," he says.

"I do, too," I say, just loud enough that I know he hears me. To give myself the cover of being heard minutes before dinner.

"Please trust us?" he asks.

And I can't answer that. Not with anything that will ease his guilt. They've broken years of carefully nurtured love and duty with the handshake of a single deal. We betray a lot of people, step on most anyone we must to get what we want, but never family. Never a Gallo.

Until now.

I open my terrace door as Father speaks again.

"Please."

"I can't," I whisper, too low to carry. And then I step outside and shut the door behind me with the softest click, ready to sneak out of the compound like I have a hundred times. Up the trellis, across the roof to the western wing that shares a wall with the garage with the openable skylight that Pat always makes sure has the expandable ladder propped beneath it, like that's where it should be stored. Inconspicuous.

"I figured you'd run."

I just barely bite down on a yelp, clutching my chest against my racing heart. "God damn it." I snap. "What the fuck are you doing out here?"

Pat sits in one of the chairs at the small bistro table, long, blonde hair pulled back in their signature perfectly smooth low-bun that somehow never frizzes, never comes undone, never *moves*. They sit with an ankle resting on their knee, their Kevlar chest binder poking out from under their crisp white collar, nude colored and doubling as a bullet-proof layer.

"Like I said, I knew you'd run." And they would know, having been my best friend since they showed me how to play cat's cradle when we were six.

I smooth my hand down my coat, not meeting their eyes in case their answer is as poor as my parents'. "Can you blame me?"

Out of the corner of my eye, I see them study me closely, leaning forward to rest their elbows on their knees. "Not really, no."

"Will you stop me?" I ask.

Pat is loyal to the Gallos, serves as house security and specifically as my personal detail. They're sworn to keep me safe, to keep my parents safe, to serve the family no matter what, when, where. We might be best friends, but Pat spoke their oath with the intent to keep it.

They rise and place a hand on each of my shoulders, leaning down to look into my eyes. "Z, you're a Gallo. You're *my* Gallo. Like fuck am I gonna keep you here for this."

For the first time tonight, the tears pricking behind my eyes flood to the front and threaten to spill.

Pat pushes my hair away from my face and brushes my cheek before they clap their hands. "Besides, who of all the Gallo Family would best understand how fucked up this is, even putting aside the whole feminist, bodily autonomy, free-will perspective?"

I let out a soft, sad laugh that threatens to morph into a sob. "You."

"Duh." They squeeze my cheeks together until my lips purse comically. It does the trick to stop the burn of tears.

I pull in a steadying breath. "Then why did you ambush me?"

Pat plucks my heels out of my hand. "To make sure you don't get yourself killed."

"I can protect myself," I grumble.

They push me toward the trellis. "You usually have better jokes."

"Fuck off, Pat." I aim a kick at their shin, but they deftly avoid the strike. Stupid reflex training.

"Yeah, yeah." They smack my ass to get me moving. "We have five minutes before the Accardis arrive."

I climb up without another word.

TAMAYO

$\mathcal{D}$arius guides the car into another alley. There's no dumpster, no stench of piss or garbage. It's three brick walls with exactly one door and one gated entryway, to which three people have the code. Darius, me, and Den of Inequity's manager.

The club's muffled music thumps through the steel door and into the cab of the car. My neck relaxes, the muscles easing as the gate rolls shut behind us. I'm back in Tamayo territory, with my people around me; the closest thing to safety we have. I don't wait for Darius to open the door, too impatient and unceremonious. I'm not a fucking princess.

He rushes past me and jabs me with his elbow. I nick his ankles with my boot in retaliation. But he beats me to the club door, which was his goal anyway. I allow him to open it for me, only so I can box his ears.

"Oh, you little—" Darius aims to flick my forehead, and I duck to slap his right nipple. Hard. He hisses and makes to wrap his way-too-big arm around my neck, but I dance out of reach with a laugh.

Directly into Angie.

She stands almost an entire head shorter than me in all her grunge glory—fishnets under ripped jeans with a cropped Nirvana tee that is definitely vintage. Her brown hair hangs in an asymmetrical bob, makeup applied with exacting perfection, and currently, one of her shaped brows arched at us in annoyed amusement. Her scarlet-painted lips twitch. "If you two are finished?"

"Sorry, Angie," Darius and I chorus with two wide grins and not an ounce of genuine remorse.

Angie rolls her eyes and shoves a wet cloth into my hands. It foams against my skin. "As requested."

"Thanks." I immediately crouch down and clean my boot as best I can.

She offers me another damp cloth to wipe off the soapy, dirty water left behind. "How'd it go?" she asks, raising both brows and not moving when I try to give her back the used towels.

"It didn't." I sigh and wrap the cleaner around the dirtier one, resigning to carrying them myself.

The stone walls keep the club's noise muffled, but the dance floor still vibrates down the bones of the building as we navigate through the basement. It's stark white down here, light reflecting bright over the interconnecting, overlapping, sometimes dead-ending maze of hallways. A protection tactic taken from a past kingdom and a past family.

"What's that mean?" she asks.

"It means Antoni broke tradition." Tradition I suppose he thought he didn't owe me, a lowly gang leader. I crack my neck. For nigh on a decade, I've brokered and smuggled and violently carved out a piece of this city in pursuit of one goal: become a Cardinal Family. They own the dirt Louredo is built on, commanding districts like fiefdoms. There has never been a space for me or people like me. It's high time they made us a seat at the goddamn table.

I make a left and then an immediate right, my boots clunking with each step. "It means the Falcones have a week to make it right."

"Fuck," Angie mutters.

I hum in agreement.

"They'll make it right," Darius reassures in his smooth baritone.

I take a hairpin turn and shoot him a censuring look. "We aren't in the business of predictions."

"Every business attempts to predict something—risk, market trends, competitors' moves," Angie says. And she would, being the manager of a night club.

"You know what I mean." I press the trick stone in the wall, and the apparent dead end ahead of us opens to reveal a stairwell.

Angie's boots clunk against the floor as Darius pulls the faux-wall closed behind us. A door opposite us leads into storage and laundry, and the stairs ahead lead to the main floor and then the private rooms and VIP box—or what Darius likes to call the throne room. I grab the railing, the bass vibrating through the building and up my arm, when Angie taps my elbow.

I pause, turning back to her.

She clears her throat with a scrunch of her nose. "There's something else you couldn't predict."

I cock a brow. "Well?"

Angie straightens, smoke-lined eyes narrowed and shrewd. "Do you know Zarina Gallo?"

The name releases the inferno I had tucked away.

I keep my face relaxed, my hand loose on the stair's railing, as the word *Gallo* shudders through my entire body. My knee flexes, and that twinge from kneeling at Antoni's head and kicking his throat settles into a bone-deep ache.

Gallo.

The family that took me, one of a hundred lost kids, off the street. The family that taught me the ropes of what it meant to hold all the power of a kingdom. The family that I have done everything in my power to cripple since they left me lying cold and broken in an alley much like the one we visited tonight.

"Why?" I ask nonchalantly, as if Zarina Gallo's name is not threatening to spark an explosion inside of me.

"She's at the front door." Angie studies me with a too-knowing look. I try to pull back the rage from where it simmers on my skin, over my face. It doesn't matter as Angie grimaces. "And she's asking—er, *demanding*—to see you."

I let a nasty grin slink across my lips. "By all means, let the princess in."

ZARINA

 *T*he Den of Inequity looks like a dump.

Black walls and black doors without a single window and a flickering neon sign with "iniquity" misspelled and *left* that way as if the Tamayo gang didn't care to fix it. A line of people wait outside, an eclectic collection of neon hair, leather harnesses, and gender-bending outfits. No one bats an eye. No one whispers about the strangeness of it. They all laugh, shoot the shit, throw compliments at each other like they're infinite and well-deserved.

It makes my heart clench in a weird, nauseous way that I don't have time or space to understand. Not when this is my only small window of opportunity.

"We should go," Pat mutters in my ear. I don't think this is what they had in mind when we fled the house. They scan the sidewalk, the street with parked cars lining the curb, the heavy traffic of the main road a couple blocks up. I know they're waiting for the moment a Gallo car pulls up and spots us. The two people corralled to the side and separated from the pack. Easy pickings.

But I came here for a reason.

"Not yet." I flick my hair behind my shoulder and match one of the bouncers—a bulky woman with a fade wearing a leather vest like she's in a motorcycle club—glare for glare. "Not until we're kicked out."

"You're not even in," she mutters.

I bare my teeth, ready to hiss insults, when a much taller, bulkier, figure ducks through the club's front door. The woman from before, short and petite with harsh, painted angles and a mouth that lacks laugh lines, slips out from behind the man and leads him right over to us.

"Zarina Gallo." She says my name like she's announcing an execution.

The man looks me up and down without a hint of attraction. It throws me off-balance. Almost every man I've ever met—except for my father—has looked at me like they want me, like they wished they could peek under my skirt and run their hands over my skin. And every single time, it makes me swallow a gag and grit my teeth.

Not this man.

I blink once, twice, and pull the mask of the mobster's daughter over my face, because I don't know how else to act. "Well?" I snip. "Take us to Tamayo."

The petite woman shakes her head. "I'll leave her to you." And then she turns on her heel and strides back into the club.

The man's eyes glide over me to Pat, stopping on their chest, their hip, their ankle. Not like he's checking them out, but like he's searching for the barest hint of a gun's barrel, a knife's hilt. He doesn't look back to me before he turns to the bouncer, with her crossed arms and stern jaw, and gestures to me and then Pat. "She comes, she stays."

Pat stiffens.

"*They* come with me, period," I snap.

The man nods at the correction. "Then they come in unarmed."

Pat stands straighter. "Deal."

He crooks a finger. We follow. The bouncer watches, as if she could lay a hand on me before Pat broke it. We duck into an all-black hallway with purple mood lighting along the ceiling and floor, house music shudders loud and heavy through the building and up my legs. Pat shadows each step, and club-goers trickle in and out of the doors.

They brush a finger on my elbow, and I slow enough for them to lean down. "Darius Taylor. Andrea Tamayo's second."

I nod as Darius leads us to the coat check, bypassing the desk with the attendant and opening a side door with a keycard. It's a bright, white room with metal shelves along the walls and baskets lining them. He pulls one out and arches a brow at Pat.

They sigh. "We invoke sacred hospitality."

"We understand and accept." Darius's voice is somehow both smooth and rough at the same time.

Pat removes their weapons, shrugging out of their jacket to take off their shoulder holster and pulling the gun out of their waistband, the knife out of its sheath at their ankle. Darius watches. I tap my foot, impatient to get to my end-goal—Andrea Tamayo.

Pat holds their arms out, and Darius pats them down. And then he turns to me, expectant.

I snort. "Excuse you?"

"Your thigh," he notes the knife strapped under my dress. "And your purse."

I suck my teeth. Normally, Cardinal Family members aren't subject to search, sacred hospitality demanding mutual trust between dons. But I'm not a don, and I'm not here with my father.

I'm just a worthless fucking princess.

I shove my purse at his chest, and he takes it, unzipping it as I remove the sheath on my thigh and slam it into the basket. Pat slips their jacket back on. Darius removes my pepper spray, like

I don't deserve to protect myself from wandering hands, and leaves the too-large wad of cash and hard drive alone without even a raised brow.

I snatch my purse out of his hands as he's zipping it closed. "Can we go?"

He places our basket of weapons back on its shelf and opens the door. "Follow me." He leads us back through the door into the purple-lit hallway. In moments, it opens to the club proper.

Okay, so Den of Inequity is *not* a dump.

Black couch-like booths spread out in an arc before a lowered dance floor with bright, blacklights hanging from the high, domed ceiling. Stairs lead up to a balcony with doors like a hotel, windows looking into the rooms. Some are opaque with frost while others are clear. The DJ spins from her booth suspended from the balcony, and the bar continues the purple-lit theme with light panels lining the rail. Behind it, a mirror made into a mosaic pattern rises from the top-shelf liquor up to the ceiling and reflects the lights back onto the teeming crowd.

And the crowd is *teeming*.

Just like the line outside, people are dressed in jarring harmony, patterns and colors that aren't usually paired but somehow work well. They use the lines of their body, the paint of their makeup, the texture of their clothes, to bend perception and force a double take. Someone wears a crop top and a belly chain with loose, ripped jeans, and it wouldn't give me pause any other time, but their belly isn't flat. Their hair isn't long and blown out. Their thighs rub together.

And they look damn good.

They smile wide, laughing bright at whatever the tall, lanky person in combat boots and a plaid dress with hairy legs and chest said, and I am staring. Pat's pushing me along, following Darius, but I can't take my eyes off them. They don't fit the mold. In fact, they blatantly ignore the mold.

And they're happy.

I swallow hard around the tangle of feelings stuck in my throat. My parents always spoke of Den of Inequity with wrinkled noses, like it gave off a stink that washed downriver. And though they never said it, it was heavily implied that I was not allowed to come here, to fraternize with *these kinds of people*. But being here now, seeing queer people in a place where they are simply people... I think it was a lot more than who owned the club that my parents disapproved of.

It's the complete lack of othering.

I want to live in it. I want to run to the dance floor and revel in it. Darius corrected himself the first time I snapped Pat's pronouns. Not a single person has attempted to run a hand over my ass only to have Pat grab their wrist and threaten to snap it in half. For once, *women* are aiming heated gazes at me.

It feels like the Upside Down, but it isn't scary. It's exhilarating.

Darius leads us up a winding staircase, and my feet hesitate to follow. What if this is the last time I step foot in Den of Inequity? What if Andrea Tamayo laughs me out of her club and I never get to experience this again?

Pat clears their throat, and I sigh, steeling myself. I know what I want. I will get it.

ZARINA

*A*ndrea Tamayo is hotter than I expected. Much hotter. Like distractingly hot.

She pours vodka into two glasses, dressed in tailored, gray bird's-eye slacks with a pressed, white dress shirt tucked in and left unbuttoned to just above her navel. I suck my bottom lip between my teeth, tracing the line of her suspenders from her hip up to her neckline. Her fade reveals the tattoos scrolling from behind her ear down the back of her neck to disappear under her collar.

Pat tugs on my skirt, and I release my lip from between my teeth, standing straight-backed, chin high, face blank. Mostly. Andrea turns, fully facing me for the first time since I entered her private room with the wall of mirrored windows looking down over the club and soundproofing foam muffling the club's blaring music. Her black hair brushes her forehead, her brown eyes like palm tree bark against the sandy tan of her skin. Freckles dot her cheeks, like pebbles on the shore. Fuck.

She hands me a sweating glass of ice and vodka and whatever else she poured in there. An orange peel floats amongst the ice. I accept it, careful to avoid her finger, because I'm pretty sure if we touched, I'd drop the goddamn drink.

"Zarina Gallo." She says my name like it's a hard candy melting on her tongue.

Fuck. My mouth goes dry. I take a sip, wetting my throat with the lemon-orange-vodka cocktail, which is delicious. And that just makes me more annoyed. I am Zarina fucking Gallo. I make men crawl and women pant, not the other way around.

I shake out my hair to cover the deep breath I take to gather myself. "Andrea Tamayo."

"Tamayo, please." She sits in the only armchair in the room, ankle on her knee, relaxed as she savors her drink. The picture of a queen on her throne. She gestures to the couch, inviting me to sit, but I stay standing.

"I don't bend the knee." Especially not to gang leaders.

"A princess through-and-through." She smirks. I shoot her a scowl, and she only smiles wider. "Tell me, has anyone ever bent you *over* their knee? Might do you some good."

Heat pulses under my skirt, but I only allow myself a single, arched brow. "Do you wish you could?"

She runs a finger over her bottom lip then lets the hand drop. Her face remains impassive, but the brown of her eyes darkens toward black. "I don't."

I scoff. "And the Earth is flat."

"I'm sure you can find a willing someone out there." She nods toward the windows, the club beyond.

I glance over at the DJ suspended over the dance floor, the black lights painting the crowd purples and neons. I lick my lips, slow and purposeful, watching Tamayo out of the corner of my eye. "I just might."

She tongues her cheek and squeezes her glass where it rests on her knee. "Why are you here?"

A trickle of relief rolls down my back—I haven't lost my touch. I turn back around to face her where she sits on her veritable throne and do my absolute best not to stare at the soft skin of her cleavage.

"I'm gay," I start.

Pat barely covers a snort-laugh behind me, and I barely hold my elbow back from jabbing their gut.

Tamayo blinks but doesn't say anything. She should know already; it's not a secret. Though when the fact of my sexuality is presented to men—specifically straight, cis men—it's usually met either as a challenge to convince me I'm simply missing the right dick, which is obviously theirs, or as a promise of a future performance for them, as if lesbians are only meant for their consumption.

This is the first time those words haven't caused a reaction.

I set my drink on the gold side table. No one else is in this room but the four of us—Pat standing behind the velvet sofa, Darius leaning against the untended bar—and yet it feels like I'm presenting to the entire club. My skin itches and my cheeks burn, but I don't slouch. This is my one shot, and I can't waste it. Not if I want to keep my freedom. Not if I want a chance to inherit my birthright.

"My parents have known I'm gay since I was fourteen. They accepted me, loved me, never pushed me to be anything else." To flirt and lead on, sure. But feminine wiles are a weapon in the social arsenal, another way to get what we want and protect ourselves from what we don't. But never before now have they asked me to change, to ignore myself so completely. "Tonight, they told me I'm to marry Marcus Accardi."

Tamayo doesn't move, face still curious yet impassive, but I catch the tension. Her eyes darken with something that echoes in the tightness of her jaw, gaze traveling from my face to my collarbones, to my fingers, where I play with the chain of my purse hanging at my hip.

I focus on the mole under her left eye, unable to watch her

watch me. "Anyway, that can't happen. And I need your help to make sure it doesn't."

"My help?" she asks.

I nod.

"What can a gang leader do for the Gallo princess that she cannot do for herself?"

I scoff. "Don't play coy, Tamayo, it discredits you."

She bites down on her bottom lip, the corners twitching up. "Ah-ah, remember—you're asking *me* for help, princess. Whether you're on your knees or not, you're here to beseech me. Not the other way around."

Pride burns through me, likely painting the skin across my chest and up my neck pink. "Fine."

Tamayo settles further into her throne, legs wider, drink perched on her knee, smug expression on her face. "So, what help do you need that only I can provide?"

"Protection."

She laughs without amusement. "All four Cardinal Families will be searching for you, and despite the fact we supply half of them with weapons, we cannot stand against them. Especially not for someone who isn't ours."

I pick up my drink again, staring at the orange cocktail and wishing I could see the future in its reflection. But it's only booze and citrus. I knock back a gulp to wet my tongue before I finally reveal the core of why I'm here, in Tamayo's club, and not with someone more powerful. "Then make me yours."

Tamayo freezes in her chair, tension spreading from her fingers up to her shoulders. She stares at me so long I wonder if she feels the urge to blink, but instead her eyes move to her second, Darius, standing at the bar. They speak without words, and I wonder what they've said.

Tamayo licks her lips once and readjusts her seat. "Excuse me?"

"You're right." I hold my glass in both hands, turning to

watch people exist in ways I never imagined were allowed on the club floor below. "The Cardinal Families will take me back home by force, and there's no one, gang or politician or outsider, who can protect me without endangering themselves and their people."

Tamayo studies me like she can't believe the direction I'm going. Apparently, neither can Pat.

"Z, what're you doing?" Pat mutters into my ear.

I don't acknowledge them, instead leaving the windows behind to slink across the room toward Tamayo. Her left eyebrow hasn't fully relaxed since I entered the room, and it makes me want to do something so surprising that the right arches up to meet it. I set my drink on her side table, leaning forward to reach it. We're so close, I can feel the heat of her licking my bare thighs. She could run her probably calloused hand from my wrist to my collarbone and through my hair if she were so inclined.

"It doesn't matter to the Council that I'm Zarina Gallo, sole heir of the Southern Districts, raised by one of the most powerful dons in the city." I straighten, fingers trailing over the arm of her throne before they fall to my side. "I can't leverage a single ounce of that power, because I'm a woman. And I can't— no, I refuse—to marry a man and act through him."

"What exactly are you saying?" Tamayo murmurs.

"I'm saying." I pause to release a pent-up breath. "I'm saying that the Council sees me as an asset to be owned, whether by my parents or by Marcus Accardi. And I would like to use that against them."

Tamayo stays silent.

I grew up a princess. Most often, I got the whimsical and spectacular things I wanted. But I'm still a don's daughter. I learned more at his knee than he intended. And one thing he never learned himself: Power is in the wielding, not the taking or having. I've spent too long sitting back on my heels, waiting for permission to rise up and be the queen I'm meant to be.

Not anymore.

"You'd betray your parents, your family?" Her voice is low in her throat, both hesitant and hopeful.

For a single moment, I allow the steel of my gaze to soften and show the pain that's taken up residence in my chest, wrapping around my heart, tickling my lungs. It's calculated, but it's true. At the bottom of the angry black hole inside me is the little girl it's protecting, and for half a second, I allow Tamayo to see her. For half a second, I'm as honest with her as I can be without words.

The last exchange with my father through my bedroom door echoes in my head. *Please trust us?* Before tonight, I did. I trusted my parents, because they didn't push me beyond the boundaries of myself, brought me into the discussion. But after tonight? After this? There is only one answer—*I can't.*

I shutter closed again. Push it all down, past the ring of angry teeth, and focus on the present, on Andrea Tamayo and her perfectly messy black hair with her scrollwork neck tattoos and a hunger in her eyes that has nothing to do with me and everything to do with my offer. With the power she can attain through me and *my* power.

I meet her gaze with a hunger of my own. Will I betray my family? My parents? Yes. "They betrayed me first."

A slow, wicked smile stretches across Tamayo's face as she leans back on her throne, legs spread and wrists lax like she has nothing but time at her disposal. "Ask the question."

I glare, biting down on my tongue to keep a shudder from my limbs.

She flicks her fingers to the floor. "And make sure it's done properly."

Kneel. The command goes unspoken, but it lands between us, flung like trash but heavy as a crown. She wants me, Gallo royalty, on my knees before a lowly gangster, begging for her help. A princess before a rogue. The fucking audacity. But I have no choice. I need Tamayo. And she knows it. My teeth grind, jaw pulsing with the ache, and that stupid, sexy grin on Tamayo's face grows wider and wider. She waits, tongue-in-cheek, as I swallow down the pride, the shame, the outrage crawling over my skin and up my throat. I straighten my back, tuck my dress tight to my thighs.

And I kneel.

Pat starts forward with a growl, and I throw up my hand to stop them without looking away from Tamayo. She doesn't mind them. As if she's confident in my submission. I bite my tongue harder while Pat curses under their breath.

Tamayo nods for me to speak, and it colors my vision red. Like I need her permission. My hands shake at the hem of my skirt. I suck in a deep inhale, compelling my jaw to relax enough to form the words.

"Andrea Tamayo"—her name is acid in my mouth—"will you marry me?"

TAMAYO

I don't think I'll ever feel more powerful than I do in this moment. Zarina Gallo is on her knees before me, begging. Her life, her freedom, rests in the palm of my hand, and I could crush it in my fist as easily as a freshly bloomed flower. I could call the Accardis or any of the Cardinal Families, and return her in exchange for a favor, more territory, a sweet deal. I could leave her broken in an alley like I was so many years ago. Tit for tat.

But that wouldn't quench the inferno of rage inside me.

The Gallos deserve worse than they gave me. They deserve to be ruined, their name laid to waste. And here their daughter sits, pretty on her knees, asking me to save her, because she has nowhere else to go. Because her parents pushed her directly into my open arms. The opportunity is too sweet to pass up. Zarina said it herself—she's the sole heir of the Southern Districts, raised by one of the most powerful families in Louredo. She has information, secrets, access that I can only dream of. And if I tie myself to her, all that becomes mine, too.

Plus, I get to ruin the Gallos's only daughter.

I tongue my cheek, raising my glass to my lips, and stare at her on the floor. Her spine is straight, jaw clenched, eyes burning. I sip my drink and set it beside hers, leaning forward to offer my hand. She grimaces at it, as if my fingers are covered in the same filth I wiped off my boot earlier.

"Pat," she says.

They stride forward without looking at me and help Zarina to her feet. Her orange dress rides up her thighs slightly before she tugs it back down.

I drop my proffered hand and sit back in my chair, taking up the whole of it. "What are your terms?"

She snatches her drink off the table and downs the rest of it, like she's washing a bad taste out of her mouth. Pat takes the glass when she's finished, and Zarina dabs the liquor from her lips. "A public claim before the Council and a three-month cap on the engagement before we *very* publicly breakup, during which you will protect me as if I'm your…fiancée."

A fake engagement, then. "What do I get?"

"You get the clout of a Gallo engagement," she says, like it's the most obvious thing in the world. "It's not a secret what you're working toward, Tamayo. You want a seat with the Council, to replace the Russos, but there's no way they'll ever recognize you as a family, as a don, as a *threat*, without some credibility."

Her words are too honest, the reality of them raking harshly over my chest. I clink my rings against my glass. "That's not enough."

She forces a calming breath through her nose. "It's all I have."

"You want me to endanger myself and my people for a fake engagement and *temporary* clout?" My voice rises at the end, incredulous despite the offer being everything I need. It's better than Antoni could give me, better than I could get myself if I betrayed Zarina tonight. But she doesn't need to know that.

"They won't be in danger." She waves my concerns away.

"Don't be coy, princess, it discredits you," I parrot her words back at her, coated with candied acid.

"They won't be *openly* in danger," she corrects.

I rub my finger over my lips, studying her. She stands tall, fully embodying Zarina Gallo, princess and heir to the Gallo crime family, rulers of the Southern Districts. She has had anything she could ever want laid at her feet. Except power over her own future.

I drop my hand to the arm of my chair. "I want thirty percent of your territory."

She reels back. "Excuse me?"

"Ten percent for each month of this farce." I raise my glass in a sardonic cheers.

"That's outrageous, Tamayo." Zarina shakes her head, arms crossed and eyes rolling. "And not only that, but I don't *have* it."

"You will, though, won't you?"

She throws up her hands and stalks over to the windows, grumbling under her breath.

"Why would you want only three months, princess?" I rest my elbows on my knees, voice low and rumbling. "What could change in such a short time?"

"The Accardis will give up by then."

"No, they won't." I push out of my chair, grabbing her empty glass from the side table by the sofa and ignoring Pat's narrowed glare as I carry it back to the bar. Darius slides fresh drinks over—two more vodka Collinses. "The Accardis have the chance to double their power, rule the South and the West. They won't let go so easily."

"What's your point?" she snaps.

"You want time." I stride over to Zarina, where she stands at the wall of windows watching the revelers below, and hand her the new drink. "Time to find a way out of this that doesn't end with you married to a man. Time to find a way to bring the Gallo Family under your command."

She doesn't turn from the view despite my outstretched hand. I wait. She chews her lip. It's like she's about to kneel again. If she agrees, she admits I'm right and yields the higher ground. And when she does, I'll have more leverage.

"Three months isn't long enough, if you ask me," I purr. "But I'm just a gang leader. What do I know?"

Zarina snatches the drink from me, and I smirk as I sip mine. She holds hers without tasting it, staring at me with narrowed eyes. "Ten percent."

Finally. "Twenty-five."

"Ten percent and a favor," she counters.

That gives me pause. Essentially limitless in scope and to be defined by me later, a favor from a Cardinal Family is more valuable than gold in Louredo. I could ask for just about anything and she'd be required to agree.

"That's my final offer." She downs her entire drink in three gulps, a trickle of citrus slipping down her chin until she catches it with her finger. She presses it back into her mouth as she shoves her glass back into my hand. "You have until midnight to decide."

And then Zarina Gallo strides out the door, surrounded in as much chaos as when she entered.

TAMAYO

*I*t clangs shut behind her and Pat like the chime of a bell keeping time. Midnight. As if this is some Cinderella bullshit and I'm not her best chance at getting what she wants—freedom and power.

"What the fuck just happened?" Darius asks the empty room.

I turn away from the window, my knee twinging again, and stride to the bar to deposit her empty glass and chug my own drink. I try not to think about the line of her throat, or the liquor shining over her chin, as she gulped the last of hers. The hem of her orange dress where it brushed her thighs. The pink tint of her lip gloss that glimmered in the light. My fingers slip on my glass, and I almost drop it. *Smooth.*

"Andy." Darius says my nickname the same way a mom says their child's full name. It's not Andrea Tamayo, it's Andy.

I drop an orange twist into the glass and take a sip. Citrus bursts along my tongue, and all I can wonder is if Zarina tastes the same. I relish another sip.

"You can't be serious," he mutters, leaning over the bar and grabbing a beer and a lime wedge to stuff down its neck with more force than necessary.

"Which part?" I ask. Before I even asked Zarina to define her terms, the moment she lowered herself to her knees before me, I knew my answer. And so did Darius. He always knows.

He shoots me his most unamused look, jaw clenched and lips tight. I can't help but grin at him, my canines catching on my lip. He levels a deadpan glower. "We cannot take on the Gallos and the Accardis and the Council while also negotiating with the Falcones."

I wave away his concerns. "The Council will honor my claim if I make it. They'll be required to."

"At what cost?" he gripes.

"You mean reward."

"I don't." He picks at the label of his beer, the same way he always does when he's worried. "We don't need to be a Cardinal Family. We're powerful enough to protect ourselves so long as we don't step on their toes—"

"And who decides if we step on their toes?" I ask.

"Andy—"

"They're proud men with more power than sense, and whatever they say goes. I can't abide that. They don't want us here, don't respect us, don't think we're worth a damn." I drag the toe of my sullied boot across the floor as if still trying to wipe it clean of muck. "We'll always be expendable, nothing but a gang playing around in their sandbox, allowed to exist by their good grace.

"So Zarina uses us as a shield. Fine. We'll use her as a stepping stone to everything we've been working toward: A family powerful enough to keep our people safe no matter what." I can't let my story become theirs. I just can't. "They deserve safety and stability—a real family."

Darius stares down the neck of his bottle, swirling the light beer before taking another drink. "The deal with the Falcones will help us, too."

If it even happens, I think. But I don't say that aloud. "Peanuts compared to the gold that is Zarina Gallo."

"And if she fucks us over?" he asks.

"Oh, I expect she will—she's a Gallo." I sip my drink and refuse to imagine her dress, her skin on my tongue.

Darius sets his drink down hard on the bar. "So, we beat her to the punch."

"Exactly." I raise my glass, and we cheers. The Gallos, the Accardis, the Capones, the Falcones—each Cardinal Family is as untrustworthy as the last. They run Louredo as if they built it, brick by brick, when in reality they infiltrated it in the dark of night and took what they wanted. Power. Money. Control.

The same things Zarina wants. The same things I want.

And for the first time since my parents forced me out of their house, since the Gallos kicked me out of their family, since I opened the doors of Den of Inequity, I can see my goal within my grasp.

Darius turns and leans back against the bar, elbows on the edge as he shakes his head. "Her parents…"

"Yeah." I clench my jaw, memories unwilling to be forgotten threatening to slither out of the shadows of my past.

"And to Marcus?" Darius's brows furrow, and his jaw grinds.

"Yeah." My own face darkens. The most poorly kept secret among the Cardinal Families is the bruises Marcus leaves on his capos, on his own mother, on the sex workers who have the misfortune of catching his eye. Zarina said her parents loved her, but if they are willing to pair their only daughter with the barbarous Accardi prince? Questionable, at best. Outright cruel, at worst.

"I feel for her," Darius says.

I blink at him. "You do?"

He shoves my shoulder. "I'm not heartless."

"Just emotionally unavailable," I tease.

He stands straight and smooths out the lapels of his jacket as if they're not already impeccably ironed. "We all have our hangups."

"Except most of ours aren't out flouncing around in Gucci and glitter." I leave out the part where he explicitly banned me from ever being a dick to said "hangup."

He yanks at the sleeves of his undershirt with too much force, shooting me a glare. I roll my eyes and push off the bar. Whatever. He can hide from his ex all he wants.

He changes the subject. "The Accardis won't take this lying down."

"I know." I stand at the wall of windows, the mirrored glass showing the club floor below fuller than when we arrived. Angie mixes drinks behind the bar with a glower, and the DJ skips to the next song too quickly. I rub the pad of my finger along the rim of my glass.

"And," Darius continues behind me, "this might fuck up the Falcone situation even more."

"I know." I scan the bar rail, strobe lights from the dance floor flashing in sporadic bursts. Orange blares here and there, but never a dress. Never paired with hair almost as dark as mine and blown out in waves.

"You're sure we're ready?" he asks, voice softer than it's been all night.

I don't turn to him, don't acknowledge the vulnerability lest he withdraw back into himself like he so often does. I straighten to my full height and square my shoulders. "We're at a precipice. We can either scrounge for scraps, beg them to deign to deal with us, and endure more Antonis, or—" Orange burns in the middle of the swarm of bodies, and I still, watching. Zarina dances with her hands above her head and her hips as inexorable as the sunset, carving arcs with each sweep. I squeeze my glass tighter. "Or we can walk out on the knife's edge and take what we want. Zarina Gallo is our knife's edge."

"And it's not just because she's a Gallo?" Darius's voice is a few feet behind me now.

The tattoo on my shoulder itches again. "It doesn't hurt."

Darius stands beside me at the window, but I don't avert my gaze from Zarina dancing. "The family deserves better than personal vendettas," he says.

"I know." But this is so much more than that. At this point, seeing the Gallos hanging from a noose of their own making is a sweetener compared to everything else we could achieve. They created their own worst enemies. Zarina, the daughter they betrayed. And me, the gangster they made. Plus... "Her parents wouldn't cut this deal if they weren't desperate."

He snorts. "Wouldn't they?"

"Kings don't sacrifice their queens. Not unless it's the only choice." Below, hands snake out of the crowd to Zarina's waist. She turns to the person and nods a moment later. Their bodies find each other in the music, their dark heads of hair coming together. The other person has short hair and wears a buttoned shirt, their long fingers digging into Zarina's hips, her waist, up under her hair to wrap around her neck. I watch. I watch as she finds their hands and squeezes. I watch as she rises on her tiptoes to speak into their ear. I watch as she plays with the waistband of their trousers. The trousers of a person with a similar haircut, similar style, similar swagger as my own.

I watch, and I smile with wet lips and sharp teeth. "I think it'll work."

"Jesus fuck," Darius mutters. And then he drains the rest of his beer. "Hundred bucks says it implodes before you see a foot of territory."

"Oh ye of little faith." I can't force my eyes away from her, from the faceless person maneuvering her until her back is to their front, her chin tilted up and head resting on their shoulder. Their lips drag down her neck. Fingertips over her sternum.

"I've known you for half my life, Andy." Darius tosses the bottle into the recycling. "You are not to be trusted around pretty girls with angry mouths."

"I'll be fine." I wave him off.

Darius buttons his suit jacket before resting one hand on the door handle. "We're fuckin' doomed."

I raise my glass without looking as he opens the door and music floods into the room. "That's the spirit."

ZARINA

A lot can happen before the bell chimes twelve.

I could lose more than a shoe. I could lose my best chance at taking the power I crave. I could lose my hand in marriage to a man. Or I could lose my clothes in one of the VIP rooms if the whispered words of the woman at my back are true. Of the three possibilities, I'd much prefer the latter. And if there's nothing to be done but wait for Tamayo's decision to come down from her throne room on-high, then by all means.

The woman presses us flush together from knee to shoulder, and for the first time in a long time, I don't want to step away. I don't wish for her hands to leave my body as soon as possible, don't feel a yank in my stomach to heave up its contents. I've snuck into clubs, pushed women up against locked bathroom stalls, even gone so far as to rent hotel rooms. But it was always under cover of shadows and poorly concocted pseudonyms. Never in the open as Zarina Gallo.

The DJ switches the song, and my partner quickens their rhythm. Their breasts press against my back. Their hands trace my arms up to my shoulders. I grind closer and entertain the thought of kissing them on the dance floor where anyone in the club could see. It'd be a first. It'd be a reclaiming of myself.

And then they disappear.

I stagger backward as the anchor of their hips leaves me unmoored in the sea of bodies. They left me. My lip hitches in a growl, offense and annoyance burning my cheeks. And then a new hand grips my elbow and slides up my forearm. I turn, frowning, and am stopped by lips at my ear.

"Dance with me, princess?"

And even though I only heard the voice for the first time tonight, only met its owner once, I recognize immediately who it belongs to: Andrea Tamayo.

Goose bumps pebble across my skin as she bands my arm across my waist and pulls me into her orbit until we're dancing flush together to a slow, sensual beat that ignores the manic build of the house music. The fingers of her free hand trail up my thigh, catching the hem of my dress in their wake before they trail across my hip, over my arm, under my chin.

"Enjoying the Den?" Her breath is hot on my ear, her nose a hair's breadth from brushing my temple.

I tense every muscle inside me to halt the shudder her voice threatens to release. There's no way I'm about to show how much she affects me after practically begging her—*on my knees* —to be my fake fiancée. Especially not when she hasn't yet accepted my offer. I release each limb, each finger and toe, until my body feels as loose as water in a storm.

"I think you are." Her nails trace the line of the teardrop ruby resting against my sternum. "I think you hate how much you love it here."

"And why's that?" My mouth runs without my permission.

Tamayo tucks my hair behind my ear so her lips can graze against its shell. Goose bumps I can't stop race down my neck. "You're free here."

I twist in her arms, and she lets me, her hands falling to my hips as I clasp mine behind her neck. My lips brush against her ear, and I think her fingers twitch tighter, her knee slipping between my legs. I scrape my thumb up the short hairs at the back of her neck. "Free for now."

Tamayo pulls us to a halt, the two of us pressed chest-to-chest in a swath of writhing bodies rising and falling to the beat. She straightens until she's holding my gaze, her hands tight, her jaw stern. The mole under her left eye draws my attention, small and brown and beautiful on her high cheek.

Tamayo curls her fingers under my chin, gentle but firm. "You have three months to take it for good."

My breath catches in my chest, stuck between an inhale and exhale. "Does that mean you accept?"

Her thumb strokes my bottom lip, the nail scraping over the sensitive skin. I lick my lips and raise my chin. A smirk tugs at the corner of her mouth. She leans in, breath caressing over my cheek, and my eyes close of their own accord.

"A million times yes, princess." Her voice tickles my ear.

And then Tamayo steps back.

Her touch leaves me, my body scorched where the heat of her kissed it. My clasped hands behind her neck break apart and fall to my sides as my jaw clacks shut before I can let out a huff. She stands with lazy confidence, black hair hanging in her eyes and suspender buckles shining in the black light. Annoyingly unruffled.

"As my fiancée, I think it's time you went home." Tamayo looks over my shoulder and nods to someone behind me. I fuel as much disdain into my glare as my short frame can hold, but she doesn't react. "Can't have you dancing with other people."

"Maybe I'd like to make you jealous."

She grins wider. "You shouldn't."

I can feel the hulking presence of Darius behind me, ready to effectively strong-arm me out of the club at Tamayo's signal. Pat materializes at my shoulder with a soft rustle of their jacket against my elbow. The crowd gives us a wide berth, an island of stillness in an ocean of movement.

I cross my arms. "And what about you?"

"I have a club to run." She stuffs her hands in her pockets.

"You have people for that."

"Be a good fiancée, hm?" Tamayo's eyes are shining with something like mischief, and despite knowing she's pressing my buttons on purpose, anger churns inside me. "Wait for me at home while I take care of business."

I raise my chin. "And if I choose to stay?"

Tamayo remains so very unruffled that I get the same urge I had upstairs to wipe the expression off her face, to do anything to force a reaction. "Then I cannot protect you when you choose to go. My people are available now or not at all. It's up to you."

Except it's not an actual choice. Not really. Not when my parents or the Accardis will find me without Tamayo's shield to keep my presence hidden until I'm tucked away safe.

And she knows that.

I shake out my hair and close the space she put between us with steps as slow as the beat she danced to with me. She follows me, eyes sharp and teeth sharper. I rest my hand on her chest, just above her heart. Our skin touches where her shirt lies open, and it sears my palm.

I rise on my toes and speak into her ear. "You're my fiancée now, too. Don't forget whose power you're trading on, Tamayo." I press my lips to the mole below her eye and scratch my nails across her collarbone as I stride away. "Keep your hands to yourself or lose them, hm?"

TAMAYO

y knee throbs, a bone-deep ache pulsing up to my hip and lower back. I yank on my compression brace, knowing it won't be enough—it never is—but it's better than nothing. The house is quiet and still so early in the morning, as if no one exists in the world but me. I breathe in through my nose and wish I had a cup of steaming coffee and no obligations for the day.

Unfortunately, those days are few and far between in this life.

I pull on my clothes, gritting my teeth when I have to balance on my left leg. Each twinge cues up another memory previously buried in a shallow grave. I've spent years visiting their headstones, paying respect to the revenge they demand, but never digging under the surface.

I stomp on their undead talons raking through my mind. There's no use in excavating them. Not today, not ever.

Footsteps patter down the hall. I frown, checking the clock on my nightstand as I tame my hair. Darius will already be in the gym. No one else lives here. The guards are relegated to the perimeter, and the capos to the inner houses.

Except we have guests now.

The memory of the silk of Zarina's skin under my fingertips, her hand on my chest, her hair against my cheek, tingles through me. I snatch up my Rolex and my suit jacket and slip into the hall. The pain in my knee fades to background noise as I stride across the wood floors of the hallway and down the stairs. I force my feet to slow as I pass the dining room, the den, and then round the corner into the kitchen.

Darius stands at the counter, pouring coffee from the carafe into two mugs. He glances over his shoulder at my entrance, but I'm checking the breakfast nook, the hallway, the deck. No one else is here. When I turn back, Darius is sliding a mug of coffee across the black, leathered granite island to me and shaking his head.

"Eager this morning," he teases.

"Can't I look forward to seeing you?" I toss my jacket over a bar stool and slip on my watch, clicking the clasp shut.

He levels A Look at me over the rim of his mug. "You can."

I lift my own to my lips—"But you don't," he says—and almost inhale my coffee with a snort.

"Would be nice if you did." He replaces the oat milk in the fridge with an exaggerated sigh. "I deserve more than grunts in the morning."

"I don't grunt." I successfully drink my coffee without drowning myself this time.

"You grunt," he insists.

"I do not," I snap. "I don't even speak."

"How is that better?" he asks.

I wrinkle my nose. "It's not fucking grunting like a caveman—"

"I need coffee before all this noise."

I snap my mouth shut.

Zarina's morning voice is gruff and a little croaky from lack of use, her hair a cloud around her face. She's wearing a huge black shirt that falls to her mid-thigh and nothing else. And while it's technically covering more skin than her dress did last night, my body does not understand the logic of my brain. I stare at the hem, at her bare feet padding over the matte-black tile, at her sleep-swollen face she rubs as if trying to encourage it awake, and grip my mug like it's the only thing holding me upright.

Darius opens the cabinet with the dishes and steps back, watching me watch Zarina. She doesn't mutter a word of thanks to him before she rises on her tiptoes to reach over her head for a mug. And the moment she does, the shirt rides up just enough to show the crest of her ass where it meets her thigh. That's the moment my brain loses all function for a full ten seconds.

Zarina settles back on her heels and pours her coffee while I squeeze my eyes shut and attempt to imprint that image in my head for all eternity. My imagination replaces Darius's shirt with mine, and I almost stagger at the thought.

Something flicks my temple—Darius. He leans close and whispers, "Simp."

"Shut up," I grumble, rubbing my temple.

Darius huffs a laugh and carries his coffee out to the deck without another word. I glare at the back of his head as he surveys the inner courtyard of our compound, which is really the combined backyards of the Sallay block where we bought every single house and renovated them into an estate worthy of a Cardinal Family. Darius has aspirations to convert the courtyard into a training ground, but I refuse to let our home become militarized like that. Home should be refuge, not warfare.

The fridge door snaps closed, and Zarina picks up her coffee.

"Good morning." I raise my mug.

She squints at me and does not return the greeting, taking a sip instead.

"Sleep all right?" I ask.

She licks her lips like she's chasing the caffeine. "Fine."

"Not a morning person, then," I say.

"Not until coffee." She leans a hip against the counter, her shirt blending into the black-on-black theme of the kitchen, and holds her mug with two hands.

"Drink up, then." I keep my gaze on her face, my hands relaxed. "We have business to discuss."

She grimaces. "At seven thirty-four in the morning?"

"Do you have any clothes?" I ask. And it's half an excuse to give in to the overwhelming urge to drop my gaze to the hem of her shirt again, to her thighs the color of honey. I linger there, imagining there are actual smears of sweet, sticky honey on her skin and—

"Whiplash, Jesus," she mutters.

I drag my eyes up again, slow enough to know it's less heated and more calculating by the time I meet her glare. "I'm trying to decide if our business should wait until you have clothes."

She arches a brow. "Is it my clothes or lack thereof that bothers you?"

I want to say that it's my inability to string two non-sexual thoughts together with her in that goddamn shirt that bothers me. But I don't. Instead, I rest my chin on my hand with a lazy grin. Her glare darkens, red flushing her neck, and I file that away for later.

"Would you prefer to be in Darius's shirt while we discuss next moves or in a tailored outfit?" I ask.

She drops a hand to the top of her thigh and bunches up the hem of the shirt in her fist. The crease of her hip lies in the shadow just beneath the heel of her palm. I can't stop my eyes from flicking down, tracing the line of her body, trying to see what might lie beneath the black cotton.

"Which would more easily bring you to your knees?" Zarina's voice is as husky as when she entered the kitchen.

Darius's shirt, hands down.

But I don't say that. This is a game, a negotiation of terms that will determine how we dance with each other in this house, in this city, in this deal. Zarina is a princess who has had the majority of her desires fulfilled at the snap of her pretty, manicured fingers. But me, I've fought and bled for what I want. If Zarina Gallo wants me on my knees, she must learn, like everyone else, that I don't bend first.

I disconnect my brain from the lust heating my skin and arrange my face into an expression of disappointment. Like Zarina Gallo is behaving badly rather than making my body pulse with the beat of my heart. I sip my coffee and watch the red at her neck travel up to her cheeks as she reads the shift in my body language. Her brown eyes are shot through with gold that hardens the longer she stands in silent defiance.

I set my mug back on the counter and raise one, sardonic brow. "Your choice, princess."

She drops the shirt and sighs. "You talk, I drink."

I nod and pull my phone out of my pocket as if I have something more important to focus my attention on than Zarina. "A pair of black SUVs have been circling since early this morning. They have Gallo plates." I slide the phone across the counter, video footage of the cars pulled up and playing.

Zarina leans over to watch, and I silently thank any powers that be that I can no longer see where the shirt ends and her thighs begin.

She hums and nods, resting her elbows on the counter.

My brain attempts to conjure up an image of her ass at this very moment, and I shut that down as swiftly as possible. "We need to nip this in the bud before they cross a line."

Zarina picks up my phone, tapping on it.

I let her. "What are you doing?"

"Nipping it in the bud." She raises the phone to her ear.

I drop my shoulders and shake my head. "Princess, that's not what I meant and you know—"

"Ssh"—she holds her finger to her smirking lips—"it's ringing."

"Zarina." I rap my knuckles on the countertop with gritted teeth. "Hang up."

"Mother." She brings the phone down to tap the screen and suddenly a very stern voice floods out of the speaker.

"—na Giovanna Gallo. Where the fuck are you?" Alessandra Gallo's voice is frigid in the otherwise warm kitchen, and the way it strikes through me feels like lightning. It's been years since I heard it, but the sound loosens the soil covering the shallow grave of my memories. I stomp on their clawing hands until they fall back, leaving scratches down my mind. Now is not the time.

Zarina pulls in a deep breath, gold-streaked eyes finding mine and holding. "It seems you already know where I am."

"What does that mean?" Alessandra snaps.

"Why are my cousins, Paul and Donny, driving around Sallay like tourists?" she asks. "There's nothing to see on this side of town."

"Apparently, there is."

"Call them off." Zarina's gaze trips over the mole on my left cheekbone, my triple pierced ear, back to my eyes.

"Not until you're safe."

She snorts. "So that's the angle."

"It's not an angle." Her mother sniffs like the suggestion is preposterous.

"Call them off, Mother," Zarina sighs, tired. I wonder if she ever calls her Mom, Mama, anything with more familiarity than the formal Mother. She stares at the coffee in her mug. "I'm more safe here than at home."

I catch my frown before it twitches across my lips.

Alessandra Gallo is quiet for the length of one breath. "Is she there?"

"I'm here," I say.

Zarina scowls. It only makes me grin.

"Return my daughter before I'm forced to wipe your little gang off the map," she demands. If I wasn't Andrea Tamayo, assured in myself and my people, I might be scared. But I'm not. Especially of a Gallo.

"Really, Mother, you're so dramatic," Zarina grumbles.

"Marcus is distraught, Zarina." Her mother tries a new tactic, and it immediately makes my hackles rise. "He fears for your life."

Zarina mock gags. "Sure, if my life is his perceived possession of my vagina."

Any mention of Marcus Accardi and this sham of a marriage is too ludicrous to entertain. I snatch the phone out of Zarina's grip. She grunts, affronted, and throws up her hands as if to say, *fine, you deal with her.*

Gladly.

I turn up the charm, hoping we don't have to resort to threats and manipulation too quickly. "I'm sorry for worrying you, Mrs. Gallo. Zarina is safe, and she's here by choice. I think you know your daughter can't be easily forced."

"Don't speak to me as if I'm your equal," she growls. "You exist by my grace. You make money, because I allow you to. You own property built on land I own. We are not equals, Andrea Tamayo."

A muscle in my eye twitches with the force of the clench of my jaw. "Even so. Zarina is here by her own choice and will remain here as long as she pleases."

"Then we declare belligerence." She says it as if speaking to a throne room full of courtiers rather than a "lowly gangster" over the phone. "The Council will call upon you to answer for your misconduct."

I chuckle. "I look forward to it."

"You're an idiot," she snaps.

Zarina steals phone back before I can so much as breathe a

reply. "Hope you have the day you deserve, Mother!" She smashes the end call button and drops it on the counter.

I stare as Zarina sips her coffee again, one hand tucking her hair behind her ear, and lean my elbows on the counter. "Your mother seems really nice."

Zarina guffaws, loud and amused, before she covers her mouth again. A grin bursts across my face.

She shakes her head. "I hate that I love her."

I get that, the push and pull of wishing a parent could be as perfect as you imagined them to be when you were younger, when they weren't fully fleshed-out adults with faults and ulterior motives. Of wishing they could love without conditions, like they said they would.

My hand stretches across the counter before I can stop it. I force it to grab my phone rather than Zarina's hand. "We don't choose our parents."

"Yeah." She straightens, thumbnail catching an imperfection on her mug.

I pull my phone over, tucking it in my pocket and clearing my throat. "Clothes, then. Give Darius your sizes, and we'll have some pieces delivered for you."

"The Council will convene soon." She ignores me and sets her coffee on the counter, back straight and chin set. "My parents and the Accardis won't let them wait very long."

This is Business Zarina. In an overlarge tee and no pants. Maybe no underwear. I pluck up my own mug and take a drink lest I drool in front of her. "What story do you want to tell?"

"The lesbian tale as old as time." She waggles her brows.

"And they were very good friends?"

She chuckles. "The other one—secrecy and shadows and pseudonyms."

I hum affirmation. "A classic."

"I need a couple things other than clothes for the meeting."

"Like?" I have to forcefully suck in my lips before I make an entire list of inappropriate suggestions.

"Hair, makeup, jewelry, shoes, purses." She rinses her mug in the sink and places it in the dishwasher, bending just enough to tease me into damn near cardiac arrest. I grip my own mug tighter, the ceramic creaking under my fingers. She continues on, as if she hasn't already listed a casual six-figure wardrobe. "And if we don't die at the Council meeting, a phone, laptop, car—"

"I didn't know having a fiancée would be so expensive," I grumble.

Zarina digs a fingernail into the skin under my collar, just beside my jugular, and scratches across my neck. "It can cost more than money, if you like," she purrs.

I take her wrist in my hand, sweeping my thumb along her pulse point in a harsh contrast to her threatening claws. I lean over, lips beside her cheek. "Really, someone ought to bend you over their knee, princess."

"Maybe later, hm?" She pats my shoulder with her free hand as I let the other slip from my grip and watch her back out of the kitchen, expression smug. "Right now, we have business to prepare for."

ZARINA

$\mathcal{A}$ rack of designer clothes rolls into my room that evening. I thumb through the garments—cashmere wool, silk, pima cotton, leather. There's a complete wardrobe with easy-to-pair pieces here. I don't know if Darius or Tamayo had any hand in the choosing, but if they did? Color me surprised.

"I walked the whole grounds, and no one stopped me at any point, though a few locked doors did." Pat lies spread-eagle on the bed behind me as I pull out a pair of cream-colored, wide-legged slacks and an orange cropped sweater so soft I want to rub it against my cheek. I try not to wonder if Tamayo chose the color palette and instead assume it's the trend of the fall season.

Despite the arrival of another rack of more androgynous pieces for them, Pat's dressed in the same outfit they wore last night. "It seems each house on the block serves as both living quarters and community space. A guard even took me to the gym—which is the entire main floor of the red house across the courtyard. It's kind of cool how they've set everything up."

"Definitely different than home," I mutter and yank off Darius's shirt, fully naked beneath it.

Pat doesn't bat an eye; nudity between us is blasé at this point. "I like it. Feels a lot more, I don't know...intimate? Like a family, not the military."

"Is it safe?" I dig into a bag hung on the end of the rack and pull out panties and a bra wrapped in gilded tissue paper. I didn't tell Darius any preferences for my undergarments, but it's as if he knew, because there isn't a thong in sight, nor underwire. It's almost as if a woman, who would understand my disdain for permanent wedgies and digging metal, chose for me.

I try not to think about Tamayo's hands touching the fabric before me, her fingers stroking the silk panties I'm currently pulling up my legs. Try and fail.

"It's safe," Pat says.

I squeeze my eyes shut and focus more on dressing and less on my wild imagination.

"They've got all the usual stuff"—they wave their hand in a circle as if to encompass all the usual stuff—"with the added camouflage of the neighborhood directly outside their front door."

I frown. That means civilians living in houses uncontrolled by the family directly outside their doorstep. "That feels more dangerous."

They crane their neck to meet my eye at the end of the bed. "It would be, if the surrounding blocks weren't full of their soldiers."

"All of them?" I blink at them.

They nod.

"How do you know?" I pull on the pants, buttoning and zipping them around my waist. They're perfectly tailored, like they were made for me and not pulled off the rack at a store as they must have been.

"They told me." They raise both their brows, their bright-blue eyes boring into mine with implication.

"They wanted you to know," I state and pull the sweater over my head.

"Exactly." They turn to study an expressionist painting of two men struggling to pull up a net full of fish with a crimson sun shining behind them. It features a bold color palette, the men drawn in blocky shapes, the fish blue and pink. "A threat is only as good as the weight behind it."

"Jesus." I tug my hair out from under the collar. It falls down my back in slightly frizzy waves. I wish I had my leave-in conditioner. "Very different from home."

Pat rolls onto their elbow to look at me. "How are you feeling?"

"Better." A shower and a change of luxury clothes has lifted my mood considerably. Especially after the debacle that was this morning. It's entirely unfair how little I affect Tamayo while the simple observation of her veined hands around a mug of coffee can make my mouth water and my core clench. Fucking ridiculous.

I survey myself in the floor-length mirror propped against the wall. The room Darius led me to last night is simple, like an elevated hotel room with distinctly Southeast Asian artwork and basic furnishings. Thankfully, there's an en suite bathroom with a clawfoot tub and a plethora of bath salts, which I took full advantage of this morning after I left Tamayo in the kitchen.

I smooth the sweater, which leaves a sliver of my stomach showing. It's a good day outfit, but it won't do for the Council. I sift through the clothes again, favoring the dresses at the end of the rack. She went all out. There are bags lining the floor marked Cartier, Christian Dior, Louboutin, and more. I wonder if Tamayo hand-picked each piece, though I can't imagine she has the time. At least, she shouldn't.

Pat rolls to lie on their side, head propped on the heel of their palm. They watch as I sort through, considering and rejecting option after option. "What's the plan, then?"

"You were there last night."

"Come on, tell me what you're scheming."

My eyes flick to the door.

They get the hint, peeking into the hallway before pushing it shut and leaning against it. "I wish we had music."

I pull out an emerald dress and hold it up against my chest. Too bright. I replace it on the rack.

"So?" Pat prompts.

"The plan is to figure out a way to save the family without marrying Marcus Ass-cardi."

They snort. "And how are we gonna do that?"

"I'm not sure yet." I take the hard drive out of my purse and hold it out to them. "But this will help."

"What is it?" They take it gingerly, as if it might explode in their hands.

I pull out a longer dress, more casual than the last, and immediately replace it. "The Gallo ledgers off Mother's computer."

Pat's eyes bug out of their head. "And you brought this here?" they whisper-scold.

"I need to understand how we got into so much trouble." To the point my parents don't think we can even keep the South without a merger.

"You think the answer is in here?" They regard the hard drive with skepticism.

I grab a gold dress. The hem is short, and the fabric shimmers with the light. It's cut low in the back, but the neckline hides most of my cleavage. Tasteful. I hang it so it faces outward on the rack. "We have three months to figure it out."

"Do we, though?" Pat counters.

"The Capones and the Falcones will side with us. They don't want a Gallo-Accardi merger." I refuse to call it a marriage. "It'd put them at too much risk and cut their power in half."

Pat tucks the hard drive back into my purse. "That won't buy you more than a month, and you know that."

I chew my lip. "I know."

"You two will need to schmooze your asses off." They lean against the door again, brows high.

"I know."

They continue as if I haven't spoken, as if they're not parroting my own thoughts back to me. "Even if the Council favors you tonight, they won't lift a finger against any Cardinal Family if Tamayo or her people are hurt."

"They will if I'm hurt."

They shoot me a sardonic look. "What, are you gonna follow Tamayo around for three months just in case she's attacked?"

"Don't be ridiculous." I dig through the clothes on the rack, searching for a skirt-blouse combo.

They cross their arms. "Good, 'cause I wouldn't have let you."

"What is it with people thinking they *allow* me to do anything?" I grumble.

"You know what I mean."

"I do." I shoot them an affectionate smile. "Thanks for always protecting me."

"Even when you're stupid," they amend.

I laugh. "Like last night?"

"If by last night, you mean always, then yes."

I shake my head, holding up a wine-colored leather pencil skirt next to a black turtleneck. "It's out of consideration for you, really—wouldn't want you to get bored."

"So, you just walk straight into danger and wave your tiny arms around"—they act out their words, making an expression like they're wearing stupidity on their face—"like you're hailing a helicopter and not a bullet?"

I swing the hanger, smacking them with the leather skirt. "They're not tiny! I have normal-sized arms."

"You're *tiny*, Z." They hold their thumb and pointer finger a hair's breadth apart. "Tiny."

"Well, you're freakishly long," I grouse.

"Thank you." They preen like a fucking non-binary peafowl, which I imagine as far more colorful than a dandy male peacock. "I worked really hard to grow taller than you."

I kick at their knees. "I will throw myself in front of a bullet just to spite you."

They dodge my assault easily. "Seriously, the tiniest *and* stupidest."

I lurch forward, intending to climb their back like a koala and make them submit. I get an arm around their neck the moment a knock sounds on the door. We both freeze.

"Off." They smack my arm, but I just cling tighter. "Zarina!"

"Come in!" I call as I scramble up their back.

The door swings open slowly, as if the person on the other side is unsure they're actually welcome. Tamayo peeks around the edge at the same time I wrap my legs around Pat's waist, a claw grasping their perfect bun.

Pat clamps a hand around my wrist. "If you pull, I swear to god, Z—"

"Sorry to interrupt." Tamayo leans a hip against the door frame, one hand in her slacks pocket, a barely suppressed smile dancing on her lips. She seems both amused and exasperated at the same time.

"No, you're not," Pat and I say at the same time with clashing tones. I'm cheery. Pat's annoyed.

"True. I'm not," Tamayo says.

"Well?" I prompt.

She holds up a piece of paper, the wax seal of the Council heavy on the edge. "We have a summons."

"And?" I readjust my grip on Pat's hair, and they huff.

Tamayo sucks her lips between her teeth to stop her smile. It has the same affect her usual unbothered air has on me—I want to make her lose control. I want to see that smile spread wide again, like this morning.

"Sunset tomorrow," she says. "The usual place."

I frown. "Mother won't like that."

"You'll need this." Tamayo pulls her hand out of her pocket, a black velvet box in her palm. She holds it out to me, and I can only stare. I know what's inside. There's no mistaking that box, what it means. What it *should* mean.

My grip loosens on Pat, and they catch my weight lest I tumble to the floor. I slide to my feet and step forward on shaky legs, plucking the box from Tamayo's hand. It's heavy. As heavy as the weight of disappointment that's been sitting on my chest since I snuck out of my childhood bedroom last night.

Tamayo stuffs her hand back in her pocket, but not before I catch her stretch it out as if it might cramp. She grabs the door handle, retreating into the hall, but she pauses. I don't look up, eyes stuck on the box in my hand.

"Wear the gold dress," she says. "It matches your eyes."

TAMAYO

$\mathcal{I}$ do everything in my power to avoid Zarina Gallo for the next twenty-four hours. It's not easy. We're both stuck in this compound, avoiding the guns circling the outer perimeter like vultures waiting for a last dying breath. Darius and I spar in the training room. I hole up in my office and actually catch up on paperwork for the first time ever. I avoid the kitchen, the second floor, any place Zarina might suddenly walk in wearing Darius's shirt and nothing else.

Like I didn't buy her the entire fall collection.

When she finally slips into the backseat of the car wearing the gold dress—the one that hugs her figure as if she was stitched into it, a slit slashing up her left thigh, and the back cut so low, it's practically missing—all that space I pushed between us snaps closed, a rubber band stretched too far. Avoiding her has only made her more potent. Her hair is shiny, and she smells of jasmine shampoo. Her red lips match her ruby necklace glinting in the low light of the streetlamps as Darius drives us across town to the firing squad. Or Council meeting. Same-same.

"Are you ready?" she asks.

I hum, not trusting my voice to be anything less than husky.

She assesses my outfit, starting at my Italian leather boots and ending at the collar of my silk shirt. "You look expensive."

I snort. "Thanks."

"And you didn't wear any weapons, right?" She fidgets with the chains of her purse, crosses and uncrosses her ankles.

"I didn't."

"Good. That's good." She chews on her lip, staring out the window before twisting again. "Make sure you kneel at the altar first. God before idols and men, or whatever."

I don't look directly at her, yet she's all I can see. "I know."

"Let me do most of the talking," she says.

I shake my head at that. "We'll both talk."

"I'm serious, Tamayo." She finally turns fully in her seat.

"So am I."

She huffs. "My mother yesterday was only a taste of what tonight will be."

"I'm not incompetent, princess." I pull my phone out when it buzzes—a capo reporting on today's weapons drop. It can wait. "I got where I am for a reason."

Zarina doesn't immediately reply, and I frown at her—her eyes are fixed on my hand where it holds my phone, brows furrowed. Headlights bounce through the cab and over her face, forcing her to blink. I tuck my phone away again.

"Your ring," she says.

I pull my left hand out of my pocket and hold it up where it catches the glow of passing streetlights. On the third finger sits a yellow-gold band inlaid with scrollwork similar to the tattoos on my neck. And set in its cradle is a large, oval ruby as beautifully cut as the one at Zarina's throat.

"Is that…" She gulps down the rest of the question.

"It is." I glance at her fists balled in her lap. Not a single ring adorns her fingers despite the heavy, black box I gave her yesterday. I want to ask, but I bite my tongue. She knows the Council far better than I do. She must have a plan.

Saint Christopher's Cathedral looms ahead, stained glass windows set in stone arches, statue saints standing guard along the parapets. We stop at the front steps, and I reach over, placing my hand around Zarina's knee and squeezing "We've got this. Just breathe."

And then her door is opening and Pat is offering their hand. Zarina takes it, her leg slipping out from under my grip as she steps out of the car. I follow after her, buttoning my suit jacket. A light drizzle patters against the sidewalk as we stride toward Darius already standing at the large, wooden double doors carved with the story of Christ.

At the bottom of the stairs, I grab hold of Zarina's hand. She frowns down at my fingers as they thread through hers. "Ready?"

She straightens her back until she's scowling down her nose at me. "Born ready."

I grin wide, canines biting my bottom lip, and lift her knuckles to my mouth. "Let's go, princess."

Darius holds open the door as we walk across the threshold to face the Council. He doesn't follow us in. Weapons are forbidden within these stone walls—no bodyguards, no guns, no knives. It is the most important rule among the Cardinal Families, borne out of bloody necessity. Our steps echo through the chamber as we cross into the nave. The ceilings sweep in repeated arches above the wooden pews, and prayer candles flicker when we pass, Zarina's gold dress glittering in their light. Saint Christopher's is the oldest Catholic church in the city, and the Cardinal Families have called it safe harbor for nigh on a century—since long before the rules of engagement were established and viciously enforced. I've never set foot in here, not allowed to attend mass or confessional as a dishonorable gang leader.

I worship a different goddess, anyway.

In the front rows sit five men. There should only be four. I toss Zarina a frown, but she's aiming a vicious glare at the dark-brown head of hair sitting in the pew beside another peppered gray. He turns in his seat, and I almost trip over the rug.

Marcus Accardi.

He wears a self-satisfied smirk that screams over-confidence as his eyes trail down Zarina's figure, stopping on the slit in her dress and the leg-ass combination it draws attention to, and licks his bottom lip. Zarina snorts, unbothered. But something like a huffed growl rumbles through my chest. I want to curl my hand around her waist and yank her behind me. I want to punch the hungry look off Marcus's face.

Instead, I wait until his gaze rolls back up and his eyes shift to mine, like he's waiting for my reaction. I offer him a lazy grin and a wink. He scowls.

In the row ahead of him sits a man with a head of hair the same color and curl as Zarina's—Riccardo Gallo. But where his shoulders are high around his ears, his neck reddening, Zarina stands tall and powerful. Every inch a princess.

At the altar, I release Zarina's hand to slip it around her waist, stroking my thumb across the bare skin of her back. The smallest gasp breaches her lips. I lean in to kiss her temple, offering my other hand to help her keep balance as she kneels before God.

I lower myself beside her. We draw the same cross before us and bow our heads toward the crucifix suspended above. I rise immediately, but Zarina stays for a breath longer. Her fingers trace the gold chain of her necklace, the ruby hung by a noose, as her eyes remain closed. She pulls in one, two, three steadying breaths before she lifts her hand. I take it and help her stand.

She turns without a glance to me, shoulders back and chin high, to address the four patriarchs of the Cardinal Families and the most powerful men in Louredo. "Zarina Gallo, daughter of

Alessandra and Riccardo Gallo, appearing before the Council of her own volition."

"Welcome, Zarina Gallo." David Capone, don of the North, sits in the front-most pew as the eldest Council member, hair streaked gray and a glorious mustache atop his lip. He wears an ill-tailored suit, the jacket too big for his skinny frame.

I step forward, standing shoulder-to-shoulder with Zarina. "Andrea Tamayo, appearing before the Council at their request."

David Capone, who just addressed Zarina with something like affection, hitches his lip at me with affronted disgust. Zarina's knuckles whiten on her clutch, but mine remain relaxed in my pockets, my face unbothered, if not slightly amused. David rakes his blue eyes up and down my body in a way that takes stock of its capital-worth rather than of its patriarchal-pleasantry.

He dismisses me without a word. "Zarina, your family worries for you."

My gaze shifts to Riccardo Gallo and the Accardis in the pew behind him—Marcus and his father Alonso.

Zarina bows her head deferentially. "Thank you. But these worries are unfounded. As you can see, I am safe and healthy."

David continues to lead the meeting despite the quiet scoff falling out of Alonso's mouth. "And yet you arrived escorted by Andrea Tamayo."

"Yes," Zarina answers.

David's eye twitches, like he wants to squint a scowl at her for impertinence. "Did Andrea compel your attendance tonight?"

Two minutes into the meeting, and Alonso's face is purpling with unsaid words, teeth clenched and bared as if he's physically stopping them from spilling out. Marcus is more collected, waiting and watching.

"Tamayo," Zarina corrects, triggering a burst of warmth in

my chest, "did no such thing. We are here together to present to the Council."

And they called us both.

"Perhaps Andrea should leave." David ignores Zarina's correction. "So that you can speak freely."

If it weren't for the circumstances leading Zarina to my club and us to this meeting on cursed ground, I might think David Capone was being kind. That he was asking the correct questions to be certain Zarina is unharmed and safe. But Marcus Accardi sits behind David, his eyes narrowed and posture relaxed, assured in the knowledge that he'll never be asked to stand here, before the Council, and answer for his sins despite his bloodied hands.

And Zarina's parents mean to marry her off to him, the city's most cruel prince. No one asked her then if she was compelled. No one pulled her aside to be sure she was safe.

I clench my jaw at the same time Zarina forces hers open. "I speak freely now," she says. "Tamayo stays."

A prickle shivers over my scalp at her words. They offer no space for dissenting opinion or contradiction, wielding subtle power over the Council. Over me.

Jimmy Falcone leans forward, elbows on the pew in front of him and one hand gentle on David's shoulder. His black hair is long enough to brush his shoulders, and his eyes are a striking hazel-green that bore into me then Zarina. "Before yesterday, you had never visited the Tamayo Family."

"Not in Tamayo territory," she says. Just as Juliet never left her tower to visit Romeo until they married.

"Explain," he demands.

Zarina returns his stare with her own. "I'm a woman, Mr. Falcone. And a lesbian woman at that."

Every single man shifts in his seat. The rage on Alonso's face contorts into disgust. Marcus's eyes alight as if this is the source of all his fantasies. And Riccardo Gallo can't even look at his daughter, like he's either ashamed of her or himself. I can't tell which. The other two, David and Jimmy, fidget as if she's just spoken about vaginal discharge, God forbid. I shift my weight back half a step and allow Zarina the spotlight she deserves. Let them choke on their hypocrisy.

"And as a queer woman"—her gaze settles on her father—"I am not afforded the same liberties to meet with lovers as you and your sons are."

David Capone scoffs in offense at the insinuation that every man in this room, including him, has a lover other than his wife. Despite its veracity.

Jimmy, though, only smirks in amusement. "So you've been meeting in secret."

"For months, yes," she lies. We agreed to keep it mostly vague.

"What prompted you to expose your relationship yesterday?" he asks.

Zarina doesn't shift her gaze away from Jimmy. "The Gallo-Accardi merger."

Alonso's clenched jaw finally unhinges. "Marriage! Marcus wants to marry you. This is not business!"

Zarina snorts, still not shifting her focus from Jimmy. "I've spent a sum total of twenty minutes alone with Marcus in my entire life. This is anything *but* romance."

"You object to the marriage," Jimmy cuts in before Alonso can sputter a retort.

She arches a brow. "For obvious reasons."

Alonso shoves to his feet with a pointed finger, spittle flying from his lips. "Your lifestyle choices don't exclude you from your duty to your family! We all make sacrifices."

Marcus yanks his father back down into the pew as he settles his gaze on Zarina with outright lust. "Our marriage doesn't have to mean you sacrifice your...proclivities."

My hands ball into fists in my pockets, and my eye twitches, my mask of indifference fraying at the edges. David shifts, wood creaking under him, and looks away from Zarina. Riccardo stares at the crucifix like he's the one hanging from the cross, nailed down and unable to change the direction of this meeting, of the decision forming among these silent men, powerful enough to stop this but not lifting a finger to do so. To them, Alonso has a point. And it seems that point is more important than the threat of combining the power of the South and West.

Jimmy leans back in his pew, watching us both like he's waiting for our next move.

Zarina must come to the same realization as I do. She blinks and affects a somber expression belied by her tight grip on her purse. "I understand that," she says. "Death before dishonor—these are the Gallo Family words. They mean we keep true to our deals, pay our debts, keep others beholden to theirs." She fiddles with the zipper, glances down at my hand still gripping her waist, and straightens again. "And they're the reason why I cannot accept Marcus's proposal."

Riccardo's head snaps up, and he finally *looks* at his daughter. She doesn't look at him, her eyes steady on David Capone's, the eldest Council member and their northern star.

"I cannot agree, because I already accepted another proposal." She unzips her purse, fingers trembling. The Council might think she's nervous, but the tension in her arms, her thighs and shoulders, speaks of her checked urge to lunge forward. I want to pull her tight against me, take the weight of her body so that she can rest. But I stand still. This is her show, her fate on the line, and I won't ruin it.

She takes out the black velvet box I presented to her yesterday and fumbles the lid. On the satin bed inside rests a large, clear ruby surrounded by diamonds and set on a narrow, gold band. It's simple, apparent wealth without being gaudy. Her mouth opens with a little *oh* as she studies the engagement ring, and I wonder if she didn't look at it until now.

For the first time since this farce of a meeting started, I step in front of Zarina. I pluck the ring from its seat, and she watches, eyes wide, as I lower to one knee, her left hand in mine, and slip the ring onto her finger. It spans the length of her first knuckle, the edges scraping her neighboring fingers. I lean forward and press a kiss to the back of her hand. She releases another gasp and swallows hard.

Someone clears their throat.

Zarina's gaze snaps up to the Council, like she forgot they were there. She squeezes my hand, still in hers, and pulls me to my feet. I thread my fingers through hers, her engagement ring knocking against my knuckles.

"I cannot marry Marcus Accardi"—Zarina speaks clearly, a hint of smugness in her voice as she meets Alonso's churlish rage then Marcus's irate indignation—"because I am already engaged. To Andrea Tamayo."

ZARINA

$\mathcal{A}$ll four dons focus on Tamayo.

As if the moment she slipped the ruby ring onto my finger, I became invisible. I am no longer Zarina Gallo, heiress to the Southern Districts and daughter of one of the most powerful families in Louredo. Now, I am only Andrea Tamayo's fiancée, inheritor of her last name and mistress to a local gangster. Bitterness coats my tongue as Tamayo stands at my shoulder, neither ahead nor behind, and slips her hand out of my fingers and around my waist.

"This is ridiculous," Alonso spits. I would like to agree, but for different reasons.

Jimmy holds up a hand for quiet. "When did this happen?" He's studied us this whole time, smart enough to see through our sham but shrewd enough to let it play out. As don of the Eastern Districts, he can't afford to cede more power. Not with the gentrification of the South and West moving half his high-rolling clientele across town.

"I asked her last month," Tamayo answers for me. For us. My shoulders stiffen, and she drags her thumb across the bare skin of my back, teasing at the edge of my dress. "She said yes."

"I would've known." Father's voice is low and strained. To anyone else, it might sound like he's holding back anger, but I'm not just anyone. I've spent all twenty-six-years of my life deciphering the tones of his voice, learning when to avoid him and his bitter, verbal lashings. "I would know if my daughter was rolling around in the mud."

I whip my head around and suck in a breath to fire back, but Tamayo physically pulls me against her side and squeezes my ribs in a grip that's both staying and punishing.

"We were forced to hide it." Tamayo stands steady, entirely unbothered by the insult heavy in Father's words. I don't know how. I could rake my nails down his face right now. She continues, "Seeing as you don't approve."

"Understandable." Jimmy brushes off his thighs and stands, adjusting his suit jacket. "It seems this meeting was unnecessary."

"Unnecessary?" Alonso sputters.

Marcus sits next to him with a darkening glower and clenched jaw, the opposite of the idiotic smirk he wore when we entered. I toss him the same smug wink he gave me then.

He growls.

Jimmy speaks before Marcus can push out of his seat. "With their engagement, it renders the Accardi claim null. As well as yours, Ricci. She's not been kidnapped, she's eloped."

"They're not married yet!" Alonso's face has progressed past tomato red into heart-attack purple, and I wish he would succumb to it already.

David Capone sits in the front pew, eyes flicking between us and Jimmy and Alonso, face wrinkled in disgust as if he's seen a cockroach scuttle across the floor and disappear beneath the baseboards. He buttons and unbuttons his jacket, like he's unsure if he should stand and end the meeting with Jimmy or if he should stay sitting and end my ungodly, improper engagement to another woman.

"Married or not, they've entered a contract. Those rings are as binding as blood." Jimmy leans a hip against the back of David's pew, mostly talking to him while answering Alonso. "A deal is unbreakable. It's our most basic law."

"We're all liars, James." Father's voice is so quiet, I can hardly hear him. His most dangerous decibel level.

"Not on the Council," Jimmy growls. "Not since the Russos."

Alonso's glare snaps to Jimmy at the mention of his long ago betrayal of the fallen fifth family. Their name is only whispered behind closed doors or when their surviving son's entry into a gala is announced to the room. They are the bloody blight threaded into the fabric of our city's history and splattered over Alonso Accardi's name. The cautionary tale to us all when deals have no merit and Louredo no keepers.

Their name serves the purpose Jimmy intended: It spurs David to his feet with a clearing of his throat. A deal made by a member of the Cardinal Families must be upheld by all of them, even if it goes against every fiber of their sanctimonious, hypocritical beings.

"You've caused quite a ruckus, Andrea," he says. As if I, a ranking member of a Cardinal Family, am not the entire reason he must hold up our "distasteful" agreement at all.

"I apologize, Mr. Capone." Tamayo sounds properly contrite. I have to lock my gaze on David's mustache to keep from rolling my eyes.

"Don't let it happen again, hm?" He winks at her, like she's a child caught sneaking candy—me—from the jar.

Alonso slams his hands on the back of a pew. "This is ludicrous! There's no proof—"

"Andrea has the marriage rite," David announces. He avoids looking at me, buttoning his suit jacket and fussing with his cuffs. "The Council awaits an invitation to celebrate with you both."

The unspoken threat thickens the air around Tamayo and me. *Don't make a fool of him, or else.*

"We'll set a date soon," Tamayo says.

"Splendid." David clears his throat and turns for the aisle. He offers Tamayo a handshake, still not looking at me. "Stay smart."

"Keep safe," she replies with the customary farewell.

And then he turns on his heel and strides away. Not one further word uttered to me. Not even a wave or a nod. Tamayo's thumb swipes over my ribs, and I almost rip myself away from her touch, too incensed to be told to calm down, whether aloud or not.

Instead I lean in to whisper in her ear, fake smile stretched across my face. "I need to leave before I scream."

"Be good." She clutches my waist tight. If I weren't fuming, my skin hot with the anger swirling inside me, I might shiver. "Straight to the car."

"Five minutes, or I leave without you." I kiss her cheek and thank Jimmy as he congratulates us—Tamayo, really—then slip out of her grip before she can draw me close to her side again.

I've spent most Sundays in this church, watching a man preach from the pulpit with gold hung around his neck as if he was a god himself. I hate this fucking place.

I stride down the aisle without glancing to my father, or to the Accardis, though I know each one of them wishes they could stop me. I don't offer them the chance. All I want is a few moments alone, without anyone watching me, without anyone undressing me with their eyes, without anyone searching for a chink in the armor of my glare. Just me and deep breaths until the urge to tear something, anything, apart finally seeps out of me.

The doors to the nave swing shut behind me, placing a physical barrier between me and the men who continuously try to rule my life. My shoulders loosen infinitesimally, and I stretch out my jaw, trying to ease the pulsing ache from the force of my clenching. Blood pumps loud in my ears, and I wish I was already back at Tamayo's, in a hot bath with a glass of wine.

The door creaks behind me.

I jerk straight again, the small relief I felt hardening into steel around my spine. When I swivel on my heel, my elbow is grabbed with a rough hand, and I'm swung around off-balance into a hard chest. Fingers grab my chin tight enough to leave a bruise if they don't loosen.

Marcus Accardi forces me to meet his eye. "You've made a right mess of things."

He's a handsome man, objectively speaking. Strong jaw with full lips and bright, golden-brown eyes. His hair is thick and curly, his shoulders broad. But he's a pig wrapped up in old power and rich silks. A pig with his hands on me.

I wrap my fist around his wrist and dig my fingers between the tendons there. He doesn't flinch. I summon my most smug expression despite his harsh grip on my chin, his nails carving half-moon imprints over my skin. "Thanks, it's my specialty."

"It's fucking stupid," he snaps.

"So was thinking you could marry me." I apply enough pressure that I think my acrylic nails might snap before they pierce his skin.

His thumb pulls down my bottom lip, pressing hard as he studies my face like he wants to paint it with something other than watercolor. "You shouldn't use such a pretty mouth for speaking, darling."

I jerk forward, teeth first, but he pulls his thumb back before I can bite it.

"Such a wild thing," he muses. "I wonder how long it will take to break you."

The words sink in, and more than his assault, more than his too-familiar touch, more than his leering glare, they send a wash of ice over my scalp and down my neck. Because he would break me, given the chance. And my parents would like to give him the chance.

I drag my nails down his arm, ripping his skin. "Let me go, Marcus."

He steps forward, forcing me back until my shoulders smack against the stone wall of the antechamber, his hands somehow even tighter on my chin and elbow. If he shifts his grip just so and applies more pressure, he could strangle me. He could pin me against this wall and force more than his hands on me.

And I can't do much about it. One mark on his pretty head, one drop of blood spilled, and it'd spark a war. But his trespassing on my body and the subsequent pain? It'd be swept away and hidden under the rug. Another woman ruined by a man.

Marcus towers over me to snarl in my ear. "You're mine to hold, Zarina. Mine to marry. You made a promise I don't intend to keep."

I refuse to be just another woman who cowers and shudders away. I wrap my hand around his neck before he can flinch and press my fingers against his carotid. "Let me go. Now."

He releases my chin finally, but only to brush over my knuckles like they're a necklace rather than a noose. I grind my teeth and squeeze harder.

"Marcus!" Father's voice booms through the entrance hall.

Marcus smirks with all the vicious intention of a starved predator. He taps the blood-red ruby engagement ring on my finger wrapped around his throat. "Until next time, darling."

He releases me and steps out of my grip, glancing back at Father. Before he can turn, before Father can stop me, before I can stop myself, I rear back and slap him with my full strength. His head snaps with the force of it, and I shove him backward hard enough to make him stumble.

My chest shakes, but my voice does not. "Touch me again, and I'll do my fucking worst, Marcus Accardi."

"Zarina!" Father scolds.

Marcus holds up his hand. "Nothing happened, Ricci." He says my father's nickname like he's speaking to a child, and it makes me want to slap him again. "Just a little caress between lovers."

"Never," I hiss.

Father stands between us, his back to me as he addresses the pig. "Marcus, leave us."

He wiggles his fingers in a condescending wave. "Good night, darling."

"Choke, Marcus." I glare as he backs away with the same too-smug, lecherous look he wore when we arrived.

"Zarina Giovanna Gallo, behave yourself," Father mutters.

The door thumps shut behind Marcus, and I snatch the handkerchief out of Father's jacket pocket to wipe it over my face. Lipstick darkens the white fabric alongside smears of concealer, and yet not a speck of the disgust crawling over my skin comes off.

"What have you done?" Father spits the words at me through clenched teeth.

I rub off the rest of my lip color before shoving the handkerchief at his chest. "I saved myself from a lifetime of abuse and guaranteed murder."

Father takes the fabric with an exasperated huff. "We know who Marcus is. We had a plan!"

"And what plan was that? Negotiate a no-wife-beating clause?"

He wrinkles his nose and looks away, and my fucking god, that *was* the plan.

My mouth drops. I can still feel the pressure of Marcus's fingers on my chin, his thumb on my lip, his grip around my neck. "No clause in any contract would ever keep that man's hands to himself. You were fooling yourself. Both of you."

"It doesn't matter now, because we no longer have the

leverage to negotiate anything." He rubs over his face, as if he can wipe away the truth. When he drops his hand, shadows line his eyes and hollow his cheeks. The signs are there—have been there for months. But I didn't pay attention.

I step closer, lowering my voice. "Why negotiate the deal at all, Father?"

He shakes his head, waving his hand.

"Please," I plead, "just tell me."

"Your mother will kill me," he whispers.

"Wouldn't be the first attempt," I say.

"Zarina."

"Father." I use the same chastising tone he does. Despite the specter of Marcus's face looming over me, his fingers digging into my skin, his breath hot on my ear, and the overwhelming urge to run out of here to scrub myself clean of all of it, I can't help but lean closer to my father. The Gallos—my family—are in trouble. I want to help.

"Please," I whisper again, "let me help."

Father stares at the handkerchief, at the makeup smeared across it, before crumpling it in his fist and shoving it in his pocket. He raises his head, and I know without a word that he's the same proud, stupid man he's always been.

"Are you really marrying Andrea Tamayo?" he asks.

I sigh. "Does it matter?"

"No," he snorts. Like this is the most unbelievable, unacceptable part of this entire sham of a meeting, rather than his failure as a father, a don, and a man. "I guess not."

Father sniffs and rolls his shoulders back, walking to the door without another glance. "Stay smart."

I watch him leave me, makeup ruined with smarting bruises forming on my chin, and wish for the first time in a long time that I wasn't his daughter. "Keep safe."

TAMAYO

y eyes follow Zarina down the aisle and out of the nave. Only when the door clicks shut behind her, when Jimmy's hand squeezes mine in an unspoken demand for my attention, do I shift to fully face him.

He wears a boyish smile that makes his eyes gleam with something on the edge of violence. "I'm interested to see how this plays out."

We glance over at Marcus, who's ignoring his father and Riccardo Gallo's conversation in favor of slipping out of his pew and glaring at me. I snort.

Jimmy turns back to me with a small chuckle. "I'd advise a short engagement."

"Easier said than done." I roll my tongue over my molars. Only the other night, one of his capos insulted me, attacked me, reneged on a deal. And now, for the first time ever, the Falcone don and I are having a tangible conversation. "Zarina and I have much to discuss. Almost as much as I have to discuss with you."

"Is that so?" He arches a brow.

I scuff my boot against the crimson rug under my feet as if there's still scum on the toe. "I met Antoni on Thursday."

Jimmy bares his teeth at the name. "He may have mentioned it. Was hard to understand, what with his broken nose."

"Oh, he's injured?" I feign concern. "Send him my wishes for a quick recovery."

"Hm." Jimmy purses his lips and runs his gaze over me, stopping on the ruby engagement ring heavy on my finger. "If you want to tell him yourself, we'll be at Casa Nostra Wednesday evening—stop by."

I tamp down a triumphant grin and keep my face subdued. "Will do."

"See you then." Jimmy turns on his heel with a wave of his hand.

"Stay smart," I call the traditional farewell.

"Keep safe," he replies.

I stand before the altar, the thunk of the heavy wooden door echoing through the empty nave. There's no tête-à-tête waiting for me; Riccardo and the Accardis disappeared without my notice. But Zarina waits for me. Mine to take home, to claim, to marry—at least according to the Council. The only ruling that really matters and the only opinion that doesn't. Fucking ironic.

I stride down the aisle, unwilling to spend another moment on the mob's hallowed ground, and push into the antechamber. Where the front door stands open with Darius fidgeting in its frame.

Darius doesn't fidget.

I pause mid-step and frown. Behind him, the night is blue-black with yellow-glowing street lamps dotting the sidewalks. The steps are empty, and on the curb, our car is the only one left. All seems well. But Darius is fidgeting.

"What is it?" My voice is a low timbre, a warning.

Darius grimaces—he knows that tone—and glances behind him like something is there. He sighs. "Something happened—"

"Where the fuck have you been?" Pat shoves him aside,

though Darius barely moves, their face pinched in anger and blue eyes bright as a flame.

I ignore them. "Darius?"

He clenches his jaw, his fist at his side. *Fidgeting.* "Something happened to Zarina."

I grind my teeth and wait. Pat's looking at me like I should already know and Darius like he would rather tell me anything else but this. I shake my head. "Well? What happened?"

"She won't say," Darius grumbles.

"Because it's fucking obvious!" Pat huffs and crosses their arms, their face covered in derision.

"We don't know anything yet," he says.

"Typical male bullshit." They scoff at him. "As if we need hard evidence Marcus laid hands on her. Her face is *bruised*, for fuck's sake—"

I shove past them.

I've heard more than enough. Pat is right—I don't need to know what happened to *know what happened.* Marcus Accardi doesn't deserve the benefit of the doubt, isn't innocent until proven guilty.

Pat calls after me to leave Zarina alone, but I ignore them and round the car, throwing open the door. Zarina sits on the other side of the bench seat, hugging her knees to her chest, forehead pressed against her thighs, shoulders shaking with suppressed sobs. I climb inside and yank the door shut in Pat's affronted face.

Zarina raises her arms up enough to hide from me, as if I cannot read the rest of her body as well as a billboard. I sigh and slide over, holding my arms open in a silent offering she can accept or reject. She leans against me without showing her face, and I take that as a silent yes, scooping her up in my arms, shifting her legs over my lap, encouraging her head to my chest.

The car pulls away from Saint Christopher's and the site of what may as well have been our own crucifixion. Zarina and I don't speak, not with words. I rub circles over her back and shoulders, stroke her hair, and ignore the growing wet spot on my shirt. And Zarina cries. It's quiet, vibrating through the cavity of my chest, the pain and anger leaking out of her and absorbing into my skin. All the while, my imagination conjures up visceral images of me cracking my knuckles open on Marcus Accardi's bones.

The ride home is taking longer than necessary, and I'm positive Pat's at the wheel, driving us around town to give Zarina time. It makes me wonder how often Pat's done this for her. How often Zarina cries. How often someone assaults her.

It takes more effort than it should to keep myself calm at that thought.

Zarina sits up, breaking up my thoughts as she swipes under her eyes. "Sorry." Her voice is thick.

I shake my head and brush the tendrils that escaped her chignon off her temple. My fingers trail around her ear to cup her chin gently and tilt her head up to the light of the passing streetlights, their glow barely enough to illuminate the darkening bruises lining her jaw like shadows.

She winces as I turn her head left then right. "Is it bad?" she whispers.

I will my hand on her thigh to remain relaxed despite the inferno of violent rage licking through my chest. I imagine finding Marcus Accardi alone and repaying him tenfold for each bruise on Zarina's smooth skin—a broken bone in exchange for each broken blood vessel—and then leaving him shattered and scarred on his father's doorstep. Sounds fair to me.

But I can't. Not without retribution. And my rage won't help Zarina in this moment.

I release her face and pass her the handkerchief from my jacket pocket. "Nothing a little concealer won't fix."

She accepts the fabric, dabbing her face and blowing out a breath as she leans her back against the door, legs still on mine.

"Who?" I ask as if I don't already know the answer. Because Pat was right—we don't need proof for this.

"Marcus Ass-cardi," she spits. The name elicits a shudder from her, and this time I can't stop my hand before it balls into a fist. She watches my knuckles whiten with the force of my grip. "Caught up to me before I left the church."

A broken bone for each blood vessel. God damn it. "I shouldn't have left you alone," I say. "I'm sorry—"

She smacks my arm. "Shut up."

"Zarina—"

"Seriously, Tamayo—shut up." Zarina throws my handkerchief back at me, and it lands on my stomach. "Despite what you think, I'm not a damsel princess. I've fended off my fair share of handsy men."

I crumple the fabric in my fist before throwing it down on the seat. "This isn't some passerby in the club playing grab-ass."

"I know." She rolls her eyes, and it makes me want to shake her.

My voice drops low again, to the tone I use with capos who think they can cop an attitude on any given day. "This is the man who stands to lose all he was promised if he doesn't find a way to marry you."

"I know!" she snaps.

I stare at her until she meets my gaze, until she sees the heavy, frightening gravity of what I am saying, of the danger Marcus Accardi presents. He will not stop. He will not leave her alone. He will not accept the Council's verdict today. And likely, he never will.

Marcus Accardi cannot be fended off. He must be destroyed.

Zarina swallows and casts her eyes down to my hand on her thigh, her face pinched with petulance. "I won't be alone with him again."

"Thank you." I let it be at that. It's not enough, not nearly, but my own anxiety to prevent something like this from ever happening again won't help Zarina, either. I breathe it out as best I can and shift to better face her. She pulls in a shaky breath and squeezes her hands into fists over and over again. I don't know what she's thinking—whether she's reliving what happened or imagining worse—but it's not good.

"What do you need?" I rub my hands over her knee, across her thigh, trying to offer what little comfort I can.

Zarina follows my touch, lip between her teeth. Her eyes zero in, like she's grounding herself in my touch rather than the swirl inside her head. "I want my power back." She raises her gaze to mine, the gold streaks in her eyes shining in the passing streetlights. "I want to feel like I own myself, my body—not him. Not anyone."

I pause my movements, unsure if she means for me to stop. "How can I help?"

She blinks at me, pursing her lips, and then she's moving. I raise my hands, confused as she pulls herself across my lap, her legs parting to bracket my hips, her ass settling on my thighs. She grabs my wrists to place them around her waist.

"Help me erase him," Zarina whispers as she drags her fingers up my arms, to my shoulders, around my neck. "Put your hands on me."

ZARINA

For one, infinite moment, I think I misread the last few days.

Tamayo doesn't find me attractive. Or she's a born flirt who doesn't actually want to bend me over her knee. Or worse, she'll say no out of deference to my tarnished emotional state, as if I don't know what I need in this moment. As if that wouldn't be another choice ripped away from me in the long list of my life.

But then she flexes her hands on my waist.

"My hands are on you, princess," Tamayo rumbles.

I arch into her fingers, but she doesn't react. She's wearing that infuriating smirk on her lips again, that unbothered air she's had since she sat on her throne and raked her burnt-bark gaze down my naked thighs. I scratch through her undercut, down her neck, under the collar of her jacket and shirt. "Touch me."

She chuckles, deep and raspy, the sound vibrating from her chest into mine. "I can't read minds, princess."

I huff and lean forward until my nose hovers over hers. I've been clear as day—erase him. Scrub away his touch with hers. What more do I need to say? My skirt rides up my thighs as her breath fans my lips. The car is warm, but the air is still cooler than the heat pooling under her hands. I drag my nose across her cheek to her ear, my lips brushing the lobe—

"Zarina." Tamayo's voice is hard as a whip. My whole body freezes on impact, a shudder rippling over me a second later. She cups my chin in a gentle hand, so opposite the grip that held it earlier, and guides me to sit straight again. She furrows her brows, searching my face. "What do you want?"

I roll my eyes, and she clucks her tongue. "I told you," I say.

Tamayo studies my face, eyes catching on the smarting bruises bracketing my chin. "You want to own yourself, your body."

"Yes." I roll forward an inch.

Her grip on my waist tightens. "You want to erase him."

"His touch, yes." I'll erase his presence from this Earth later. For now, this will do.

Her fingers smooth over my jaw to thread in my hair, and she leans in, in, in. Until her lips graze my cheekbone. Until her heartbeat is pulsing through her chest into mine. Until the distance between us is a sliver of space that feels too close and too far. Her words brush against my cheek. "So take what you want, princess."

I frown and try to pull back, but her hands hold me in place. "But I want you to do it."

Tamayo chuckles under her breath and settles back against the seat again, her fingers leave my hair and trail down my arm to rest on my waist again. Unbothered again. "I don't think you've earned that yet, hm."

"Tamayo." I harden my voice.

She arches a brow. "Take what you need."

This has never happened before. "Seriously?"

"Sorry, princess." She rolls her tongue over her molars. "I only fuck good girls who use their words."

"I did!"

"If you had…" Tamayo murmurs. She hasn't moved, still laid back against the seat as if Zarina Gallo, mob princess with curves wrapped in gold and sin, isn't sitting in her goddamn lap. I don't beg. Not for anyone. Her fingers dig into the top of my ass, pulling the fabric of my dress and making my skirt bunch up even more. At this point, my panties are on full display. And so is the darkening wet spot I would very much like Tamayo to take care of. But she stays stubbornly in place and keeps talking. "I might've skimmed my hands up your legs, under your pretty dress."

Her nails scrape up my back, skimming over fabric until they meet skin. The small tease has me arching my back again, wishing it was everywhere.

"I might've brushed my thumbs along the crease of your thighs, played with the hem of your panties."

My hips roll forward of their own accord.

"How do you prefer it, princess?" She helps me rock, forward and back over the harsh fabric of her trousers, eyes lidded as she smirks up at me. "Slow and teasing? Hard and fast?"

"Tamayo." My voice is more of a whine than I intend.

"I think you like to tease, be teased. Like to push buttons until your partners snap." She scratches up my spine as I hold tight behind her neck. My hands burrow under the collar of her shirt again, seek out what little skin I can find as her thumbs slip under the edges of my dress, so close to my breasts that it's more maddening than igniting. I circle my hips until I find the exact right spot, pressing down and dragging my clit over the seam of her slacks.

Tamayo keeps talking in that low, taunting voice, the timbre vibrating through my body, down to my core. "And when they snap? You lie back while they do all the work. A princess playing at being queen."

"That's—no—not true." I shake my head, breath stuttering.

Sweat dapples my brow and gathers at my nape, and my thighs are burning with each undulation of my hips. All I want is her hands on me, flicking my nipple, clutching my ass, finding their way under my dress. Just the thought of it sends shudders through me.

"Look at you." She scoffs, lifting a hand to brush my hair behind my ear, patronizing. "You barely know what to do without me. Don't you wish I'd take over?"

I don't want to agree, but gods, *yes*. It's not enough. I need faster, harder, *more*. I try to snake my hand out from under her collar to do what she refuses, but she presses back and traps it. I try to lean closer, legs widening, body searching for friction, but Tamayo's hand slides up to grip my hair in a fist and hold me at a distance. I bite down on a whine.

She forces my gaze to hers. "Use your words, princess."

"Your hands," I breathe.

"They're on you." She traces her free hand down my back.

"No." I can't hold back the whine this time, chin dropping in frustration.

"Head up. Look at me." Tamayo holds my gaze, her pupils blown wide, black swallowing the brown. She tugs my hair, and it sends shivers through my scalp. We're inches apart, my hips circling, tension gathering in a whirlpool but never cresting into a tidal wave. She guides my face closer, fingers teasing the top of my ass, inches from where I want her. "You look so good riding my thigh. All you ever have to do is ask, Zarina, and I'm happy to help."

I can't hold back anymore, can't stop the word from spilling out of me. "Please."

A wide, satisfied smirk spreads over Tamayo's face. "Please what, princess?"

I dig my fingers into her skin, trying to pull her closer. I've never begged once in my life, not for anyone, but it tumbles out of me, desperation and want cracking my voice. "Please help me."

She doesn't budge. "Help you what?"

I press my clit harder against her thigh, and it jolts up my body, into my throat. "Can't come, not enough."

"Good girl." Tamayo closes the distance between us for the first time since I climbed in her lap and presses a kiss to my cheek. She speaks into my ear, "And what do I do with good girls, hm?"

"Fuck them." My pussy clenches in anticipation.

Before I can register what's happening, Tamayo's lifting me off her lap and maneuvering me to turn around and sit, my back against her chest. She wraps a hand around my throat without an ounce of pressure, simply guiding my head to rest against her shoulder as her fingers drag up, up, up the inside of my thigh.

"That's right." Tamayo bites my earlobe, and my ass presses into her. She holds me close as she swipes up the seam of me over my panties, the fabric soaked through. My breath hitches. Her teeth skim the skin behind my jaw. "I fuck them."

And then she finally, *finally* touches me.

If I couldn't stop myself begging, there's no hope to quiet the moan that falls from my mouth. Tamayo's grip twitches on my throat, like the sound is affecting her more than anything else I've done. She circles my clit, and I roll forward into her. I grab her wrist with both hands and ride her fingers, biting down on another too-loud moan.

"Ah, ah." She adjusts her grip on my neck, pressing her thumb on my chin until I give in, mouth falling open with a mewl. "That's right, princess. Let me hear you."

My body twitches of its own accord.

Tamayo hums in my ear, fingers stroking harder, my hips setting the pace.

Her grasp on my chin keeps my mouth open, and words

tumble out, broken and breathless. "Ooh, yes, Tamayo. Fuck me, please."

"Good girl," she rumbles. Her lips find my neck as she releases my chin, fingers slipping down to my chest. She licks below my ear at the same time she scrapes her nails over the thin fabric of my dress covering my nipple. My body shudders and throbs.

"Harder." I don't know what I mean—her hands, her teeth. I just *need*.

She answers. Her hand presses harder, rubbing faster over my clit; her teeth dig into the column of my neck; and her fingers pinch my nipple and pull, making my back arch and shooting sensation straight to my core.

And the whirlpool finally crests into a tidal wave.

I go taut as a bowline pulled tight in a storm until it snaps with the force of the wave, and then I'm tipping over, swirling under, lost at sea. My orgasm washes over me. Tamayo doesn't stop, holding me tight by my chest, teeth in my neck, fingers ushering me through like a lighthouse. My jaw drops wide, and a high mewl trembles out of me.

Small pecks litter my neck, and nails tickle up and down my arms. My chest heaves. I turn my face into Tamayo's ear, and a kiss lands on my forehead. Something warm soothes through me. Something unnerving in its unfamiliarity.

Tamayo's fingers leave my panties, drifting up my dress. I crack my eyes open to watch as she opens her mouth, her gaze holding mine captive. My wetness glistens over her knuckles, and when she brings them to her mouth to lick them clean, a sound unbecoming of a mafia princess crawls up my throat.

I look from her lips to her fingers and back to her lips. They're shiny with spit and *me*, beckoning me to lean in. She's inches away. The space is negligible, the distance between us simple to close. To taste myself on her tongue. I reach forward—

A knock cuts through the dense fog of lust.

I snap backward. At some point between when we started and when I finished, the car stopped moving. At some point, I forgot we were in a car.

"We're home," Pat's voice calls through the window.

Tamayo takes my weight under my elbows and helps me move onto the bench seat. I let her, yanking my skirt down like she didn't just have her hands on my pussy, on my breasts. I glance back to the door then to Tamayo reaching under the seat and pulling out a packet of wet wipes. She holds them out to me with a blank look, no longer smug nor lidded nor anything. It's worse than the unbothered smirk.

I wave off the offer. "What does this mean?"

"It doesn't have to mean anything." She takes a couple for herself, cleaning her hands then her pants. "We're consenting adults, and we both wanted this."

"And we're fake engaged."

She stuffs the dirty wipes into her pocket and slips the packet back under the seat. "This doesn't affect our deal."

Deal. Like what we did was just business. Detached and impersonal and nothing.

"So we just sweep it under the rug?" I ask. "Never speak of it again?"

Tamayo cocks her head. "Do you want more?"

I swallow hard. No. Yes. Maybe. "I don't know."

"Let me know when you do." She leans across me and opens the door without another word.

Pat stands on the other side, face blank except for the stern set of their jaw. I sit still for a moment, panties cooling against my skin, somehow both arousing and nasty at the same time. I don't know why, but annoyance simmers under my skin. This wasn't nothing. It was something. I just don't know *what.*

All I know is the black hole inside me that craves without

logic gnashes its teeth, just as greedy as it's always been. And it wants so much more. But I'm not sure if it should.

"Fine." I twist out of the car to stand on shaky feet.

"Good night, princess," Tamayo calls after me.

I roll my eyes and stride out of the garage, Pat on my heels and Darius's watchful gaze following me like I might turn around any moment and crack Tamayo across the jaw. While that might feel good for a moment, it wouldn't help the cum still wet in my panties. Or the echo of my orgasm thrumming in my veins.

Marcus who? My body can only think of Andrea Tamayo.

TAMAYO

’m drinking a vodka Collins again. Orange prickles across my tastebuds, but despite its tang, despite the heavy pour, it’s not enough to burn away the memory of Zarina’s cum sitting heavy on my tongue. Even multiple mouthwashes haven’t erased the taste of her. All I can think about now is giving in to the overwhelming urge to capture her lips in mine the next time I see her.

Kissing is not a good idea.

Hell, the Gallo princess coming on my thigh like it was a goddamn throne made for her pleasure was not a good idea, either. Not when I can’t get the taste of her out of my mouth, the smell of her off my fingers. I let a sip of my drink sit on my tongue, trying to burn away the memory of her.

A knock sounds on the office door. I call for them to come in, and Darius steps inside. He arches a brow as if drinking before Sunday mass is somehow more condemnable than all the other sins we commit. I scowl at him and take another gulp out of spite.

“We need to increase security around the shelter. Rita will hate it, but she’ll get over it.” I don’t turn to face him as I speak.

"Same with the Den. Tell Angie to suck my left big toe if she complains."

"Both are already done." He lowers himself into one of the comfy chairs in front of my desk as I mumble thanks.

"We need to discuss Casa Nostra later, too. And the properties in Gachico."

He hums in affirmation, staring at me.

I frown at him. "What?"

"Are we just not gonna talk about it?" he asks.

"About what?" I turn back to the window, because I know perfectly well what he means.

Apparently, he's out of patience anyway. "About you fucking the Gallo princess in the back of the car."

"Jesus." I fumble my glass and almost drop it.

The corner of his mouth twitches. "I don't think he has anything to do with it."

I set my drink on the desk, rolling my eyes and swiveling around to face him. He spills out of the chair, all limbs and muscles, and tamps down on the teasing smile threatening to form on his lips. I wipe vodka Collins off my hand on my very expensive trousers. "We didn't fuck."

He snorts. "Semantics."

I rest my chin on my palm, fingers on my cheek, and breathe in. Nope—they still smell like her. Like she came on them moments ago and not on the other side of a layer of fabric a night ago. I grind my teeth. "It doesn't matter, anyway."

The amusement coloring Darius's expression sloughs away. "And if it brings us to the edge of implosion?"

"Don't worry." I wave him off. "It didn't mean anything." And it won't. Not with both of us using the other, whether it's to forget the pain caused by our parents or protection or power. Feelings have no place between us. But fuck if I wish clothes had no place between us, too.

"Not yet," Darius mutters.

I raise my glass with a shake of my head. "Ye of little faith."

"Me of vast experience and observation." He leans forward, elbows on his knees, and stares at me with that stupid, blank face he wears when he's worried because he doesn't want me to know that he's worried but is unwittingly blaring loud and clear that he is, in fact, *worried*. I sip my drink and wait. Because there's no making Darius say it, there's only giving him space to.

His brows scrunch. "Andy."

"Darius," I mimic his serious tone.

He groans, falling back further in his chair. "How does this bring us closer to the goal? The fake engagement, the fucking, the stupid business deal—it's all window-dressing."

"I'm not explaining it again," I sigh. "You were there."

"And I still don't get it." He spreads his arms as if to encompass the lack of logic filling the room, his navy suit stretched to its limit across his chest and arms. "Get the princess out of town and take the meeting with Falcone."

I set my glass down too hard. Despite being mostly empty save for the ball of ice and the orange twist, liquid spatters over the desk. "Do you think we'd have this invitation without her? Do you think Jimmy Falcone would even *speak* to me if I wasn't engaged to Zarina fucking Gallo?" I rein in the glare I want to aim at Darius—this isn't about him. It's about the futility of years of plotting and battling my way to this exact moment, only to have the daughter of the family I swore to tear asunder, brick by brick, be the reason I finally achieve it. And worse, it's about the way that same woman has sunk into my skin like a goddamn perfume, no soap strong enough to erase her.

I scrape my hands over my face and let them drop to the arm rests. "Don't be purposefully dense. Zarina was right—her family name, as much as I fucking hate it, brings us respect. The most we could have expected from Antoni's idiocy was a meeting with another capo, not with the don."

Darius wrinkles his nose. "You don't know that."

"It's what I would have done." I slump back and stare at the ice melting in my tumbler, wishing it was full again so I could gulp it down. I push out of my chair and grab the belt and waistcoat I hung up earlier, unwilling to be so restricted while I pouted into my drink.

Darius crosses his arms. "There's nothing keeping her here or from crossing us."

I yank on the deep-violet waistcoat over my collared shirt. "Except the threat of a forced marriage to a savage prick?"

He scoffs like that's not so big a deal as to make Zarina run away from home and strike a deal with a gangster she'd never met. I want to smack him upside the head. But he speaks before I can reach him. "And after all this is over?"

He means after Zarina is gone.

I clamp my mouth shut, eyes on my fingers buttoning my waistcoat. When the Accardis and their cruel son are no longer a threat, Zarina will leave. With less territory and more information on the Tamayo Family. Which means Darius isn't wrong —she has no reason to stay, to keep our secrets—and that's infuriating. Even more so because I don't have a back-pocket solution that will solve this problem. And that's unacceptable.

I push it down into the well of my brain where it can steep longer in the muck until a solution will rise fully formed. "A lot can happen between now and then."

"That's what worries me," he sighs.

I button my cuffs. "Not much we can do about it now."

"You could not fuck her and make her hate you?" he snaps.

My hands pause, and I turn to study him fully. He fidgets with the ring on his right pointer, twirling the diamond around and around. He watches his fingers, eyes unfocused and brows furrowed.

I speak softly. "Not all relationships end in heartbreak, Darius."

His shoulders bunch as if bracing for impact. He forcibly

relaxes them, his hands falling to his lap and his face fumbling for unaffected nonchalance. "So it's a relationship now?"

I let him change the subject and pull my jacket off its hanger. "Didn't you hear? She's my fiancée."

He groans, his head rolling back on his chair. "You know what I mean!"

"You're a worrywart," I tease as if I'm not at all.

"Yeah, I'm fucking worried!" He shoves to standing and crowds in front of me. "I'm worried Zarina will fuck us over, and I'm worried your need for revenge will push this too far, and I'm really fucking worried that you're not worried at all!"

I stuff my hands in my pockets and stare at him with all the anger of a woman willing to murder and steal and deal her way from broken in a back alley to the inner sanctum of Louredo's crime families. I didn't get here by being an idiot, by miscalculating. Darius knows that. He's been with me since before the beginning. My best friend, my right hand.

And sometimes he thinks that allows him certain privileges. Like insulting me.

"It sounds like"—my voice rumbles through my chest—"you think I'm being careless and stupid."

Darius has the good sense to back the fuck up. "Andy—"

"The goal is the same as it's always been, Darius." I prowl forward as he stands completely still, muscles tense. "Whatever it takes to become a don, to become a family with a seat at the goddamn table, to protect our people and give them a piece of the pie. We will use Zarina Gallo as a stepping stone to more territory, more power, more respect." I roll my shoulders back, breathing through my nose and dialing down the simmering boil in my gut. "We're already set to make good on respect, now it's about garnering the other two. I can't do it alone—I need Zarina."

Darius takes my jacket from where it's tucked between my arm and hip, shaking it out and holding it open for me. An olive branch, which I accept. I thread my arms through, and he smooths down the sleeves as I adjust my wrist cuffs.

His hands fall away. "And the revenge?"

My knee twinges at the mention. "What's more demeaning than watching your only daughter and appointed heir defy your orders, run away from home, and marry the head of a gang so far beneath Zarina's station that her parents are threatening to stop the wedding before it can ruin their reputation?"

"I know you, Andy. That's not enough."

"No, it's not." I grab my handgun, double-checking the safety before slipping it in my waistband. "They left me broken. I plan to do the same."

"How?" he asks.

"Mine Zarina for every bit of affluence I can while ruining her for anyone else, especially anyone considered powerful enough for the Gallo name. She'll always be my castoff, always be the weak, spoiled princess who couldn't close a simple deal with Louredo's only lesbian gangster." And by the time this engagement is over, that will be true. We'll be more than a gang. We'll own a true piece of this city and keep growing, swallowing up streets and buildings until we're as fat and powerful as the Cardinal Families sitting at the top of their towers not noticing the foundations are rotting beneath them. Not noticing I'm eroding them like water, slow and steady. "The shame of her failure will infect the Gallo Family, hanging them by a noose of their own making. Even the Accardis will refuse to deal with them."

Darius snorts. "You're an idiot."

"What?" I whip around to look at him.

He shakes his head with amusement. "You really believe you'll be able to use her and leave her?"

"I'll do what's best for the family," I snap.

He sucks in a long-suffering breath. "Idiot."

"Don't make me shoot you," I growl.

Darius giggles—actually giggles. "I'm upping my bet." He grabs a pen and sticky note off the desk and writes it out. "A grand says this implodes before we see a foot of territory."

I smack his hand away with a scowl. "I'll do it. You'll see."

He crosses out the number to write a new one. "Five grand."

"Get out." I stomp over and yank open the door.

"Don't spend my money." He tucks the paper into my breast pocket, and I catch his wrist, twisting it back, but he breaks my hold easily.

"Out."

He pulls down his sleeve. "I got my eye on this watch at Cartier—"

I kick at his ankles until he dances into the hall to evade me. He's laughing as I shut the door behind us, turning the key to lock the deadbolt and shaking my head. "Moving *on.*" I punch his kidney without much force. "Casa Nostra."

We walk down the hall past the bedroom doors to the top of the stairs, and I have to work to stop my gaze from drifting to Zarina's door, my mind from wondering what she's doing, where she's at, how she is.

Do you want more?

I don't know.

"When do we infiltrate the devil's lair?" Darius rests his hand on the banister as he descends the stairs.

I stretch my jaw. "Wednesday."

ZARINA

$\mathcal{I}$ refuse to attend mass. Not after last night, standing before the Council where they sat in Saint Christopher's's pews, reigning judgment. Not after having Marcus's hands on my neck, on my chin. Not after Tamayo's touch pushing me over the edge. I can imagine the confessional now: *Forgive me, Father, for I have sinned. And I refuse to repent.*

I sink lower in the bathtub, bubbles up to my neck and body submerged. The shower I escaped into last night didn't do a thing to scrub away the feeling of Tamayo's touch, the sound of her voice in my ear. And this bath isn't helping either. Especially not when each brush of water feels like more.

My bedroom door clicks shut, and I glare at my unlockable bathroom door.

"Z?" Pat calls.

I sigh, shoulders easing. "In here!"

They step inside, checking the room as if someone might be hiding under the bubbles with me, and close the door behind them. They lean against the vanity with their hands stuffed in their pockets, the mirror reflecting their perfectly coiffed bun as they peer down at me with bright-blue eyes that may as well have X-ray vision. "So we're hiding."

"I'm soaking." I lift my hands out of the water with a pointed *duh* look.

Pat snorts. "You took an hour-long shower last night. Not clean enough?"

"Not after sharing a bed with your nasty ass."

They cross their arms with a squint. "Mmhm."

"Shut up." I slide down until my chin touches water.

"My mouth was closed."

"And yet sound still escapes," I grumble.

They take in a calming breath, like I'm the annoying one. "You've had twelve hours."

"For what?" I ask.

"To process. Now, explain."

I wish I had wine, but it's ten in the morning and I refuse to leave my room until Tamayo leaves the house. "Explain what?"

They blink without amusement. "Zarina Giovanna Gallo."

My full name? "Jesus."

"He's at church," they quip. "And I assume we're not meeting him there."

"Fine! Fuck, just—" I stand without decorum, bathwater sloshing onto the tiles and bubbles clinging to my skin. I can't be so exposed for this conversation. Pat hands me the towel off the hook before I can reach for it, and I murmur thanks as I wipe myself mostly dry before slipping into a fluffy robe.

"Start with the easy part—the Council." They hug their waist, opposite elbow resting on their wrist and knuckles under their chin. Their blonde hair is bright in the gray sunlight, and I focus on that rather than meet their gaze.

I snort. "Sure, the easy part."

They arch a brow, their lips twitching. "We can start with the end, if you prefer."

"I do not prefer." The mere mention of the end of last night sends a shiver straight to my core. I let my hair down from its messy bun, finger-brushing through the strands, and ignore my body's inability to control itself.

"The Council, then," Pat prompts.

"Four stodgy old men with more power than sense." I shake my head and explain what happened—how Marcus Accardi was overconfident, how David Capone was a sexist dipshit with a bad tailor, how my own fucking father wouldn't even look at me until I pulled out Tamayo's engagement ring. The same ring that made me invisible to every man in that godforsaken church the moment it was slipped onto my finger.

None of them see me as anything other than a pawn to be owned. Not even Father.

"And Marcus?" Their voice is soft, like the utterance of his name is a trigger.

I pick through the basket on the vanity stocked with high-end face lotions, serums, body butter, and even genderless body spray. I pull out what I need. "He's never seen me as more than an object."

They watch me in the mirror. "You know that's not what I meant."

"I know." I ghost my fingers over the light-red bruises dotting my chin. Pat doesn't move, doesn't reach to comfort me. There's no need. The void lined with greedy teeth inside me has already gobbled up all the pain, and all that's left is cold, calculating rage. I drop my hand to the counter and turn away from my reflection to grab the body lotion. "He's the same barbarian he's always been. Not much to tell."

They wait as I open the body butter and moisturize my feet, my calves, my knees. But I don't continue. I move up my body, feel each inch and remember it's mine. Only mine.

"Are you okay?" Their voice is quiet, but it still bounces off the walls, reverberates in my ears.

"I'm fine, Pat. Really." And I am. The unfortunate reality of being a woman, especially a mafia princess, is getting used to unwanted advances and gendered trauma. And finding ways to cope, whether healthy or not. Exhibit A: last night in the backseat of the car.

They sigh. "Okay. I'll drop it."

"Thanks." I swipe toner across my face.

They hum. "Tamayo will need to be vigilant."

"What about you and me?"

Pat grabs my wet towel off the floor and hangs it up to dry. "What can we do other than rely on Tamayo and her gang to protect us? That's the whole deal." They don't say it, but all I can hear are the unspoken words, *the deal* you *made*, ringing through the room.

"I'm not holing up in this house and never leaving." I rub serum into my cheeks, my fake engagement ring bright red like blood.

Pat leans against the wall behind me with a smirk. "Even if Tamayo fucks you dizzy?"

"Patrizia Ann Marino!" I shoot them a glare through the mirror.

They snort. "You think partitions are fucking soundproof?"

I cover my face with both hands.

"It's not like it's the first time," they needle.

My head hangs heavy, and I mutter to myself, "This isn't happening. Nope. No one heard anything. No one at all—"

"You were a lot more whiney this time, though—"

"Pat!" I turn and smack them in the gut. They don't even grunt, let alone *shut up*.

"Usually you're the one taking control."

"Oh my god, how do you know this?" I snap.

They roll their eyes. "I have ears, Z, come on."

"Ew." I wrinkle my nose and squeeze a small dollop of sunscreen onto my fingers.

"So"—they waggle their brows—"was the top finally topped?"

I shudder. To Pat, it probably looks like disgust, my currently wrinkled nose adding to the effect. Except it's not. Because the question only reminded me of Tamayo's hands maneuvering me where she wanted, of those damnable words she whispered to me: *Good girl.*

"We're not having this conversation," I snap.

"Tamayo," they draw her name out, whiny and long and mocking. "Please, help me," they beg nasally.

I punch their arm. "I don't sound like that!"

"Similar, though."

I shake my head, rubbing the sunscreen in with far more pressure than necessary. Pat is right. Which is the problem. In the past, I've always led the tryst, always demanded what I wanted and gotten exactly that. No one's ever treated me like Tamayo did.

"Are you a bottom now?" Pat asks.

"No." I sniff. "I was having a moment."

They snort. "That's called an orgasm."

I replace the products in the basket and narrow my eyes at them, chin lifted haughtily. "How would you know, seeing as you and orgasms are distant acquaintances?"

Their mouth gapes in open offense. "Cheap shot, Z!"

"Whatever gets you to shut *up*," I grumble.

Pat giggles, high and breathy, and it makes a smile pull at the corners of my lips. They never laughed much at home, even if we were alone. The other soldiers and capos used anything they could as evidence of Pat's weakness. Evidence that they didn't belong because of their anatomical gender. Every day was a struggle to earn their place among them. And I don't think they ever really did.

Pat shakes themself and steps up to the vanity beside me. "It didn't mean anything right?"

"No," I say. Because it can't. Like Pat said, this is the deal I made. A deal to give me time and space to figure out just how fucked the Gallo Family finances really are and why my parents were willing to sell off their only daughter to fix it. A deal I agreed to in part to prove that I can be a better don than my father, than my mother who uses him as her puppet. A deal that doesn't allow for more than passing lust for Andrea Tamayo. "No, it didn't mean anything."

They study me as if they can see straight through me. "Don't catch feelings, Z. We're not u-hauling with a gangster."

"Ew, I could never." I fake gag.

"Good. One more thing"—they lean over and swing the bathroom door almost fully closed, lowering their voice—"I overheard something interesting."

I turn on the faucet and let the water run.

Pat nods, still speaking low. "Tamayo secured an invite to Casa Nostra."

My body stills. Casa Nostra is the mafia gentleman's club and another neutral zone. Where Saint Christopher's is the overwrought, dramatic setting of Council meetings, the dizzying arches meant to prop up the Cardinal Families as if they wield benevolent power from its pews, Casa Nostra is the seedy underbelly of Louredo dressed in polished mahogany and steeped in cigar smoke. The most powerful men loiter in its lounge, negotiating law, business, and criminal deals over poker and whisky.

And of course, besides paid escorts, only a select few powerful women are invited inside its sacred walls. Which now seems to include Tamayo.

"Who invited her?" My voice is as low as Pat's.

They shake their head. "Not sure, but she's going on Wednesday."

Three days from now.

Pat leans in closer, as if they don't want to allow the smallest chance of anyone overhearing their next words. "Doesn't the Birdwatcher spend most nights at the poker table?"

A slow, conniving smirk spreads across my lips. "Yes. Yes, they do."

TAMAYO

I would like to throw my phone into the ocean.

Unfortunately, the largest body of water beside me is my fucking toilet. I could fill the tub in the hopes that the *plop-sink* would satisfy the depths of my frustration in this moment, but I think only the blue-black waters of the Bend River would be enough. The damned thing vibrates in my hand, Angie's name on the screen, and I don't have to answer it to know what kind of news waits for me on the other end.

Assault. Robbery. Vandalism. Narcs and moles. Take your fucking pick.

It's been four days since we left the Council meeting, since Marcus laid hands on Zarina, since I had her in my lap, and I have never had so many fires to put out. Homophobic slurs were spray painted across the Den on Sunday. A slew of small businesses that lease from the Tamayos in Sallay were hit Monday and Tuesday. And if my capos hadn't swept the fucking area before unloading the weapons shipment, we would have walked right into a goddamn police raid.

I almost don't answer the phone. Soldiers have been instructed to tighten ranks, halt recruitment, and keep all street activity legal, but we can't play shield for much longer without revealing a chink in the armor.

I swipe my wet hair out of my face and finally answer. "Angie." I can't summon an even tone.

Neither can she. "We've got thugs harassing the line."

"Fuck." It's not even ten at night on a Wednesday.

"This is out of fucking hand, Tamayo." Angie is one of the few people who's earned the right to talk to me like this. And it's mostly because she's right more often than not.

"No fucking shit," I mutter.

"We can't operate like this," she says.

"I know that, Angie." I yank a brush through my hair with more force than necessary, glaring at my reflection.

"I think we should shut down."

"Absolutely not." I throw the brush at the tile, and it clatters across the floor without breaking. I wish it was my phone. Or Marcus Accardi's skull.

"They're slinging slurs, Tamayo." She breathes heavy as if she's running around the club, trying to put out fires she didn't start. "Customers are walking away, and they're for fucking sure telling others to stay away."

"We can't shut down." I pick up the brush.

"Then what the fuck are you gonna do about this?" she snaps.

My voice lowers in warning. "Angela."

"Don't take that tone with me," she scolds, like she's my fucking mother, not three years my junior and reporting to me. "The paint over those tags is barely fucking dry, and now this? The Den is supposed to be a place for our people to be themselves, to feel *safe*. It's theirs as much as it is yours."

"I know that." I spit the words through grinding teeth.

"So take it the fuck back," she says.

A pause as long as the distance between me in my compound and Angela in Den of Inequity stretches out in silence. I know she's worried. I know she's right. I didn't open the Den just to sell drugs or launder money, though those are added benefits. I established it for the exact reason she said—safety in queerness. Whether they're part of the Tamayo Family or not, any queer is welcome in the Den.

No one should be punished for who they are.

I close my eyes and breathe in deep. "Okay. Get everyone inside quickly—no cover tonight. I'll send a team to remove the delinquents and keep a rotation out there to escort patrons when they exit. If news is spreading, I'm not worried about capacity, but if it becomes a problem, call me."

She doesn't speak for a long moment. "That's barely enough."

I glance to the suit hanging on the door, waiting for me to step into it and out the door to Casa Nostra, where the most powerful people in the city gather each night. "I'm working on more."

"Fine. But I will shut our doors to protect our people and the Den if I see fit."

I release a heavy breath. "Fine."

"Fine." She hangs up.

"God damn it." I immediately dial the capo in Sallay and instruct her to take her most trusted to the Den to remove the Accardi pests. They won't be Accardi soldiers, though. Not even Gallo soldiers. None of the attacks have been directly linked to either family, most of the assailants are desperate people who were likely paid inadequate sums to harass the Tamayo Family into submission.

As if some run-of-the-mill harassment is enough to scare me, us. I've spent my life functioning in a shitstorm to the point that clear, sunny days are abnormal. And my family is made up of people like me. People who deal with inconvenience bordering on violence every goddamn day. Church protestors spent months picketing outside the Den of Inequity when it opened. Slurs have been painted, stamped, and carved across

Tamayo Family businesses since their inceptions. It will take a whole lot more than this to intimidate us.

But the frequency is beginning to piss me the fuck off.

I rub across my fade, the texture soothing me. The Tamayo Family crow tattoo on my back carries a noose in its beak, the ink and its obligation heavy on my shoulders. As soon as I'm ready, Darius and I will leave for Casa Nostra. Which is hopefully where the "more" I promised Angie—and myself and my family—will finally come into play.

I apply pomade to my hair, towel tied around my hips, bathroom choked in steam from my shower, as my brain flips through strategy for tonight. Part of me wishes Zarina were coming, too. This is her world more than mine, much as I loathe to admit it. She knows the players, understands the game in a way I don't yet.

But I can't afford the distraction that is her, and Darius had a point on Sunday. Zarina will know too much by the time our deal is up. Anything I can do to limit that knowledge is in the best interest of myself and my family. I swipe mascara over my lashes and dab a bit of concealer under my eyes to hide the puffiness from a lack of sleep. I pull on my briefs then my gray suit and button it up until it feels like I'm dressed in chainmail.

I stride out of my bathroom, slip on my Doc oxfords, and stuff my gun into my waistband before taking the stairs two at a time.

Darius stands at the garage door. "Angie called."

Of course she did. "It's taken care of."

"For now," he says, like I need a reminder.

I sigh. "For now."

We push into the garage, the lights already on. "Ready for tonight?" he asks.

"Ready as I can be."

"Reassuring," he deadpans.

Energy skitters through me, and I wish I could dispel it by

throwing a punch. Move my body in a way that will ground me inside it, keep my mind from racing and my worry from growing. Casa Nostra is more than an opportunity to schmooze the créme de la créme of the city, it's the only real chance to protect my family through this fabricated storm.

Darius rests a hand on my shoulder, large and warm. "Hey." He gently pulls me to face him, and his dark-brown eyes hold mine. "You've got this. We're all behind you."

I find his hand and squeeze it hard. "Thanks."

"Now get in the damn car." He play-shoves me toward the sedan, opening the door, and I chuckle as I slip into the leather seat.

"Good evening," a voice purrs beside me.

The same voice I last heard in this exact spot, but much breathier, much whinier, and much, much more welcome.

Zarina Gallo.

In the corner of the garage, Pat darts out from behind a tall shelf. Darius jerks toward them as if he has a chance at stopping them. Pat winks, already leaning against the passenger door with the grace of a barely-restrained tiger. Darius huffs.

My smile sours as I consider Zarina in her emerald-green dress and crimson lips with her brown-black hair falling in waves. "Where are you going?"

"With you, wifey." She smiles sweetly.

The nickname churns my stomach, and I'd much prefer to get to the fucking point. "Where do you think *we're* going?"

She smooths her hands down her body, ruching the fabric under her fingers like she's trying to direct my attention. "Into the belly of the beast."

I don't take the bait. "Zarina."

"Hm?" she plays innocent.

"Get out of the car," I growl.

She simply settles further into her seat, the threat in my voice barely registering. "No, thank you."

"You cannot come with me." My hands slide to rest on the outside of my thighs, and I have to force my gaze to remain on her face.

She picks invisible lint off the silk of her dress. "Do you think you garnered an invite into the most exclusive criminal gentleman's club by virtue of anything other than *my* name and *my* audacity?"

My fingers twitch again, and the urge to gnash my teeth grows. And I know why. It's not because she's doubting me or insulting my pride. It's that she's right. She's one thousand fucking percent correct and it kills me.

"I'm coming with you." She tilts her head, coy and pretty, as if she didn't just slap me with the truth. "Whether we present ourselves as united in power or separated in turmoil is up to you."

I study her. She's dressed to slay a man in his seat without a single cut to his person. Casa Nostra is exclusive, but its patrons are the same people she and her family have known and entertained her whole life. What does tonight mean for her that she must attend? I mimic her, cocking my head. "What are you up to?"

Her gaze smolders with anger. "I won't be relegated to the shadows simply because I'm fake marrying you."

I hum, unconvinced. "Shadows are the least of your worries. No one will be able to take their eyes off you."

"If by no one, you mean yourself, then I believe it."

I keep my tone light. "I could forcibly remove you."

"You could try." She lifts a single brow, as if in challenge.

We stare at each other, two boulders unwilling to give way against the current. Zarina needs something at Casa Nostra, something that will likely help her along in annulling our fake engagement and therefore demoting my status from Cardinal Family member's fiancée back down to notorious queer gangster with a target on her back.

How badly do I want to stop her?

I dart for her wrist, drawing my gun with my other hand, but Zarina's quicker. She snatches my arm and pulls me close. Sharp, cold steel rests against my jugular as the edge of her knife threatens to slice me open. Goose bumps shiver down my spine.

A devilish grin unfurls across my lips. "Wouldn't have thought you were into knife play."

"When the occasion calls for it." Her hand is steady, no hint of a tremor, of hesitation.

"What are you gonna do, princess?" I lean into it, the blade an ounce of pressure away from breaking my skin. "Cut me?"

She smirks slow as honey. "I'll let you choose where."

"You forgot about my other hand, hm." I aim my gun for her gut, my fist resting on my knee.

She laughs, bright and short. "Death before dishonor, Tamayo." She winks. "Whether you like it or not, I'm worth far more to you alive than dead. You, on the other hand..." Her eyes rake over me, down and up, and come back as if she's found me wanting. "You, I can spare."

I reach out with the fingers of my captive hand and brush the green silk of her dress, right above her navel. She presses her eyes closed a second too long to be a simple blink, and her smirk loses its shape.

I sigh and replace my gun in my waistband. "All right, princess. You can come."

She stares at me without removing the knife from my throat or her hand from my wrist, like she's unwilling to believe my words. I get it. I'm not sure why I'm agreeing either. Path of least resistance? Devilish curiosity? All I know is I don't have time to lollygag.

"Try to behave, hm?" My gaze slinks down her dress, to the seam of her thighs, to her hands around my wrist. "Wouldn't want anyone to think you've been ruined by a gangster."

Zarina holds completely still, like she might topple if she gives a single inch. I wish she were closer. Wish her shoulders would loosen and her posture would melt back into the leather seat. Wish it was Saturday again and the space between us would vanish.

"Darius, let's go." I don't move my gaze from hers as I speak or as Darius grumbles, pushing the door shut with more force the necessary. My knuckles draw patterns like hurricane paths over her dress as Darius and Pat slide into the front seats. His words the other night hang between the front and back of the car. *There's nothing to keep her from crossing us.* Zarina adjusts her grip, and it nearly nicks my neck.

"Unless you're planning to use it, can you sheathe the knife, princess?" My voice is soft and rumbly.

She flicks her hair over her shoulder. "There's always a possibility."

I can't help but chuckle. "I'll keep that in mind."

ZARINA

Casa Nostra is like a speakeasy without a secret password. The host triple-checks our name on his list, like he can hardly believe street urchins are allowed to darken his precious doorstep, let alone the lounge he leads us to. I scan the dimly lit corridor, the too-muscled security standing in front of an emerald velvet rope blocking the stairwell, the well-worn hardwood with its polished sheen and creaky floorboards, the three closed doors we pass that are entirely too silent. And then we enter the lounge.

Unlike the Den of Inequity, it's exactly what I expect.

My shoulders remain straight and tall despite the sigh that whistles out from under my tongue. The place is all bronze finishes and overstuffed leather chairs and whisky poured into neat tumblers with cigar smoke choking the air. Men, all of whom likely have a room in their ornate mansions or penthouse apartments that looks eerily similar to this, gather in besuited huddles and speak too loudly.

I keep my face neutral to hide my distaste. "The most powerful men in Louredo are in this room," I murmur, "and all they can imagine for themselves is the same thing men have imagined since the invention of the wheel."

Tamayo hums, leading us to the bar. A few patrons narrow their eyes as we pass, while a few more crane their necks to get a better look. "Whisky, leather, and cigars."

"And women." I spy the handful dotting the crowd, bright gems glittering in the smoke. Each of them hangs off a man's arm or sits on a man's lap. Always near power, but never grasping it. The hungry teeth inside my chest grate at the thought.

"I can't fault them there." Tamayo swipes her thumb across the small of my back, making my skin prickle with a shiver.

"I can," I growl.

"Remember, *wifey*"—she throws the horrid nickname I used back at me—"behave."

I run my hand up her arm, onto her shoulder, and play with the shaved hairs at her neck. She leans a hip against the bar and orders for us—as if I am no longer an autonomous person who can order for myself, fuck you very much—and ignores me. I press closer, my chest against her arm and my nose at her ear. "What are the parameters, hm? What does it mean to behave?"

"It means"—her fingers fiddle with the chain straps of my dress, yanking one like a church bell—"use that pretty mouth to say only pretty things and don't leave my side."

I scratch my nails a little too hard over her nape. "That's a tall order. What's in it for me?"

She doesn't turn, still. "Casa Nostra."

"A poor deal." I want to ruffle her hair just to see if she'll do something about it, but I know this isn't the place.

"Unfortunately"—she pays the bartender with far too much cash, which she insists he keep—"your knife was checked at the door."

I chuckle, more breath than sound. "As if that's the only weapon I keep."

She finally turns to meet my eye, sliding my drink toward me as she arches a brow and smirks. "I'd love to explore your arsenal."

"Maybe." I wrap my fingers around my glass and hold her gaze. "If you're good."

Her smirk brightens into a pleasant smile.

"Tamayo!" Jimmy Falcone approaches with a small entourage. "Welcome!"

"Jimmy." Tamayo turns to shake Jimmy's hand, my fingers leaving her nape and hers my back. I stand against the bar behind her and take a sip, playing the part of an ornament. Orange citrus lights up my tongue and sense memory slams into me—Tamayo on her throne, me on my knees, and Den of Inequity's music vibrating up through the floor, into my legs. Another vodka Collins on another night risking too much for a chance to grasp at my own power.

Jimmy offers me a hand with a fond shake of his head. "Zarina."

"Surprised to see me?" I tease. Despite his status as a cis man and a rival don with a penchant for chaos, I don't mind Jimmy Falcone. He's never expected me to be small, unlike every other man in this business.

He laughs, full and hearty. "Not even a little."

"Good."

"Come"—Jimmy waves for us to follow him, turning and walking away without checking if we're behind him—"we're sitting with Logan Anderson."

Louredo's district attorney.

Tamayo slips her hand around my waist again, lands a kiss on my cheek as if I'm incredibly dear to her, and whisper-growls, "Behave."

I would like to shove that damned word down her throat.

We follow Jimmy across the room to a group of low, leather arm chairs already occupied by a handful of men. Pat and

Darius stand against the wall, scanning the room. Casa Nostra is another neutral ground where most weapons aren't allowed, save for soldiers and personal guards. Pat holds my gaze, their blue eyes bright despite the hazy air, and offers me the slightest tilt of their lip. I shoot them a wink.

Jimmy snaps his fingers, and three chairs open up, men jumping out of them as if bitten on the ass by rats. Jimmy settles into the seat beside Logan, Tamayo across from him, leaving the seat empty beside her. But she told me to behave, to stick by her side.

Which is exactly what I do when I sit in her lap.

Air huffs out of her, hot against my arm, and I wiggle backward until I'm fully seated in the nook of her thigh and hip. Her hand snakes around to grip my waist, the other landing on my thigh. She shakes her head and lands another kiss on my jaw, murmuring against my skin, "Brat."

The men laugh as if I've performed the most uproarious prank.

"Can't leave an inch of space between the two of you?" Jimmy teases.

"That's what it's always like in the beginning." Logan waves a hand with a shake of his head as if to say, *look at these naïve lovebirds in their honeymoon phase.* So cute. So silly. Two youths in love and doomed from the start. Fucking hilarious.

"You can't be speaking from experience?" Jimmy's laughing and rolling his eyes, his long hair swept aside. "You haven't kept a woman longer than the beginning!"

"For good reason!" Logan roars, and really, calm the fuck down. My ears ring as they laugh themselves hoarse, their men chortling around them, and I hide my annoyance behind a sip of my drink.

"And you, Tamayo?" Logan leans back in his seat. "Is Miss Gallo the first woman you've kept past the beginning?"

Tamayo squeezes my thigh, and I pretend I don't want it higher. "Not the first, but she's the last."

Logan chuckles, his eyes stuck on her fingers splayed over my skin. "Smooth."

"Or she knows I'll kill her otherwise." I smile sweetly.

"Careful, Tamayo, the Zarina I know doesn't make promises she won't keep." Jimmy leans back in his chair, considering me then Tamayo then me again. He points at me, still holding his typical scotch. "I remember when you were sixteen at whatever gala and you almost cut some poor boy's balls clean off. Who was it again?"

I cut a pointed look at Tamayo. "Billy Fawkes."

"Right!" He snaps his fingers. "David's nephew. Such audacity, you might as well have worn his balls for your own."

I shrug. "He was getting handsy at coat check and wouldn't *stop.*"

"You rendered him infertile." Jimmy shakes his head.

"Weak boys like him have no business procreating." I sniff. The insult is for them, not me. If I could tell the truth without losing the smallest bit of respect they've shown me, I'd tell them Billy Fawkes was a rapist and deserved worse than he got. If I were speaking plainly, I would tell them I was aiming for his gut, aiming to kill, but my hands shook and fumbled and the knife tilted wrong. But I can't say that. Not me, Zarina Gallo, mafia princess and soft woman in a den of ravenous wolves.

Tamayo rubs her nose over my shoulder and pulls me closer as if I've slid too far down her legs. "Your ferocity is exactly what I love about you."

"Careful it doesn't come back to bite you in the ass," Jimmy warns with a dangerous grin.

Tamayo matches him tooth-for-tooth. "Might be fun."

Everyone laughs, Jimmy and Logan and their men and Tamayo. I sip my drink.

Logan wipes at his eyes despite no apparent tears falling.

"Only someone as crazy as you would take on the Accardis and the Gallos."

"A fool for love." Tamayo's hand leaves my legs to raise her glass.

"A fool, indeed." Jimmy crooks his finger, and a man with two bruised eyes, the skin mauve tinged with yellow, peels himself off the wall. He shuffles forward with his head hanging low until he stands before us. "Antoni, I believe you've met Andrea Tamayo."

Tamayo sips her drink, but her grip on my waist tightens and her gaze narrows on Antoni.

"Yes, boss." Antoni nods without looking up.

"Well?" he prompts.

Antoni turns, chin pressed to his chest, and clears his throat. "Ma'am—sir—Tamayo, please—"

"Do it proper." Jimmy's voice has lost all warmth.

"Boss—"

Jimmy kicks out the back of Antoni's knee. I snake my arm behind Tamayo's neck, sneaking a glance at her face. She remains impassive, wearing that annoyingly unbothered mask she dons when she doesn't want anyone to *see*. I wish I could study it closely now that she's aiming it at someone other than me; mark the tension in her jaw, the wrinkles at the corner of her eyes, the set of her brow. But this is a show, performed by Jimmy to be viewed by Tamayo and me for god knows why, and to ignore it would be tantamount to slapping him in the face.

I lift my chin and look down my nose at Antoni on his knees.

His hands shake where they rest on his thighs, and his voice is strained as he speaks. "Tamayo, please forgive me."

"For what, Toni?" Her voice rumbles in her chest, limned in violent threat.

He glances at Jimmy who arches a brow. "Mr. Falcone, um, he didn't order me—"

"No." Tamayo sets her drink on the side table and lets her

hand fall on my naked thigh. The cold condensation from the glass beads up between our skin, and she draws patterns with the droplets. "For what am I forgiving you?"

Antoni frowns, which makes him wince. "I don't understand."

"What did you do, Toni," she asks, "that requires forgiveness?"

He gulps. "I double-crossed you."

"Hm." Her fingers trail further up my thigh, and only now does it hit me, full force with her knuckles teasing the hem of my skirt, that the last time I was in this position—sat on Tamayo's lap as she touched me—was Saturday, when I begged her to fuck me. Red burns across my chest, up my neck, and I try to hide it with the raise of my glass and a gulp of my drink.

Tamayo's touch slips just under my skirt. "And what will you do to earn my forgiveness?"

Antoni glances to Jimmy, who doesn't offer an iota of help. "What do you want?" he asks.

Tamayo sighs, as if the question is loaded and there's any way this won't end in screaming. And with the way her fingers won't stop drawing paths of condensation over my skin, I'd very much prefer my screaming to Antoni's. She doesn't spare me a glance, though, staring at the man on his knees. "I want what all men want—respect."

Antoni's face scrunches in confusion as he tries to understand what that physically equates to, how he can provide something so abstract to Tamayo. He glances to Jimmy, who watches Tamayo, who waits for Antoni. And I—with Tamayo's hand two knuckles deep under my dress on the outside of my thigh—chance a roll of my hips disguised as a shift in weight.

Tamayo's mask slips for a millisecond, her eyelids drooping and her nails digging into my skin. I hide a smirk behind a sip of my drink.

She sighs dramatically, disappointed. "What's the cost of disrespect to your boss, Toni?"

His eyes widen, and he sputters the answer. "Broken bones."

Tamayo hums, her hand sliding around to grasp under my thigh and drag my body further into the nook of her hip. Her fingers don't leave, digging in just below the crease where my thigh meets my ass; the action merely an excuse to retaliate. I wish I could grin. Instead, I'm scanning the room, looking for the true reason I came to Casa Nostra in the first place—the Birdwatcher.

I find them playing poker, their long legs stretched out under the table and a long finger resting against their cheek. Their tawny skin burnishes in the low lamplight, rich amber in a crowd of chalky white. I've seen them twice before. Once when I was twelve and they visited Father before he and Mother closed a deal with the mayor, and again three years ago when they caught me fucking someone outside one of the only queer clubs downtown. They smirked, tipped their nonexistent hat, and continued on their way. And I just pressed the faceless woman harder against the alleyway wall.

My sexuality was never a secret to be weaponized.

Rough movement pulls my attention away. Darius has hold of Antoni's shoulder, the poor capo's feet struggling to find purchase as he's dragged over the thick, wool rugs. Tamayo taps her fingers against my upper thigh, and Pat catches my gaze. I unfreeze on Tamayo's lap and flick my hair. Pat glances to the Birdwatcher and back to me with a nod.

Jimmy sighs and settles further into his chair. "Thank god for the basement."

"And even more for the second floor." Logan raises his glass to the infamous bedrooms on the upper floor of Casa Nostra.

"Not that Tamayo will make use of it." Jimmy's grin is wide and teasing, his brows raised.

The district attorney looks us up and down as if we're the

beginning of a very interesting porn storyline he wishes would unfold more quickly. "Unless Miss Gallo were interested—"

"I have a bedroom at home, thank you." I wrinkle my nose in disgust.

Logan's grin adapts a lascivious slope. "Not like this."

I frown, leaning back into Tamayo in discomfort.

She turns an unimpressed gaze onto Logan. "We have dungeons at the Den."

"The Den?" Jimmy asks.

"My club, Den of Inequity." She presses a kiss to my shoulder as Jimmy and Logan exchange a loaded look.

"Baby." I relax further against Tamayo and pout, blocking her view of the lounge. Without looking, I know Pat is picking their way through the lounge toward the Birdwatcher while I do my part. "I need to use the lady's room."

Tamayo's fingers crawl further up my thigh to graze the edge of my ass. "I'll come with."

"Can't be separated for even a second, hm?" Logan taunts. "My assistant informs me that's called 'simping.' Is that right?"

"Fuck if I know." Jimmy pins Tamayo with a calculating stare. "I have business to discuss with you, but if you need to go…" The implication is heavy in his silence, in the shrug of his shoulders, in the judgment clouding his gaze.

Even if I truly had to use the toilet, I would insist Tamayo stay here. She came here for a reason—multiple reasons, if Pat's reports about the escalating assaults on Tamayo businesses are true. She needs alliances and deals. She needs to stay.

It just works in my favor this time.

I drag my hand down her arm, to her wrist at the edge of my skirt. "Stay, baby. Order another drink, talk business." I wrinkle my nose like the idea of it bores me. I'm a princess, after all. This is what they expect of me—beauty, no brains. Violence, no business acumen.

I kiss Tamayo's cheek, dragging my lips over to her ear. "I won't be long, I promise."

Logan cracks an imaginary whip, the sound effect snapping out of his mouth.

Tamayo's jaw ticks, but her gaze doesn't leave mine. "Take Dar—"

"He's busy with what's-his-face." I wave my hand toward the hallway where the guard stands outside the stairwell.

She grumbles. "Pat, then."

"Thanks, baby," I say as if I wasn't already planning to take Pat with me.

"Five minutes, princess," she growls.

I adjust her collar, which isn't crooked at all. "And if I'm longer?"

She grabs my wrist in one hand and raises it to her lips, pressing a kiss to the pulse point there. A promise. "I'll come get you myself."

I chuckle as I rise from her lap, her hand still holding my wrist like I need balance because she's left me off-kilter. I refuse to acknowledge the too-wet feeling between my legs as I adjust the hem of my dress and nod to Jimmy and the district attorney with a wink. "Have fun, boys."

I can feel Logan watching my ass until I'm out of sight. Disgust coats my skin like slime. I want to turn back, grab the man by the taint, and twist until he screams. But I can't. So I walk through the lounge, past the poker table without so much as a twitch toward it and the Birdwatcher sitting there, and into the dimly lit hallway. The burly guard protects the staircase, which leads down to the bloody basement and up to the sinful second floor. I ignore him, aiming for the powder room with gilded mirrors and tufted chairs that precedes the restroom. And I wait.

Thankfully, the Birdwatcher is prompt.

They stride past us and directly into the restroom. And I

follow straight after. The room is ornate, the surfaces shining, the lamps glowing gold, the mirrors unmarred. As if a wealthy man's shit deserves better treatment than a poor man's life.

They stand at the vanity, arms crossed and dreads tied back loosely. "Miss Gallo."

I stand with my back to the door and wrinkle my nose at the name—it's diminutive. Like I'm a little girl without twenty-six years of violence and crime staining my manicured hands.

They either don't notice or don't care. "You secured yourself an invitation to Casa Nostra. How conniving of you."

I wave away their words. "I don't have much time."

"No, you don't." The way they say this implies far more than the promise of Tamayo coming to find me. "Everyone's all atwitter with the news of your...impending nuptials."

"To whom?" I tilt my head.

They mirror my movement. "That remains to be seen."

I don't have time for riddles. "My family—we're in trouble."

They don't speak, head still tilted and eyes trained on me. I'm not sure who gave them the moniker, the Birdwatcher. Maybe it was them, maybe it was a client or a victim. Whoever it was, they chose well. The Birdwatcher doesn't get involved in the muck of gaining and losing power, the violence of crime and punishment. They watch. They wait. They remember.

I take in a steeling breath. "I need to know the trouble."

They twirl their wrist. "I believe your mother would know far better than I."

"She would," I agree.

They tuck their hand back into the crook of their arm. "I assume she's not speaking to you."

"Why assume when you already know," I deadpan.

They flash a cheshire grin.

"What's your price?" I ask.

They stare at me with wide, unblinking eyes, and I wait on pins and needles, apprehension growing with each breath I take.

I know they don't deal in money, but rather in a currency more sinister and dangerous to a mafia don's daughter—secrets and favors. I already promised Tamayo a favor, something that weighs heavier than the ruby at my throat. What will the Bird-watcher deem worthy enough to spill the information I need?

They push off the vanity and drop their hands, stuffing them into their trouser pockets. "I require three secrets."

I suck in another fortifying breath. "From the Gallo Family?"

They stare at me and their grin grows a millimeter at a time, each sharp tooth revealed stirring ominous dread inside my gut. Finally, they shake their head. "No, Miss Gallo. From the Tamayo Family."

TAMAYO

The district attorney is half a second away from feeling my hand around his throat when he finally unsticks his eyes from Zarina's ass. He swivels his attention back to Jimmy then me, and I cock my brow. He just grins with a shrug. Like I caught him with his hand in the cookie jar rather than visually assaulting my fake fiancée.

My grip tightens around my glass.

Jimmy settles further into his chair, the leather ready to swallow him whole, fully relaxed in this place that has always welcomed him. "How're you holding up?"

"We're fine," I lie. There's no way to answer honestly without yielding something—the way we're spread too thin, the properties we own, the length of our reaching fingers. I've spent years buying up plots of land and commercial property under various shell companies to keep the Cardinal Families ignorant of my movements. Especially the Gallos. They can't know the way we're creeping into their territories, choking their income streams in a slow, imperceptible stranglehold. Not yet.

"'Fine.'" Jimmy ruminates on the word, studying me. "That's one way to put it."

I glance to the archway leading into the hall—still empty.

Jimmy heaves a long-suffering sigh. "Zarina is fine." His voice is on the edge of a snap.

I adjust my body to give him my full attention, knowing I am here by the grace of his invitation.

"You need friends, Tamayo. That's why I invited you here."

I rest my drink on the arm of my chair, fingers loose around it. "What are you proposing?"

"Business, of course. The only sacred thing left to men like us." He gestures at Logan and then me.

I hum, barely withholding a snort at the irony of my being man enough for business but not man enough for much else.

"The Accardis are reaching too far, digging too deep." His voice is low, meant to be heard by Logan and me only. "And with the way Marcus and Alonso can't keep their dicks in their fucking pants, war is too likely for my taste. I need guns. And you need legitimacy."

"Isn't that why I'm marrying a Gallo?" I ask.

He shakes his head before I finish speaking. "That might be enough if you were a man. It was for Ricci."

Irony strikes again. Not man enough to marry into a Cardinal Family. Unlike Riccardo, who married Alessandra Gallo and took on the role as don without an eye batted.

"If you can call him a man." Logan pulls a face in disgust. "Would you do the same, Tamayo? Would you take the Gallo name?"

If it were another name, I might. If it weren't the family that broke and abandoned me. My knee twinges, the ghost of an old pain pulsing deep in my bones. It hurts when it rains. It aches after a long day. It swells if I pivot too quickly. All thanks to the Gallos.

I ignore Logan's question and look to Jimmy. "So, you want to cut a deal."

His lips twitch, fighting a smile. "I do."

"And what do I get in return?" I drag a finger through the condensation coating my glass.

He snorts. "My money."

"Seems unbalanced to me." I lift my drink and hold Jimmy's gaze over the rim. "If the war you believe so inevitable breaks out, you could use my own guns against me."

He shrugs. "The deal is the deal." He says it like it's inscrutable. Like selling him the very weapons that could spell mine and my family's destruction if the mockery of my engagement is revealed isn't the exact definition of absurd. A few days after the Council meeting and already we're dealing with vandalism, assault, harassment, robbery, and trespassing. And he distills that into a shrug, unbothered because he doesn't have to be.

Angie's words during our phone call earlier echo in my ears. *The Den is supposed to be a place for our people to be themselves, to feel safe, and it's theirs as much as it is yours... So take it the fuck back.*

I set my ankle on my knee and consider him. He's worried about the Accardis, about their too-greedy hands digging into dirt not meant for them. It's been a quarter of a century since the Russos fell, but it seems Jimmy hasn't forgotten what led to boundaries set in blood-soaked asphalt. He wants me to bear the brunt of the oncoming storm while he sits safe in his shelter.

I'm here to tear the shelter down.

"You're right, Jimmy." The compliment releases the smirk ready on his lips. "I need friends. I can't do this alone."

He nods, pleased with himself. "I knew you were smart."

"But I need more than money."

His smirk tightens into a frown.

"My family is taking the brunt of the backlash, and money only goes so far." I let my shoulders slump just so, my body curl inward as if dejected. I play into what they expect of me, a girl amongst men—incompetent, silly, more nurturing than cutthroat. "I need help."

Jimmy squints at me. "What kind of help?"

"Nothing...loud." I swirl the dregs of my drink, ice tinkling against the glass. "There's been an influx of crime around the Den—my club. Just tonight, men were intimidating and harassing the line, scaring my customers, yelling slurs."

Logan shakes his head as if this is the saddest thing he's ever heard. "That's horrible, Tamayo."

"I know." I meet his performance with my own, pained expression covering my face, a tremble in my chin. "Unfortunately, it's not uncommon. Queer people are still targeted in these modern times, attacked for existing." I scoff. "A handful of stores under my care were vandalized this week. Hateful words painted over their windows."

Jimmy and Logan meet each other's eyes, a loaded pause passing between them. I watch without looking, my gaze focused on my hands as if stuck in the recollection of a painful memory. But inside, I'm reveling in their reaction. Nothing makes privileged people more uncomfortable than being faced with the product of their oppression.

Jimmy nods and pats Logan's knee. "We can't allow such prejudice to run rampant, my friends. Our city is better than this."

Logan leans forward in his seat, finger jabbing into the supple leather of the arm rest. "This is *exactly* the kind of crime I'm trying to highlight in my reelection campaign. Everyone deserves to feel safe on the street, especially people like you, Tamayo."

I clamp down on a spiteful reply, keeping my face pathetic.

"Of course"—he leans back again, adjusting his suit jacket— "I can't get the word out alone. It takes a team to campaign, money to fund, man-hours to investigate and increase vigilance in the area."

Jimmy waves his hand with a fond shake of his head. "For the safety of the people, money is no object."

"Hear, hear!" Logan raises his drink, smiling too wide.

I clink mine to his. "To new friends."

"And to Louredo." Jimmy joins his glass with ours.

We all drain our cups. The last of the liquor hits my tongue, bitter as it rolls down my throat. I set it on the side table and watch as Logan pulls a case of cigars out of his breast pocket and taps it on his knee.

"When's the party by the way?" he asks.

I frown. "Party?"

"The event of the season, Tamayo! Your engagement!" Logan spreads his arms with a laugh. "I'm keeping an eye out for my invitation."

"Right." I clear my throat.

Jimmy throws me a bone. "It's expected of a Cardinal engagement."

I want to snort—the Council would have never accepted my engagement to Zarina if the threat of consolidated power wasn't a knife at their necks. "Invitations are going out this week."

"Great. I'll speak to my friends at the precinct—we'll find these bigots and serve justice." Logan pulls the cigars out one by one and cuts them before passing them around. "To the ol' ball and chain! At least she's pretty, eh?" He chuckles as if he's made the best joke.

I accept the cigar, leaning toward the lit match Logan holds before my face. Not for the first time, I wonder if men even like women. He lights his own last and melts back into his chair. His suit is Tom Ford, his shoes shined to gleaming, his hair styled. He likes his things, cares for them. And yet I wouldn't be surprised if he treated women worse than the objects he owns.

They chat about things I don't care about—Logan's reelection campaign, the state of the potholes on the street, the women in the room. I smoke my cigar and try not to cringe with each deplorable comment, offering a remark here and there. Suspicion grows in my gut, tangling around my heart and lungs. Zarina's been gone too long. More than the five minutes she promised. There's no way it's not purposeful. But for what?

Darius stands at the archway and tilts his head. Time to go.

"Jimmy, Logan, thank you for tonight." I snuff out the last of my cigar in the ashtray and stand, buttoning my jacket. "But the ol' ball and chain has been gone too long."

Jimmy breathes a puff of smoke. "Zarina's a big girl, she can take care of herself."

"I know, but I can't." I wink with a grin bordering on indecent.

Logan guffaws, going so far as to slap his knee. "She's got a date in the bathroom! Let her go, Jimmy."

I let the grin widen as if he's right, as if I'm unable to hold myself back from meeting Zarina behind a locked door and slipping my hands beneath her dress. Like I haven't already gone multiple miserable days without having her in my lap, moaning my name and begging me to fuck her. But these men don't understand self-control, only seizing.

I waggle my brows. "Can't let my princess sit on an inferior throne."

Jimmy laughs too loud, head thrown back. "At least take her home!"

"Or upstairs!" Logan teases.

"I'll leave my card." I shake Jimmy's hand then Logan's. "See you both at the party."

"Looking forward to it." Logan puffs on his cigar.

Jimmy flicks ash on the ground. "I'll be in touch."

TAMAYO

*D*arius waits as I stride through the lounge. He's unruffled despite his time spent in the basement with Antoni. When he finishes scanning the room around me, he flicks his eyes left, like he's pointing behind him. I pass pockets of men with women draped over one or two like pretty shawls and stop beside Darius.

"It's done," he rumbles.

I nod. "Zarina?"

"Pat's outside the bathroom."

I hum, looking down the hallway opposite the lounge. "Leave my card with Jimmy's man and the district attorney." I brush past him without another word. I don't have to specify which card or which of Jimmy's men, because Darius knows. It's his job to know. And I have more important concerns to attend.

My jaw tenses and my steps staccato as I aim for the restroom. I asked one thing of Zarina before we came—*behave*. Stay with me and don't offend anyone. Of course, she couldn't honor even that simple request. The only time she listens is when she's half-gone, flushed red with my fingers knuckles-deep inside her.

Fuck. That train of thought is not helping.

Pat tries to stand in my way, blocking my path into the powder room and to the door behind them. "She's still inside."

"I know." I push past them.

They scoff and sidestep to beat me to the door. "Can't a girl have a bowel movement?"

The force of my glare would make every single one of my people cower—even Darius—but Pat rolls their eyes like they're not inviting violence with the action.

They cross their arms, and all I want to do is grab their wrist and twist. "Just wait a minute, and she'll be out."

"It's been fifteen," I say through clamped teeth.

"All the more reason to wait." They must be severely confident to stand in my way without fear.

"Pat." It's my last warning. "Move."

"You're not my don, Tamayo," they snap back.

"Half the underworld's most powerful people are here." I rest my hand on their shoulder, my thumb in the crook of their neck and my voice dripping with honeyed threat. "Don't cause a scene."

"And what are you doing, then?" They meet me octave for octave.

"To these people?" I bear my canines. "Taking what's mine."

Pat curses, and I don't wait for them to step aside, reaching behind them to grab the door handle, push it open, and slip past. They let me.

The door swings closed behind me as I stop two feet inside the room. It's too large for its intended purpose, the toilet behind textured glass and the lighting dim. There's a vanity with a huge, gilded mirror hanging above it and a sink across from it. Zarina leans toward her reflection and rubs her lips together as she caps her lipstick. She dabs at the corners, the crimson color as bright as the rubies at her neck and on her finger. She doesn't spare me a glance as she replaces the tube in her purse and adjusts her hair like it isn't already perfect.

"Impatient, much?" She scowls at me through the mirror.

The gold chains across her back glint in the low light. "I told you—five minutes."

"How long's it been?" she asks, too innocent.

"Longer." I press my hand into my pocket and slouch into nonchalance.

She pouts into the mirror, her eyes on mine. "Poor baby. Can't survive without me, hm?"

Without conscious choice, my feet carry me further into the bathroom until I'm arm's length from her. "You said you'd behave."

She smirks. "I didn't."

"That was the deal." My teeth grind.

"I don't keep promises I don't make, Tamayo." She snaps her purse closed and finally twists to face me, wearing that imperious look she learned at her father's—no, likely her mother's—knee. "You told me to behave. I took it under advisement."

I crowd closer until the distance between us could be closed with a deep breath, my chest expanding to brush the silk of her dress. My voice drops to a rumbled whisper. "Why'd you come to the bathroom, princess?"

"To use it, Tamayo." Condescension coats each syllable.

I tilt my head. "With the door unlocked?"

She shrugs, and it makes her dress tickle my shirt. "I forgot. Pat usually stops the trash." She looks me up and down, heavily implying I'm said trash.

My hand rises of its own volition, my body acting as if it's separate from my mind, and yet I have no objections when my fingers brush hair. And neither does she. "We're in the belly of the beast, as you put it. You shouldn't be unarmed and alone behind unlocked doors."

"I don't know if you heard"—her voice hardens to steel—
"but I can take care of myself."

I drop my hand, and it smacks against my thigh. "Fuck's
sake, Zarina, can you set aside your pride for one goddamn
minute?"

"Oh fuck you, kettle," she scoffs.

"Would it make you fucking *behave*?" I growl.

"Excuse me?"

"Logic doesn't. The threat of violence doesn't. What will it
take?" I unbutton my suit jacket and rub at the back of my neck.
The memory of Zarina pliant in my lap won't stop running
through my head. It was the only time she's softened, stopped
butting heads like a bull charging the matador. "Is that what it
takes?" I murmur to myself. "Will a good fuck help you behave?"

Zarina rears. "Jesus Christ, fuck you, Tamayo—"

"I could pin you against the vanity." I press forward until she
backs into it with a jolt. The basket of complimentary products
wobbles. My gaze rakes over the flush of her cheeks, down to
her neck, her heaving chest. Her body reacting without her
permission. "I could pull your pretty straps down, watch your
nipples harden."

"Tamayo." She tries to warn me, but it's more breath than
censure.

I lift my gaze to hers and let a smirk slink over my lips
because it makes her eyes dilate. Every time. "I could lift you
onto the counter, put your legs around my waist. Make your
skirt ruck up just right." I rest my hands on the counter on
either side of her, our noses millimeters apart. "You'd play with
the hair at my neck that you like. And I'd play with your nipples
until you arched real pretty."

She swallows too loud. "The door isn't locked. This is inappropriate."

I chuckle, more breath than sound, my mouth at her ear.
"That's what you like, though, isn't it? Somewhere a little public.

Someone on the other side of the door, of the partition." I drag my nose down her neck and pull back to look her in the eye again. "Maybe I'd turn you around, make you watch in the mirror as my fingers skimmed your dress. Hold your throat tight as I fucked you. Right here. In the belly of the beast. All those men outside who wish they could have you but never will."

Her breath hitches, eyes blown black and skin flushed red.

"Do you want that, princess?" I ask. Because fuck, I do. My hands tighten on the marble countertop with the force of the desire coursing through my muscles. "Want me to fuck you pliant?"

Zarina's narrows her eyes. "It won't make me behave."

My smirk only widens. "I'd like to test the theory."

"What changed your mind?" she asks. I know what she's referring to—the end of our last tryst. When I told her to find me when she figured out what she wanted.

And I could provide a litany of reasons, not least of which is her in that dress and my own frustration. But I bite my tongue. I'm not sure I did change my mind. I'm not sure I've made a conscious choice since I let the bathroom door closed behind me. I'm running on instinct and desire and the throbbing ache pulsing under my skin. We stand quiet, my thumbs brushing the silk over her ass and her fingers playing with the lapel of my jacket. Both waiting for the other to move first. To choose.

My chin falls closer to her lips.

Her fingers fist around my lapel.

I drag a hand up her spine, cup her neck with my thumb at the corner of her mouth.

"Tamayo," she says on an exhale.

And then a heavy knock cracks on the door.

"Time's up," Darius calls.

Zarina leans back at the same time she pushes against my chest. Her face, so open and expectant a second ago, closes off again, a scowl scrunching her brows. I consider telling Darius and whoever's waiting outside to go fuck themselves, but I can't afford the insult. Not yet. Instead, I swipe my thumb across Zarina's bottom lip before she can stop me. Red lipstick smudges across her chin.

She huffs, jerking back. "What the fuck?"

I transfer the red on my thumb to my own lips. "An excuse for our delay."

"You're unbelievable." She pushes me further out of her orbit.

"Thanks." I put more distance between us as she checks her reflection in the mirror, but doesn't fix her makeup. Darius knocks again as I unbutton my shirt and re-button it wrong. "Coming!"

Zarina grumbles, and I could swear I hear something like, *hopefully someone is.*

ZARINA

*T*he entire drive home, I sit with my legs crossed and my hands stuffed between them. If I release them, I know they'll wander. If I uncross, I know I'll slide over the leather seat and directly into Tamayo's lap. And god-fucking-damn her for it.

We pull into the garage, and I don't wait for Pat to help me out of the car, nor do I wish anyone a good night. I shoot out of the back seat, striding inside, up the stairs, and into my room without a word. I don't trust my mouth to say anything other than *Tamayo* and *please*.

I kick off my shoes as my back crashes against the door and slams it shut. My skin crawls, heat burning me from the inside out, sweat clinging to my dress below my chest, above my ass. My panties are uncomfortably wet, and sitting twelve inches away from the person who caused the mess for twenty stupid fucking minutes, with her scent stinking up the car, her words echoing in my ears and tingling down to my core without doing anything, did *not* help.

I yank my purse over my head. It lands on the floor with a clatter as my hands skim the satin of my dress, rucking it up my thighs and slipping under the hem. Goose bumps tingle up my stomach to my nipples, which tighten into pointed buds.

I could pull your pretty straps down—Tamayo's voice whispers in my ear as if she's here right now—*watch your nipples harden.*

A pathetic whimper escapes my throat, and I haven't even touched myself yet. I clamp down, willing to bite through my tongue to keep her cursed name out of my mouth. My fingers trace the edge of my panties, my other hand holding my skirt out of the way.

Put your legs around my waist. Make your skirt ruck up just right.

My breath quickens, and the silk is rough against my skin despite feeling soft as a kitten all night. It pulls and scratches over my sensitive nipples. I can't help it when my back arches into it. I can't help it when I dip into my panties and find the fabric damp, my fingers wet.

I'd play with your nipples until you arched real pretty

I apply the slightest pressure to my clit, and my jaw drops open, a moan deep in my throat. I clap my free hand over my mouth. The door is cold on my back. My own words float back to me. *The door isn't locked. This is inappropriate.* But I don't stop. I circle my fingers and clench my jaw, palm muffling any noise I can't hold back. Anyone could be walking past, hear my heavy breath and see the shadow of my feet. Pat could try the handle. Tamayo could pause to knock, hoping to catch me before bed.

Somewhere a little public. Someone on the other side of the door. A whimper, high and whiney, climbs up my throat. I do like it. The chance of discovery, but more the idea that my pleasure can't be contained by physical barriers, too big and too loud for something as silly as walls. My hand eases away from my mouth until it falls to grab the door handle. Tension bubbles in my gut, gathering from my chest, from my knees, from everywhere silk fizzes over my skin and leaves prickles behind. My fingers quicken, and a fully formed moan drops out of my mouth unhindered.

Footsteps pause in the hall.

I don't cover my mouth. It could be Pat or Darius—it could. But it's not. Because Pat would yell at me for being lewd. And Darius would keep walking as quickly as possible. And that leaves one person outside my door. One person now walking, slow and clipped, until she's so close, I can feel the heat of her body through the wood between us.

My fingers never stop.

The tightness in my core burns hotter. I can't feel my feet, so cold they're numb on the floor. My thighs are shaking from holding me up, from squeezing tight around the phantom waist they're meant to hold. My chest heaves faster, and my other hand grips the handle so hard, it should break.

"Princess?" Tamayo's voice calls. It seeps around the jamb and into my skin.

I quicken my pace.

"I can hear you, princess." Her voice is so deep. Right in my ear. "Are you watching yourself?"

I wish the mirror was facing me. I wish my hands were hers, one on my clit and one on my throat and our eyes meeting in the reflection as I come apart cradled against her. A whine puffs out of me.

Tamayo spits a whisper that sounds like a curse. Something brushes against the door—fabric? Knuckles? The tension inside me is too tight, champagne braced to pop before it's uncorked. My whole body contracts, a mewl pushed out of me. The release is right there. A just-right flick of my wrist, and I'll burst.

Tamayo's voice sounds closer, the timbre of it vibrating into my chest despite the barrier between us. "You sound so pliant, princess."

I finally erupt. My core clenches over and over, and my thighs clamp together as if trying to crush the cause of this painful pleasure, and a long, deep, unstoppable moan tumbles out of my chest. I can't stop my fingers on my clit; they circle harder and harder, pushing myself from floating effervescence into a freefall orgasm that takes hold of my throat and silences me as effectively as Tamayo's grip around my neck.

My hand falls away, finally, and I rest against the door, breath slowing one inhale at a time.

"Next time, princess"—Tamayo's voice is deep and commanding, the one she uses when she expects to be obeyed—"you'll come on my fingers or not at all."

And then her footsteps carry her away from my door and down the hall.

I scoff. "We'll fucking see about that."

ZARINA

The next morning, a shopping bag sits on the floor outside my room. I glance around the hallway, like the person who set it here is waiting around the corner. The place is empty, the house quiet. It could have been anyone who set it here—a soldier, Darius, even Pat—but all I can recall is Tamayo standing on the other side of this door last night, her hands brushing the wood. She likely left it behind. Maybe it was the whole reason she came to my door at all.

The bag is white with a familiar, silver logo in the shape of an apple on the front. I peek inside and find a new laptop, the box apparently unopened. Doubtful. I bring it into my room, upturning the bag onto my bed. There's a phone and a pair of the latest over-ear headphones. Everything is sealed, the hardware still sporting their protective films. Either Tamayo and her people are really good at hiding their tracks, or she's stupid. The latter is unlikely.

All it takes is opening the activity monitor application and a simple keyword search to find it—malware. It's pretty basic, and it likely requires a password I don't have to delete it. Easier to simply create encrypted pathways instead. I set to work, fingers tapping over the keyboard, and wonder if it was her or the techs on staff who underestimated me and which presentation gave me the upper hand—spoiled princess, high femme, or simply having a vagina. Either way, their loss is my gain. I start the tedious process, wishing I'd grabbed coffee before settling in to code what I need to keep my family's secrets out of Tamayo's hands.

The exact opposite of what I promised the Birdwatcher.

I pull my necklace up to my lips, the ruby resting between my teeth and the chain tightening around my neck like a noose. That's three promises now. None of which I know how to keep. Tamayo wants territory and a favor. The Birdwatcher wants secrets. And I only want time. To understand what the fuck has my family running scared toward the precipice of extinction. If this deal they've struck with the Accardis ever comes to fruition, there's no other inevitable conclusion. The Gallos will be swallowed up whole and disintegrated into acidic nothing.

But I don't have secrets to give the Birdwatcher. Or territory to give Tamayo. Or power to fulfill a favor.

I spit out the ruby pendant and grab my hair in fistfuls. "Fuck."

The Birdwatcher didn't even give me anything but a place to start. *I don't trade without a deposit, but I'll offer a show of good faith,* they said. *Look at properties in the Gachico neighborhood.* It's not much—it's almost nothing—but it's better than sifting through decades of records to find the rotting mold in a Scrooge McDuck–sized pile of gold. At least I have a direction, even if the direction is "generally south."

The door squeaks open, and Pat trudges in, sweat soaking their clothes. They collapse on the floor with their limbs akimbo. I don't spare them a glance as I continue typing. They groan. I ignore them. Their hand falls with a dramatic thump. I roll my eyes.

"I'm dying," they complain.

I hum. They got their own room on Monday, but they always end up here, whether to sleep or to shower or to bug me. I'd find it adorable if it wasn't always at the most inopportune moments.

"Darius is trying to kill me," they grumble.

"And yet you're alive enough to annoy me," I mutter.

They grab the duvet and pull themself up the bed to sitting, hand stretching to my toes. I pull my foot under my knee, in case they get any ideas about tickling. Their hair is still annoyingly smooth and flawless despite having spent likely hours in the gym with Darius.

"I see you got your phone, too," they say.

"It's like you have the gift of sight," I deadpan.

"What's got your panties in a twist today?" Their voice is clipped with impatience, their sweat rubbing off on my sheets. I wrinkle my nose, and Pat huffs. "Jesus, what is it? Mad you had to fuck yourself instead of letting Tamayo do it like you want?"

I gasp and grab a pillow, smacking Pat in the head with it hard enough to mess up their always perfect hair. Smug victory fills my chest before they jump to their feet and rip the pillow out of my hand.

"Admit it," they demand.

"No," I say as sternly as possible. "Don't hit my face or the tech."

They narrow their eyes, bright blue darkening to a stormy cobalt. "Admit it, Zarina."

"Pat," I warn.

They raise the pillow above their head.

"Don't you dare."

"Admit," they say through grinding teeth, "it."

I throw up my hands. "Oh my god, fine! I want Tamayo to fuck me!"

A knock echoes across the still-open door, and I lurch

forward, yanking the pillow back at the same time I shove Pat away from the bed. They stumble with their face stuck between a smirk and grimace. I jump from the bed and wind my arm back, pillow heavy in my hands.

"Princess?" Tamayo calls, still standing in the wide-fucking-open doorway.

"What?" I snap, because it's less embarrassing this way.

"Can I have your ear for a moment?" she asks like I didn't just *scream* that I want her to fuck me.

I twitch my arm, and Pat doesn't even flinch. "Only if coffee's involved."

"Join me in the kitchen." Tamayo turns on her heel and leaves me behind.

I drop the pillow and stick my tongue out at Pat. "Use your own shower, heathen."

They pout, their eyes wide and lip heavy. "But yours has better pressure."

"Whatever." I pull the door shut harder than necessary.

Tamayo's already halfway down the stairs as I follow her, still dressed in my pajamas. At least this time I have shorts on under Darius's oversize shirt. When I enter the kitchen, Tamayo's sliding a mug of coffee with a dash of oat milk across the island toward me. I hold it between my hands, the smell nutty and wonderful.

Tamayo leans her hip against the counter. "I was—"

I hold up a finger, taking my first drink and savoring the taste. Coffee isn't a jolt for me, the caffeine not often affecting me. No, for me it's the taste. It's the routine of waking up and enjoying a moment without the rush of the day bearing down on me. Tamayo bites her lip like she's clamping down on a smile, something soft in her brown eyes. I don't try to translate it for once. I simply enjoy my coffee for as long she'll let me.

She's dressed more casual today in jeans and a plain white

tee. I wonder if she plans to stay on the compound, leave the business to her capos rather than pull on her suit of armor to deal with it herself. Her hair is swept to one side, revealing her undercut. Soft. She looks soft.

"Can I speak yet?" she asks, voice quiet as if to protect the moment.

I hum for her to continue.

"When I spoke with Jimmy last night," she says, "he mentioned the expectation of an engagement party?"

I sigh, the familiar frustration of the dons being up each other's assholes rolling through me. "I was hoping we could put it off until we break up."

Tamayo purses her lips. "That might've worked if I hadn't told him and Logan invitations are going out this week."

"Damnit." I rest my chin on my mug. It's not Tamayo's fault, even if I'd really like to blame her for it. These gossipy old men don't know how to keep their big, stupid noses to themselves. "If they were asking about it, waiting wouldn't have worked. Not with an engagement as contentious and scrutinized as ours."

"Almost like they think it's fake," she teases.

"Weird, right?" I snort.

We smile to ourselves. Tamayo's staring out the wall of windows into the shared backyard, and I'm staring into my coffee like it's tea leaves that can show me the shape of my future. There's no avoiding it now. Not if Tamayo said the invitations are going out this week. It's Thursday. The week is basically over.

I chew my lip. I want them off our backs as quickly as possible. I know Tamayo's taking the brunt of the backlash. I know the Accardis and my parents aren't as quiet as they seem. The sooner we confirm our engagement, the more time I'll have with my laptop.

I set my mug on the counter. "Two Saturdays from now."

"Halloween weekend?" she asks.

I hadn't even realized. "Why not? We're playing dress up anyway."

She checks her phone then locks the screen. "I'm free. What do we need for this?"

"I know someone." I wave my hand. "You won't have to plan a thing, but I'll need your credit card."

She squints at me, hand already reaching for her back pocket. "Are you trying to steal my identity, princess?"

"Please, you think I want to be anyone other than Zarina Gallo?" I waggle my fingers, palm up, as she pulls out her wallet.

"Fair point." She holds out her card.

I snatch it from her hands and stuff it in the waistband of my shorts, lifting the shirt just enough to show a slip of skin. "You'll need to pick a charity—it's customary to accept donations rather than gifts."

"Sounds fake, but okay." She lifts my coffee and takes a sip before setting it back down.

I immediately pick it up and hold it against my chest. "Is that it, then?"

"Not quite." Tamayo's face morphs from amused skepticism into the smug, satisfied look she wears that I always try—and fail—to break into pieces. She stalks around the island toward me, and I can't help but back away until I hit one of the stools. She stands in front of me, hands in her pockets and a foot of space between us. Even so, I feel as if I'm caged in, small.

Her voice drops an octave. "I heard you want me to fuck you."

Heat warms my cheeks, but I don't duck my head. Pat got me to basically yell it to the whole damn house, and last night, I was ready to let Tamayo shove my skirt over my hips in Casa Nostra's only bathroom. It's not a secret, as much I'd like it to be.

My chin juts out. "Depends."

"On what?" She tilts her head, listening.

"What changed your mind?" I ask the same question I did last night.

Her eyes roam my cheeks, my lips, the collar of my shirt slung over my shoulder. "My mind never needed changing, princess."

I frown. "You said—"

"Do you want more," she quotes herself.

"That it doesn't affect our deal," I argue.

She frowns, like that's the part that's the most clear. "It doesn't. It won't."

"How can it not?" I scoff.

"Easy. We don't let it." Tamayo inches forward and raises her hand, achingly slow, to pinch the sleeve of my shirt and pull it back to center. Her gaze follows the line of my collarbone, my neck, up to my eyes. "*Do* you want more?"

I wrinkle my nose. She asked this in the car, too, and I didn't know how to answer. It was too abrupt then. But now? I've had a moment—several days of moments—to think about it, to watch Tamayo, to come to a decision. And even then, it was never a choice to be made or a conclusion to be reached.

Wanting Tamayo was a reckoning, simple as that.

I lick my lips, the buzzing under my skin pleasant and welcome. "You heard me earlier."

"If I'm gonna fuck you..." She leans closer, only a few inches taller yet towering over me. My coffee is clasped to my chest and the edge of the counter digs into my back and her words do what they've always done, spark a fire that is cold heat—and all this without a single touch. She holds my gaze with dark brown eyes. "Truly fuck you, then I need you to speak up."

I gulp and try to hide it with a snap. "I practically yelled it already."

"Then it should be nothing to say it again." She tilts her head, and this time, she's so close her hair almost brushes my cheek.

"Tamayo." I try to make it a warning, but it sounds more like begging.

Her eyes darken, and her voice hardens. "Say it, princess."

I scowl at her, but inside I'm reveling. This dynamic we have, the way she speaks and the way it lights me up, it's like nothing I've experienced before. She promised it won't affect our deal, and I'll hold myself to the same standard. Because I want it. I want more.

I want to trace the scrollwork and floral tattoos winding out of her collar and up her neck. Better, I want to be *invited* to touch them, to touch her, for more than the performance of it. For me. For her. And I want everything she's said to me, nasty and nice and in-between.

So I lean into it, like I haven't truly allowed myself since I got on my knees before her in the Den of Inequity. I drop my voice low and fill it with the craving I feel. "I want you, Tamayo. Want you to fuck me pliant."

She smiles, wide and wicked. "Good girl."

I roll my eyes like that doesn't do something to me. "Thanks, daddy."

She laughs brightly, her eyes shimmering. "We can discuss eye rolls and titles later."

"Wait, later?" I narrow my eyes at her. "What're you doing now?"

"I have work to do." She lands a kiss on my temple like I'm a patient person and not a spoiled brat who hates waiting. The way she dances backward too quick for me to grab her suggests she knows and she's using it against me. "And you have work, too. Call your event planner friend for me, hm?"

My mouth hangs open. "Are you fucking kidding me?"

"No, princess." She pulls her phone out of her pocket, already fully distracted from me. *Me.* Half-dressed and fuckable and willing. Tamayo starts down the hall toward her office. "I'll fuck you later, hm?"

"You missed the opportunity!" I shout after her. "The door to this pussy is closed! For good!"

"We'll see," she says barely loud enough to reach me.

TAMAYO

The television blares the ten o'clock news in the living room, Darius standing in front of it with the remote in hand. Logan Anderson speaks at a podium in front of a cluster of microphones with reporters and cameramen scattered through the room in front of him. He's answering questions about the rising crime rate in Sallay neighborhood and the targeting of queer people. He doesn't say hate crime, but he might as well spell it out.

"This is of highest priority to our office," he says. "No one should be in danger for their indelible identities, whether that is religion, race, gender, or sexuality."

Darius snorts. I sip my beer.

"What steps are being taken to prevent further crime in the neighborhood?" a reporter asks.

My ears perk up, waiting for the answer. Despite being the person Logan is supposedly helping, I have no idea how he and Jimmy plan to leverage this to muzzle the Accardis. Logan stands at his podium in his luxury suit and slicked-back hair and dimpled chin, and all I can see is a priest preaching about loving the sinner and hating the sin and damning both in one breath.

Which is exactly what he does.

"We'll be increasing patrols," he answers—the worst possible answer. "Working together with key community members to identify suspects, and utilizing the full scope of the law to bring them to justice."

I gulp a third of my beer. *Fucking idiot.* Increased patrols won't help anyone but him and his optics. God damn it.

"Have any arrests been made?" another reporter asks.

"We have two people in custody, who we believe are responsible for the hateful vandalism on a local LGBTQ+ club, Den of Inequity." At least he didn't fumble the acronym. And who the fuck is in custody? He continues, "We cannot release more details at this time."

Another reporter asks, "The Den of Inequity has been the focus of protests and harassment the past week. What will your department do to keep the peace?"

"Police officers will be employed to keep patrons and protestors safe." Logan says it like he's doing a service for the community rather than endangering them.

"Jesus fuck." I slam my beer on the table.

Darius throws his hands up. "How is this supposed to help?"

"Fucking law dog can't be trusted." I scrape my hands down my face and *think*. Logan is using me as much as we're using him. He wants to appeal to a wider base of voters while appearing like the law and order candidate. Plus, he doesn't want to actually offend the Accardis lest they turn their targets on him.

We have two people in custody. I pull out my phone and shoot a message to Jimmy, asking for their names. If those people aren't Accardi affiliated, then what's the point of any of this?

"This is not what I had in mind," I grumble.

"What *did* you have in mind?" Darius asks.

"In my wildest imaginings?" I pick up my beer again and take a long pull. "A RICO sting that brings in half the Accardi Family for questioning and ties them up in scrutiny and court proceedings for fucking months, if not years."

He drops onto the other end of the couch. "And all we got was more cops and more problems."

I don't disagree.

He falls back against the pillows. "I'd rather our people took care of this. They'll actually keep the Den safe without scaring off half our customers."

"We'll make it up." We have to.

"Will we?" He mutes the television and drops the remote. "This is just the beginning. Hell, it's not even the worst that'll happen. Can we handle this?"

"We can." And I fully believe that. The Tamayo Family is more than capable of taking on the brunt of the Accardis' wrath. Especially if it means garnering a place among the Cardinal Families.

My phone buzzes with Jimmy's reply. *Marcus's snake and Alonso's weasel.*

"Holy shit." I sit up straight.

"What?"

I pass the phone for Darius to read. Jimmy's speaking in code, but it's part of my job to know who these people are and to whom they matter. Marcus's snake is his favorite cousin, Dan, who's well known as the devil on Marcus's shoulder. And Alonso's weasel is Frank, his favorite crash and dash man, the one who "accidentally" stumbles into the wrong hotel room that just happens to be where a key councilman is having an affair with his mistress.

Not big fish, not crippling to the Accardi Family, but a kick aimed right for the gut. The wind knocked out of them.

"Okay, maybe he's not the *worst*," Darius grumbles.

"We'll have to thank the DA." I take my phone back and

shoot a reply to Jimmy then tap it against my chin. "And with more than votes and an invite to the engagement party."

Darius groans. "Are y'all really having a theme and *enforcing* it?"

"Yes." I snort, quite sure the main reason we have a theme at all is because I refused to fuck her the other day. "And unless you want Zarina to twist your balls off with her bare hands, I suggest following it."

"Maybe I'd like to see her try," he muses.

I bite down on a laugh, the story Jimmy told about the handsy boy in coat check coming to mind. My gaze drifts up to the ceiling as if I can see through walls and into her room.

"She's been awfully…absent," Darius murmurs.

I've only seen her once since Thursday morning, the morning I had to walk away from the most tempting offer because my consigliere called and I couldn't ignore it. Now it's Saturday, and Zarina hasn't left her room except for food, coffee, and to rip Darius and I new assholes when we pushed back on the theme for the engagement party—Wonderland. Fucking White Rabbit, Mad Hatter, and Cheshire Cat *Wonderland*. And while I might be looking forward to seeing the four most powerful men in the city dressed in costume, I am not keen on wearing one myself. But Zarina informed us both that anyone off-theme that is not security detail will be denied entry and neither of us were exempt.

"What's she been doing on her computer?" I pick at the label on my beer bottle.

Darius shrugs. "Tech says she's planning the engagement party and binge-watching *Sense 8*."

I furrow my brow. "For three days?"

He doesn't think much of it, grabbing the remote and turning off the TV. I watch Logan fade to black and glance back up to the ceiling, to Zarina, the two of them somehow linked in this fucked up play we're performing. One whose curtains never would have opened if Zarina hadn't sought me out at the Den that night and struck a deal.

All to buy time. All to find a way out of her betrothal to the most brutal mafia prince in Louredo. And she's just planning a party? Watching television?

I set my beer on the coffee table and stand, phone in hand. "We're going to the Den."

"What? Why?" Darius is dressed in sweats and a T-shirt, a direct reflection of my own outfit, both of us having thought we were in the for the night.

I shoot a message to Logan, inviting him out. "Multiple reasons. I want to keep an eye on the cops and the protestors, check in with Angie, and show District Attorney Logan Anderson our gratitude."

"Ugh fine." He pushes up off the couch and stretches, back cracking without much effort. I shake my head, and he aims a kick at my butt before I dance out of reach. "I'll change and meet you at the car."

"Zarina is coming, too." I toss my bottle in the recycling, already knowing the pained and unamused expression Darius is wearing without looking at him.

He pulls in a long-suffering breath in an attempt at being patient. It fails. "Sure, keep an eye on the 'cops' and 'protestors,' not Zarina's ass."

I don't deign replying to that, walking toward the stairs already. "We'll leave when she's ready."

"If she wants to come." He sock-slides across the floor to catch up to me.

"She will." The ghost of a smirk twitches over my lips.

Darius sees right through me. "Don't elaborate one fucking word."

"Yes, sir." I salute.

"Ugh, gross." He elbows me out of the way and races up the stairs ahead of me.

I chuckle, using the railing to ease some of the weight off my knee. It's not aching, but it's stiff today. Too much time sitting at my desk doing the most boring part of my job—reviewing and signing. I stop in front of Zarina's door and knock, speaking without waiting for her to answer. "You're coming with me to the Den. Be ready in an hour."

"No, thanks." Her voice is closer to the door than I expected. Like she's standing directly behind it.

"Wifely duties, princess." I draw my finger down the wood frame as if it's the curve of her waist. "You're coming or I'm carrying you out."

"I'm heavier than I look!" she snaps.

"Just the way I like it," I murmur. "One hour!"

ZARINA

I can't believe I put on a corset for this.

If Pat hadn't broken into my room and literally shoved me into the shower, I would likely still be in bed, blue-light glasses perched on my nose, hair in a greasy top-knot, researching every property my parents own in Gachico and trying to figure out a pattern. But I haven't deciphered anything yet. And it doesn't help that they own the entirety of Gachico— at least until the last few years. I shift on my stool in Tamayo's throne room above the Den of Inequity's dance floor and signal the bartender for a third drink. My frustration at my continued failure sits heavy in my chest. Pat knows me well, knows I wouldn't have left my room of my own volition if they didn't make me. But for this?

Tamayo and Logan stand at the window, the latter surveying the people below like he can pluck someone out of the crowd at his leisure. I wish everyone down there would see through him, see him for the lecherous, narcissistic turd dressed head-to-toe in bloodstained Tom Ford that he is. His eyes have stuck to my ass so often tonight, I've debated forcing a long, loud fart just to offend him.

Another uber-fancy cocktail I don't know the name of slides across the bar. I pass back my empty glass and thank them for the drink. Pat stands by the door, allowed to carry their weapons inside this time and playing guard while Darius does whatever he's doing in the club. I sip my drink and wish I was back in bed, minimally dressed and organizing the last decade's worth of Gallo business dealings so that I can finally make sense of the information I stole.

"Miss Gallo!" Logan waves me over to join them, and I shoot the nastiest side-eye into the mirror behind the bar, not moving an inch. This isn't Casa Nostra, and I'm not a fucking dog, happy to come at his beck and call. The bartender shares a knowing look with me, and I pop the fancy dragon fruit garnish into my mouth as if I don't hear Logan.

He tries again. "Join us, hm? We're lacking for feminine energy."

I almost choke.

"Yes, Zarina"—Tamayo's voice is teasing—"it's far too masculine over here."

I tap the bar once and shoot a pointed look at the bartender, who nods in understanding. I don't think I can do this without alcoholic armor. My wine-red leather pencil skirt slides up my thighs as I slip off the stool. "Of course, gentlemen."

Both Tamayo and Logan watch as I pick my way around the couch and chairs to the wall of windows overlooking the club. While Logan's eyes attempt to mark the dips and curves he would like to claim, Tamayo's gaze is shared amusement.

Logan's hand hovers at the small of my back, millimeters from touching me. "What do you think of Tamayo's little club?"

I step closer to her, and she wraps her arm around my waist, blocking the heat of his too-forward-hand. "I love this place," I say honestly. "It's actually where we met."

He tucks his hand into his pocket, no longer able to almost

touch me. "Surprising—I could swear we've all attended the same parties before."

"And yet we didn't shake hands until this week," Tamayo says.

"You got me there." He points a finger at her.

"You could say Tamayo and I shook hands here for the first time, then." I insinuate whatever Logan wants to infer for himself.

He laughs with his whole belly. "I can imagine."

I bet he is. Thankfully, the bartender delivers my replacement drink, which allows me to cover my disgust with the chug of the rest of my glass to exchange it for the new one.

Tamayo leans into my ear. "Slow down, princess."

"Bite me, gangster," I whisper back through a gritted smile.

Her hand tightens on my waist.

"It's much nicer than I expected." Logan sips his scotch, staring at the platforms suspended over the dance floor with blown pupils. Each one hangs at a different height, holding a dancer dressed in leather—harnesses, bikinis, bodysuits, thongs —their bodies thrumming to the beat of the music. The Saint Andrews cross is pulled out tonight, a professional dominatrix offering a demonstration and, for one lucky submissive, domination. The dance floor isn't as full as the night I proposed to Tamayo, but it's definitely not empty.

Logan's gaze flicks between one specific dancer—they're topless with scars below their nipples, leather pants hugging their hips, long hair pulled up in a messy knot—and the domme at the cross wielding a long plastic wand that produces small sparks of electricity whenever it meets skin.

Logan clears his throat and shifts to face us again. "Do you host nights like this often?"

Tamayo's nails dig into my side like she can see the smile twitching on my lips. "A couple times a week. We like to give our community a safe space to explore."

"I see."

"Are you interested?" she asks.

"Oh—no! No. Not at all." But he answers too quickly, with an almost panicked glance to the cross and back to Tamayo. "No, thank you."

"You're welcome any time, Logan." Tamayo's hand doesn't leave my waist as she angles herself between me and him, like she wants to be as clear as possible that the club is open to him, but I am not. I bite my bottom lip as she nudges him with her elbow like an old friend. "We have private rooms so you can enjoy in peace, without…prying eyes."

"Oh?" He doesn't bother averting his gaze from the dominatrix ghosting her electric wand along the inner thigh of the person hanging on her cross.

Tamayo grips his shoulder, speaking low like she's weaving a spell. "I've prepared one for you this evening. As a token of gratitude."

"Ah, that's not necessary." He sounds wholly unconvincing.

"I insist." She massages his shoulder, and I can't help marveling at how easily she manipulates him without using her sexuality. It makes something in me flicker and burn.

Tamayo keeps her voice in that low register. "You work hard, Logan. You deserve to relax."

"It has been a long week…" he trails off.

"Please, make use of our services." She glances to the stairwell, where Darius is climbing up to us, and turns back with a theatrical smile. "We've even prepared something special for you."

Logan finally breaks his gaze away from the cross below to frown at Tamayo. "Special?"

"Of course." She claps him on the back. "We've prepared one of our second-floor rooms for you."

"A second-floor room…" He studies the club again like he

missed the balcony walkway surrounding the dance floor with doors evenly spaced along it.

Tamayo finally releases me to rest her hands on both his shoulders and steer him around. "It's quite private, with access to the club, bottle service, and a couple of my most trusted entertainers."

"Tamayo, this is too much!" He feigns protest. "I wasn't expecting all this—"

She waves him off. "Is there such thing as too much among friends?"

"Ah." He tries to groan convincingly, but he's already emptying his glass and setting it on the side table as Tamayo guides him toward the door. "You make a good argument. I don't want to inconvenience you, but it'd be rude of me to reject your kindness. It seems I must accept."

Tamayo chuckles. "Darius will personally escort you to the room. Feel free to take your time, walk the floor, enjoy all the club has to offer." She pauses with her hand on the door. "I must ask that you treat my people with the utmost respect. Though, I think Mistress Davina will hold you to task."

"Mistress…" Logan puts two and two together. He somehow both gulps and laughs at the same time, the sound coming out more choked than anything. "I'm not—I don't—"

"I have no idea what you mean." Tamayo opens the door with a flourish and hands him off to Darius waiting on the other side. "Please enjoy yourself, Logan. You've worked hard."

He coughs. "Yes, it's been a stressful campaign."

"Let off some steam." Tamayo winks, shaking his hand.

"Uh, yes, thank you." He barely returns the handshake, neck half-craning toward the dance floor and the occupied cross. I struggle to hold back a snort.

Darius sweeps his hand out for Logan to follow him. "This way, please."

Logan practically trips down the stairs in his haste. I shove my fist in my mouth to soften the burst of giggles clogging my throat.

Tamayo holds her ingratiatory expression until the door clicks shut, and then her face falls into a stormy frown while I finally bend over in a fit of laughter. She shakes her head at me, striding to grab her half-full glass and drain the rest of it in a few gulps. She sets it on the bar a bit too harshly. "I fucking hate that man."

I slip onto my earlier stool, my own drink almost empty again. "Who is Mistress Davina?"

Tamayo signals the bartender for another vodka Collins. I wonder if she ever drinks anything else. "A dominatrix."

"And Logan wants to be dominated, not do the dominating?" I frown, recalling his gaze on the Saint Andrews cross, on the dominatrix caressing her submissive.

"Naturally."

"I would have thought him too...toxic to be dominated." I pluck the dragon fruit off the rim and bite into it. Juice trickles over my chin.

Tamayo watches the trail, fingers gripping the edge of the bar.

I catch the liquid on my thumb and suck it off, pointedly ignoring her gaze. "How'd you find out?"

"I have wiles," she says. The bartender delivers her drink, and she thanks them, carrying it over to the seating area. She sinks down onto her throne-like chair, legs spread wide and shoulders sagging.

"Are you filming the room?" I pop the rest of the fruit in my mouth.

She tilts her head, studying me for a long moment. "You're conniving, aren't you?"

"Duh." I drain the rest of my drink. The alcohol is warm in my belly, tingling over my tongue. I know that when I stand, the feeling will spread over my limbs and buzz pleasantly in my fingertips. Just the right amount of buzzed with all the loosened inhibitions, but without the nausea. I stretch my hands over my head to feel how they float. "Are we done, then? We can leave?"

Tamayo doesn't answer, instead massaging her temples like she's annoyed and burdened by my presence. I glower at that. I didn't drag myself here against my will, she did.

I cross my arms. "Let me rephrase that—I'm done. I want to leave."

"Patience, princess," she says with a long-suffering sigh.

"For what?" I snap. She told me why we're here on the way over—to reward Logan Anderson for arresting Dan the Snake. And she's done that. What else is there? "All I've gotten out of this field trip is borderline sexual harassment and a buzz."

Her hand falls to the arm rest. "Another reason I fucking hate that man."

I snort, derisive and pissed off. At least I was doing something productive at the house, in my room, away from her, before she knocked on my door. I try not to think about it, but every day, time ticks further. We're almost a month into this haphazard Band-Aid of a fake engagement, and all I am is closer to failure. Failing to save myself and the Gallo Family. Not my parents, but all our people. The soldiers, the capos, their families. Our friends. Tamayo calls me princess all the time, but what use am I as a veritable royal if I can't save us from extinction?

And with all that weight on my shoulders, here I am, wasting my time playing arm candy for my fake fiancée and a shitbag attorney. I shake my head, lip curling. "When are you gonna stop letting them piss all over you, your people, your things, and start demanding respect, Tamayo? You want to be a don? Fucking act like one."

She shoots me a confused look. "What's got your panties in a twist?"

My face heats with anger, at her, at myself, at everyone who has ever used me for their own gain. "You dragged me here to be a fucking worm wriggling on a hook in order to lure the district attorney in and keep him on the line."

"I brought you here to present a united fucking front and keep up appearances," she snaps back.

"Plenty of dons do business without their wives."

She scoffs. "Would you prefer me to conduct myself like other dons? Would you like it if I kept you at home with a credit card and the kids and fucked you when I wanted without a thought to you?"

"I'd rather you be honest with me and yourself about what you're using me to achieve and how!"

"And what are you using *me* to achieve, princess?" Her voice is quiet, reminding me of a dog growling in its throat before it snaps off a finger. "You've been locked away in your tower for days. I know you're doing more than watching TV and planning an engagement party you wanted to avoid."

"How do you know what I was or wasn't doing?" I challenge. Because she wouldn't know a damn thing if she didn't have spyware installed on the computer she gifted me.

She scrunches her nose and sits back, cornered.

I lower my voice to match hers, smoke-like venom coating my throat. "At least my secrets don't involve being paraded in front of predatory men who would just as likely assault me as they would compliment me."

Tamayo holds my fiery gaze with one of her own, both of our blazes stoked higher with each word. I refuse to douse mine. This night is on her. She brought me here for more than she's saying, and she knows it. She fucking *knows* it.

Something relents in her, and she deflates, scraping a hand over her face. "You're right."

"Excuse me, I didn't hear you," I say, because I'm petty.

She throws me a deadpan look but doesn't comment. "I'm

sorry," she says. "I won't use you like this without your consent again."

"Great." I'm still too mad and riled up to be gracious. "Can we leave now?"

She sags back in her chair. "Not until he does."

"Fine." I slip out of my chair and readjust my skirt to sit just right. "I'll be downstairs."

Tamayo levels a hard glare that pins me in place with the force of it. "Absolutely not."

"I don't recall asking." I take one, singular step.

She cocks a brow at the movement. "Neither do I."

We glare at each other for so long, I think minutes have passed. Tamayo sits too relaxed, legs wide and shoulders loose, as if she is confident in her ability to control me with twenty feet between us. And I might believe that picture if I couldn't see her fingers on the arms of her throne, white with the force of her grip. Like she's holding herself back from pushing out of her seat and keeping me here by force. I think about testing the theory, about whether I can make it to the door before she grabs my wrist and pulls me back, about how much energy it would take to evade her and slip down the stairs to the dance floor.

And the thought itself exhausts me.

I release a breath, and with it, my fight falls out of me. It's more than Tamayo's stubborn ass weighing my limbs too heavy to keep going. It's my lack of progress. Even if I were to leave right now and sit in front of my computer into the early hours of the morning, I'd find as much in my parents' ledger as I have over the last few days—nothing.

I sink into my seat at the bar again, and the bartender offers a sympathetic frown, saying enough without a single word. I rest my chin on the heel of my palm and chew over all the times I've been in this exact situation—a pawn in someone else's game and unable to further my own. How often have my parents asked me to flirt my way into a man's good graces, to wear a specific type of dress in order to play distraction to a man's ego. Almost every gala, party, or business dinner, I've been trotted out like the most delectable morsel of meat that no one can have. Always allowed to sit at the table, but never allowed to be anything more than a set of curves drawn just right.

And the one time I have the chance to make my own moves in a game of my making—one that will not only keep me free, but my family, too—I'm failing.

Tamayo's elbow rests on the bar beside me, her body inches from mine. I ignore her, tracing the rim of my empty glass and grinding my teeth. She waves off the bartender in the middle of mixing my drink, and they immediately set everything down and stride out of the room through the back door. I watch them leave, lip curling in annoyance.

"We have a couple hours to kill, princess." Her fingers inch toward my wrist out of the corner of my eye. I flinch away. Tamayo is just another distraction from my ultimate goal. As much as I want her, she's my pawn. I can't become hers.

She sighs. "Would you prefer to spend it sulking?"

"I tried to spend it dancing, but you're a stubborn ass." I watch her in the mirror behind the bar. Her eyes are on me, trailing over my hair where it falls down my back, over the profile of my face, pausing on my lips turned down with irritation. At me, not her. Because I can feel her gaze traveling over my skin like a physical touch, and fuck, do I want to melt into her.

She sidles closer without touching me. The inches between us crackle with tension. Her face is so close to my ear that each breathy word brushes over my scalp with a shiver. "Dancing with someone else, their hands all over you."

"That's the point." I try to sound unaffected, but my voice cracks.

I can see her smirk in the mirror as she inches her fingers closer. "To lose yourself in the music?"

"In the crowd," I add.

She slips an arm over the back of my chair. My spine tingles with awareness. The whole left side of my body, so close yet so far from her, heats up as she cages me in. I can't stop staring at us in the mirror, at her annoying smirk and the sharp edge of her jaw and the heady focus of her gaze on me. She lowers her lips closer to my ear. "You can lose yourself up here, princess."

I clench my hands into fists on the bar to keep from closing the distance between us, from grabbing hold of her. If I do, I'm failing again. Right? I can't get caught up in her, in the pleasure she can give me. *I can't.*

"What would you do if I said no?" I ask. "Gone downstairs anyway?"

This time, when her fingers inch toward me, I don't move away. This time, I hold still as prey sensing danger while she skims her nails from my wrist, up my arm, and into my hair, where she brushes it over my ear and curls her fist around it. I suck in a breath, heart beating loud in my ears. I should say stop. I should push away from her. But instead, I wait as my blood simmers in my veins. Pinned without a fight, unable to move my head, and imagining Tamayo leveraging her grip to make me wait, make me beg, make me *kneel.*

Her lips are still at my ear. "Downstairs doesn't have what you want, hm? What you need."

Pat curses behind us, and then the sounds of the club crash into the room for a moment—the door opening as they step out —and then muffle again. Despite watching the mirror, I don't see them go. I only see Tamayo, her arm flexed across my body, the back of her neck long and graceful. I don't know why, but the line of it makes something inside me itch with a need to touch, to be touched.

She tilts my head and drags her nose along the length of my jaw, back up to my ear. "Stay with me. Let me lose myself in you."

"I should leave you hanging like you did me." I should leave, period. This is different than before. I'm not coping with Marcus's putrid touch. I'm not distracting Tamayo from the fact I met the Birdwatcher. There's no ulterior motive between us this time except plain *desire*.

She smiles, her lips brushing my lobe. "You don't want to leave."

"How do you figure?" I arch a brow, as if that's not the exact struggle within me. Give in or get out?

Her teeth nip my neck, making a shudder sizzle down my back and shaking my resolve loose. "Hmm, it's the way your legs keep pressing together, princess. The way goose bumps pop up wherever I touch you."

I ball my hands into fists on the bartop in an attempt to steel myself. If I push away now, I could walk out. I could do it. "What do you want, Tamayo?"

Her hand resting on the back of my chair slinks over the distance between us to my spine, down to the waistband of my leather skirt, and plays with the seam. "I want a lot of things. I want to watch your skin pinken under my hands, want to taste you, want to give something for that pretty mouth to do other than argue."

I sit in the chair, surrounded by her body, the smell of vodka and citrus heavy on her breath. And all I want is to be swallowed completely. Devoured until there's nothing left of me except what she deems necessary. The black, greedy abyss inside of me sated, because she would deem it so and that would be enough. I would be enough. Just me.

Her forehead rests against my temple. "Will you let me?"

"You made me wait for days." My voice is barely audible. My hands are loosening, and as they do, my convincing logic as to why I should leave jumbles into discordant need.

"Why wait longer?" She turns my head until our noses brush, our lips millimeters apart. I gasp, small and quiet. We haven't kissed yet, not once, despite my coming on her fingers. Despite her pinning me against the bathroom vanity. This will be the first time, and I want it more than I want her hands on me.

She must know, because her smirk widens the moment I try to lean forward. The movement pulls my hair in her fist, her hand not moving, and the slightest pain tingles over my scalp. Giving in won't affect our deal or my goal. I can take what I need from her and still do what must be done. Just like my parents, like the Accardis, like Tamayo herself. She might be a gangster, but I'm a mafia princess. My nails are claws and my curves alluring bait, lethal and unassuming.

"Tamayo," I huff, wanting more, more, more.

"Hm?"

"Kiss me."

And she does.

ZARINA

She's soft at first, our lips slotting together and mapping out each dip and curve. I stop holding back, my hands latching onto Tamayo's arm across my chest, digging my nails into her skin, between her tendons. And when her tongue begs entrance, I grant it. Each press together, every pull apart, builds the flames inside me.

I turn in my seat, and she steps forward between my legs, my leather skirt riding up to allow her entrance. Her free hand digs into my waist at the same time she sucks my tongue into her mouth, and I groan. It's like the sound flips a switch. One moment, I'm sitting in the chair, one hand in my hair, her other on my waist, and the next, I'm lifted up onto the bar. I grab her shoulders for balance as her touch roams from my waist to my thighs, hooking my knees to wrap around her.

Her lips slip down my neck, over my chest. My corset top pushes my breasts up to greet her mouth.

I arch into her. "Jesus," I breathe.

"I prefer Daddy."

I snort, eyes rolling. "I'm not calling you daddy."

She pulls back, lips slick and pink, and somehow the

debauched look only serves to make her unamused eyebrow raise more sexy. "I recall saying we'd discuss eye rolls and titles at a later date."

"Is right now the right time?" I snip. Despite the desperate need to have Tamayo's hands all over me, her mouth devouring me. I won't yield easily. I don't know how. And doing so would go against every instinct inside of me.

Tamayo shakes her head. "You're a brat."

"Well spotted."

Her hand wraps loosely around my throat, her thumb propping my chin up uncomfortably high. "I only have so much tolerance, princess. You push me too far, and I'll have to stop. Do you understand?"

I swallow hard. "I understand."

"Good girl." Her thumb finds my lower lip and presses down on it, exposing my teeth. She stares for a long second, brown eyes hooded, and then lets go. "We'll use the stoplight system. If you're good, you're green. If at any time you want to slow down, you say yellow. If you want to stop, red. And if your mouth is otherwise occupied, pinch me. Understand?"

"Is that really necess—"

Her nail scrapes over my jaw. "Do you understand?"

"Fine," I concede without grace.

"What's yellow?" she asks.

"Slow down," I grumble.

"Red?"

"Stop."

She nods, her free arm circling my waist. "And if you can't speak?"

"Punch you?" I hazard, voice bright with faux innocence.

She sighs. "Good enough." And then she undoes the busks at my back, unwrapping my corset from my torso as if I'm a gift. My breasts relax, free from constraints, and immediately her tongue traces their curves from collarbone to areola and back again. I arch into the heat of her mouth as her fingers dig into my hips like she might be ripped from me at any moment.

It's too late for that now. Now that I've given in, I don't want to stop. I find the buttons of her shirt and undo each one until I can slip it down her shoulders and reveal her white tank, her tattoos scrolling over her skin like filigree. The sight of it has me licking my lips, mouth dry like I need a drink and the only one around is Tamayo.

But before I can sate my thirst, her grip shifts to press me back, back, back to lie across the bar, hair and ass hanging off either edge. My knees are lifted until they rest on her shoulders, and her mouth carves a spit-slicked path from my tummy down to my thighs. My panties are wet with want, my core tight and impatient. I try to grab her head to guide her where I need her.

Tamayo tuts. "Don't top from the bottom, princess, or I'll have to put you in your place."

"And what's my place?" I don't remove my hands. My skirt is scrunched up around my hips, my breasts are puckering in the cold air, and Tamayo is *not* touching me.

"Keep running that mouth, and you'll find out." She yanks me forward by my hips, and I yelp, off-balance and scrambling over the smooth wood to find somewhere to hold on. Her forearms band across my stomach to keep me in place as she presses kisses along my inner thighs.

I hold my breath in anticipation as hers caresses my skin, my lips, my clit, but never coalescing into the pressure of her tongue against me. "Tamayo." I barely keep the whine out of my voice.

"Hm?" The sound huffs against my skin.

I almost grab her head again but clench my fists and release an irritated sigh instead. "Touch me."

"Say please." Her words shiver over my clit and up my spine.

I groan and fall back against the bartop. She spent time and energy convincing me, but now she wants me to beg. Me, a

Gallo. I don't beg. I try to raise my hips, to press my clit to her mouth still hovering over it, just out of reach. Her arm over my stomach clamps down harder, holding me in place. I wriggle harder against her grip.

Tamayo's fingers dig into my inner thigh. "Patience, princess."

Without thinking, I reach for her head to push her back where she's most useful.

She pulls back out of my grip. "Hands to yourself."

"Just—" I flop back with grunt. "Touch me!"

Tamayo throws one of my legs over the other and lands a smack on my lace-covered ass. Sweet-stinging pain reverberates through the cheek, up my back, and out of my throat with a breathy groan. And then she lands another. And another. Each one punches a moan out of my chest, the sound uncontrollable. Her rough callouses soothe over the sensitive skin. "Want to try that again?"

Maybe it's because I can't see her face or she can't see mine, but I don't control what comes out of my mouth next. "Which part, the spanking or the laying there, bored?"

Her hand, so gentle a second before, scratches harsh enough to rip lace. She hauls me off the bar and throws me over her shoulder as if I'm weightless. I slap her ass, which is directly in front of my eyes, and she reciprocates with her own, far more effective spank.

I bite down on the groan clogging my throat.

She lowers me to the ground, our bodies sliding against each other until my feet touch the ground and my face is staring at her tattooed neck now. Tamayo stands annoyingly unruffled and overdressed, whereas I stand topless in my rumpled skirt, hair frazzled, and panties soaking through. Heat flushes over my chest, up to my ears.

And her face is dangerously stern. "Bored, huh? Show me how it's done, then."

"What?"

She runs her hands up my arms to the tops of my shoulders and applies gentle pressure, the signal clear: *On your knees.* But I wish her grip was back in my hair, pushing me downward with force, not allowing me the choice. And it wouldn't matter, because I'd want it, too.

Tamayo smirks, her gaze darkening like she can hear my thoughts. Or maybe it's the defiant tilt of my chin, my narrowed eyes, the telltale signs of refusal before I say a word that makes me so obvious. She steps back, feet meeting her throne-like chair and removing her hands in her own refusal to meet my challenge. "Show me what exciting oral is, princess, and I might make you come after."

"Might?"

She cocks her head. "Depends if you're a good girl or a cheeky slut."

"Can't I be both?"

"Not when I'm riding your face."

A visceral shiver runs the length of my body, my nipples tightening and clit pulsing. It's not even for me, but the image that paints itself across my brain removes all rebellion from my limbs. It's Tamayo sitting on her veritable throne, legs wide, hands tight in my hair as she uses my tongue to make herself come. It's my knees and jaw aching, her uncaring as she chases her pleasure. It's the saliva building at the back of my mouth and trying to spill down my chin.

"Good," she praises as I lower myself to kneeling before her. Her gaze roves over me, my body red and rumpled, as she removes her belt. She folds it in her hand and drags it over my jaw, my chest, my shoulders. I ignore the way my body shivers with each caress of the leather and focus on the last barrier between us. I unbutton her slacks, pull down the zipper, and slide her pants and briefs down her legs. They drop to her ankles as she lowers herself to sitting, legs wide, and picks up her glass that was abandoned on the side table. As if she's about to hold a meeting rather than receive head.

She stares at me over the rim. "I'm waiting."

I trace the flat plane of her stomach, follow the path from her navel to the core of her. Her pussy is pretty folds framed by trimmed, black hair. It looks soft and wet, beckoning my mouth to drink from her. I drag my hands up her legs. Soft hair whispers against my palms.

Tamayo shakes her head. "What did I say before?"

I frown for a moment before I realize—*Hands to yourself.* "Seriously?"

"Last warning."

I don't remove my hands from her knees. "Or what?"

She flicks her belt lightly against my knuckles. "I render them useless."

Another image of my hands tied behind my back as Tamayo holds me in place, grinding against my face, pops into my head. And it heats me so deliciously, I almost push. I almost walk my fingers up her thighs until she snaps, pins my wrists together and does exactly what she's promised. Almost. I'll play good girl this time. Because her previous words leave a loophole.

Hands to yourself. Yes, ma'am, will do.

I settle them on top of my thighs and lean forward, biting and kissing my way from each knee toward the seam of her. She stares down her nose at me, taking sips of her drink as if she's bored waiting for me to perform. And I should know by now that I can't force a reaction, yet I still vow to wipe that bored expression off her face.

I dive in.

My tongue is almost as wet as her lips as I gather up as much of her sweetness as I can. I may want Tamayo to devour me, swallow me whole until I'm nothing but an exposed nerve, but fuck, I want to do the same to her. I want to eat her out until she's a trembling mess and know that I was the cause. That I made her mask finally slip and shatter. I suck and lick, finding a rhythm that at least has her hips flinching every so often.

But she's still drinking. Her face is still impassive. She even checks her fucking watch, like this is taking far too long. "This is your best?"

I huff through my nose, hands clenching into fists with the urge to pull her lips apart, to slip a finger inside and stroke her to madness. Instead, I suck her clit into my mouth and flick it with my tongue.

"Don't hurt yourself, hm." She sets down her empty drink and reaches forward to brush back my hair. And finally, *finally*, she wraps it tight in her fist and pulls. The movement detaches me from her, arches my neck at an awkward angle. I breathe heavy, Tamayo's arousal dripping over my chin.

She offers me a mocking look of pity. "A for effort."

"Fuck you," I spit.

Her condescension morphs into dark intention. Like she expected this, maybe even hoped for it. "Tongue out. Open wide."

A fizzle of arousal sparks through me. I don't hesitate, mouth wide open and tongue wagging.

Tamayo yanks me forward, hovering above me as she drops a line of spit into my mouth. "Don't swallow," she says. And then she's guiding my head by my hair to settle back between her thighs. Her spit slides over my tongue and lands on her clit as she presses herself against my face. "See, princess, I need pressure."

Her fist is tight in my hair as she pulls my head forward and simultaneously grinds her hips hard. A moan tumbles out of me and vibrates against her pussy. She hums at that, like I did well. But I'm not doing anything. I'm just a tool, wielded by her harsh hands and burning up with arousal tinged with a hint of shame.

"And you—you're more about the rhythm." Her breath is heavier now. I stare up at her, eyes wide open as she uses me to find her pleasure. Her hair falls across her eyes, gaze hooded while she watches me watch her. "Do you know how I know that?"

I hum a no. My jaw is starting to ache, my scalp prickle.

"Because I pay attention," she whispers like it's a secret. Her hips jerk, her clit drags over my tongue, and I sit still like a good girl who wants to be used.

"I listen." Her pace quickens, pressure harsher than before. A long moan drops out of her mouth. "But I can't listen if you don't speak up."

My chin is sopping with my drool, with her wetness. I try to meet her thrusts, and she tugs my hair harder, a warning to stop. Finally, she's falling apart above me, but it's not because of me. I'm barely doing anything. And yet her chest is flushed, her body trembling on the edge of release, her movements losing all structure and devolving into a chaotic pursuit of pleasure.

My own clit is throbbing in my panties. *Hands to yourself.* I know it's not what she meant, but I can't hold myself back. Not when she's moaning so deep, not when she's so sweet on my tongue, not when each pull of my hair travels down my spine like static shock.

"Fuck. Yes, princess." Her head is thrown back, the line of her neck perfect, and I have to relieve the pressure. My fingers slip over my panties, one single finger flicking over my clit. And just that amount of stimulation is enough to have my arousal climbing higher.

She rides my tongue while I find a rhythm that has my own hips jerking in small little jolts in an attempt to find more. The pressure isn't fizzling, it's building. Almost as quickly as Tamayo's, her other hand grasping hold of my hair while her hips surge forward so hard, my teeth almost clack against her pelvis.

And then she's coming on my tongue.

Sweetness floods over my tastebuds, over my lips and chin.

A groan tumbles out of my throat as I lap up everything I can. My fingers quicken over my own clit, lifting me higher toward a crashing crescendo. Tamayo sags back, hands loosening in my hair as I kiss along the crease of her hips, her inner thigh.

And then her hands tighten in my hair with a punishing grip as she yanks me away from her pussy. "Hands," she snaps.

I grin and lick over my cum-stained lips, my fingers continuing their pattern over my clit. I'm strokes away from hurtling into an orgasm. And with the look Tamayo's shooting me—a glowering challenge—a few more will be enough.

Tamayo twists my head until I'm awkwardly watching her out of the corner of my eye. "Come once now at your own hand and no more for the rest of the night, or," she says through clenched teeth, "put your hands on my knees. Now."

My body tightens, teetering on the edge. I could topple. I could give in to this one, guaranteed burst of pleasure. But I know Tamayo doesn't utter empty threats. She'll edge me, just like she's done the last week using only her words and the prospect of more, and not let me come again. But if I relent... Maybe in the future I'll test her patience more, but today, I want to more pleasure than pain.

I force my fingers off my clit, splaying them over each of her knees, and affect innocence. "You said keep them to myself."

She tongues her cheek.

My palms slide up her thighs, her skin soft like suede, reaching as far as her grip in my hair will let me. "I was just following directions."

"Cheeky slut." Tamayo shakes her head and stands, pulling me up with her. Each shift tugs on my scalp, and my hands fall off her body until they're hanging at my sides. Her shirt hangs open over her chest as she steps out of her pants and shoes, forcing me backward. She rakes her gaze over me and licks her lips. My skirt is bunched around my waist, panties still on and likely glistening, breasts covered in goose bumps and nipples erect. And my face is covered in spit and cum. But she looks at me like I'm a painted Madonna, golden halo around my head.

"What were the consequences to using your hands?" she asks.

My breath catches. "You render them useless."

She raises her free hand and opens it, her belt unfurling from her fist. "Color?"

I roll my eyes.

Her grip tightens in my hair. "Color."

"Green."

"Good girl." Her voice is like a purr.

And goddammit, I hate that my body reacts to those words. My clit pulses with need, and desperation claws its way up my ribs. The feeling only heightens as she twists me around by my hair, releasing it to hold my wrists behind my back with one hand as she wraps her belt around them.

A shiver rips up my spine.

She hums, like she noticed, and the sound travels over my heated cheeks. She pulls the belt tight around my wrists, the leather soft and forgiving. Like with my hair, she uses it to move me, yanking me flush against her chest as she presses her fingers under my chin and captures my lips. I moan into the kiss, touched with pleasurable intent for the first time since she laid me out on the bar top.

My fingers yearn for her skin beneath them, reaching and seeking where they can. But she holds them in place against my lower back and does what I wish I could do to her—explores my body, travels the dips and curves of my neck to my collarbones over the swell of my breasts and down the slope of my stomach. Yet she avoids the core of me. She digs into my hips, my inner thighs, but never where I want her most. And all the while, she steals the air from my lungs with her kiss until my chest is heaving with the effort to breathe.

And then Tamayo is guiding me forward until my thighs hit

the arm of the sofa and pressing me over it. I go without thinking, high on her kiss. My face falls into the leather, no way for me to hold myself up off the seat, my cheek pressing into the soft material and my hair falling over my face uncomfortably. She leans over me, lips dragging up my back and her body encompassing the whole of me as she traverses up my spine over my shoulders and sweeps my hair back for me.

Her lips pause at my ear, tongue flicking the lobe. "What to do with you, hm?" Her breath against my skin is both warm and cool where she licked. "How were you both cheeky and good? It baffles the mind."

I breathe to answer, but the moment my mouth opens, she stuffs two fingers inside it.

"Ah-ah," she chastises. "No more cheek, princess. I've had enough, I think."

I swirl my tongue around her fingers and grind my ass back against her. She chuckles. "Still not learning, hm? Patience."

I don't stop—my hips or my tongue—and Tamayo sighs. "Fine, then."

She pulls out of my mouth, spit trailing down my lips and over the sofa, and stands straight. Her hands leave my wrists, my body, and she steps away from my legs. I try to twist around to find her, but I can't. The way I'm lying across the arm of the couch, my wrists tied behind my back, I don't have the right leverage. Not without rolling half off the seat.

A smack lands on my ass. Hard.

I gasp. The spot stings and then dulls into a burn. Tamayo grabs each cheek, massaging and rubbing. It both soothes and deepens the feeling, driving it out of my ass and straight to my pussy, making me clench around nothing.

She spanks me again, in the same spot, and this time a moan is punched out of my lungs. Her fingers play with my cheeks, squeezing and then dropping them as if to watch them jiggle. I hide my face in the couch. But then she swipes up the seam of me, and I jolt, finally touched after so long.

She snorts, almost condescending. "You're so wet. You like this, hm? Cheeky slut likes it when I spank her."

My body is a blushing mess. I do like it, and I don't know why.

"Is this why you don't listen to me?" Her nails scrape over my skin, right where she smacked me twice. "You know you don't have to act out. All you have to do is ask."

Without thinking, I press back into her grip. Immediately, she spanks me once, twice, thrice. I shudder as the sharp bite of her hands twists into heightened sensitivity. The leather couch against my clit, my breasts, my face is like rough hands now.

"See, just ask." She presses a kiss to the dip of my lower back, just below my bound wrists, at the same time she pulls off my panties. Cold air brushes over my wet pussy, and a whimper leaves my mouth without permission. Tamayo's lips follow the path of my panties, kissing and licking down to my knees. She lifts each foot out of them, heels still strapped to my feet, and stands straight again.

Her hands dig into the meat of my ass again, thumbs pulling my cheeks apart, putting me on display. Shame wriggles over my skin and swirls into the cocktail of arousal, pleasure, pain, and growing desperation.

"Tamayo." I draw her name out on a whine, like I'm asking for something. My hands try to find hers, but she swats them away as she yanks my hips back from the couch and kicks my legs apart. Spread wide open, face pressed into the seat, wrists tied, I can't do a damn thing. I have barely enough leverage to tilt my hips, let alone press forward to find friction against the sofa.

And then she lies across my back, weight heavy but not suffocating. My hands are pinned between us as she threads her fingers through my hair and turns my head, not allowing me to hide anymore. "Did you like it when I used your face to make myself come? Did you like being treated like my toy?"

Another whimper escapes me without permission.

She kisses my cheek. "Speak up, princess."

God damn it. "Yes. I liked it."

"What else do you like?" She drags her nose along my cheekbone and back again.

I swallow hard. "When you spank me."

Her nails scrape over my scalp. "And."

I lick my lips. "When you fuck me into the sofa."

She pulls back with a glint of mischief in her brown eyes and a smirk. "I'm not sure cheeky sluts deserve to be fucked into the sofa."

"Tamayo." I do my best to salvage what little dignity I still have.

A featherlight touch ghosts over my clit. "Beg."

"What?" I frown.

Her fingers circle the tight bud for a heavenly moment before stopping again. "Beg me to fuck you."

I grit my teeth. "Tamayo."

She smacks it lightly, and I jolt with a choked moan. "Beg, princess."

I bite my tongue and try to push back against her hand, but I can hardly move with her still lying over me and my legs too wide apart. Tamayo chuckles in my face, grip in my hair unrelenting as she simply waits. I cannot move without her. Not in any way that I *need*.

Tamayo dips the tip of her finger between the lips of my pussy and drags the wetness up to my clit, circles it once, and then pulls back. To land another smack on my ass. I choke on air.

"You can't top from the bottom, princess," she says. "Beg."

"God, fine!" I snap. I want to bury my face into the sofa again, but Tamayo's grip is too tight. She watches with that stupid fucking smirk inches away from my nose as I finally give in with a whisper. "Please fuck me."

She furrows her brow, pretending like her ear isn't inches from my mouth. "What?"

I huff. "Please fuck me."

She yanks my head back until my neck is craned, my face no longer touching the seat, and asks again. "What?"

"Please fuck me!"

"You only need to ask," she teases.

If I could growl, I would. "Oh, fuck off—"

She shoves my cheek into the couch again, using it as leverage to remove her weight from my back, and slips two fingers inside me. My mouth pops open, but all sound is stuck in my throat. Tamayo doesn't tease anymore. She does exactly as I asked and fucks me into the sofa.

Each stroke drags against that sweet spot inside me. Shudders start at my core, twitching my hips what little they can and climbing as little whimpers out of my throat. Tamayo's hold doesn't allow me to throw my ass back into her hand, to bury my face to hide from the overwhelming build of pressure, to adjust my chest as my nipples rub against the leather. All I can do is give in to the pleasure, let it swallow me whole and spit me back out whenever it's done with me. Whenever Tamayo is done with me.

She adds another finger, and I can't muffle the guttural groan that drips out of my mouth.

"No more cheeky comebacks, princess?" Tamayo's voice is low and dark, as tangible as her hand in my hair. "Needed to be fucked quiet, hm?" She quickens her pace. My pussy is so wet, I can feel it on my thighs, hear the filthy *squelch* each time she thrusts inside. And after weeks of teetering at the edge of giving in, tortured by the possibility of more than teasing touches and lilting smirks, I am close to finally falling.

"Tamayo." Her name unfurls out of me on a moan. "I'm cl— I'm gonna—"

"Come, princess."

As if her permission was the last push I needed, my orgasm washes over me. My pussy contracts so hard it reverberates around my spine until I'm arching against her fist in my hair. Goose bumps erupt over my skin as if I'm cold, but all I can feel is melting heat devouring my body whole as I shudder through the onslaught of pleasure.

And Tamayo doesn't stop.

Her fingers quicken even more, and her thrusts sharpen their aim.

My orgasm morphs into overstimulation. Her hand in my hair yanks, and the sting fizzes over my scalp, down my neck. My body can't relax, every muscle pulled tight against the pleasurable pain. Even though my feet barely touch the ground and Tamayo's pinned me down, I'm still trying to crawl up the sofa and out of reach of her punishing fingers.

A whimpered keen drags out of me. "Wait, wait—"

"Yellow if you want me to slow down, princess," she offers me an out.

And yet I don't take it. Because I want exactly this—this all-encompassing, brain hazing, logic-devouring feeling of letting go. Pain and arousal fight for dominance inside me. It sounds like I'm sobbing, but I don't know if that's out loud or in my head. Her fingers don't let up, determined and sure as they stroke inside me. Tamayo's pushed me over the brink once, and already I'm dangerously close to crashing again, all without touching my clit. It's been left alone to open air, chilly and wet and tight with its own heartbeat.

"Tamayo," I beg. For her to stop or keep going, I don't know.

"You can take it, princess," she says, quiet and encouraging.

And then she finally presses my clit, and it's like a fucking detonator. Everything explodes. Again.

I can hardly comprehend anything outside of my own body, but I think I hear Tamayo whisper, "Good girl."

TAMAYO

My hands move without much thought, my mind preoccupied as I unwind my belt from Zarina's wrists, massage the pink marks left behind, and ease her feet out of her heels. All I can think is, *I just fucked Zarina Gallo*. Mob princess of my enemy who I've promised to wipe off the face of Louredo's map.

And damn, it was good.

I smooth my hands over her arms and dip to kiss the dimples of her spine. "One second," I murmur against her skin before I dart away to slip my pants back on and grab a couple towels and water. When I turn back to the sofa, Zarina is curled up on her side with tangled hair flipped over her shoulder. My mouth twitches. I fucked Zarina Gallo and it was good and I want to do it again.

I dip the towel into one of the glasses and cup Zarina's face. "Cold?"

She nods as I wipe away cum and drool and smears of makeup until she's barefaced, save for mascara and eyebrow tint. The way I'm used to seeing her at home. A little more vulnerable, a little less masked. I press a kiss to her temple.

And she snags the towel out of my hand. "Turn around."

I chuckle. "You're naked, and we just did very nasty things to each other—"

She pushes my face away with a glower. "And I would like to clean the evidence of that without an audience."

I shake my head, turning on my good knee, and shrug off my shirt. My tank is more than enough when she's bare. I raise it behind me, and she snatches it out of my hand. I have to bite down on my laughter. The towel lands with a wet smack on the coffee table.

"May I turn around now?" I ask

"Bring the water with you."

"Yes, princess." I lift myself onto the couch, scooting back to sit beside her, and press the glass into her hand. She's pulled her skirt, previously rumpled around her waist, back down, and buttoned up my shirt. It strains over her chest, meant for my slimmer frame and barely able to accommodate her delectable curves.

She tilts her head back to drink, and all I can picture is her face under me, tongue out, neck arched. I squeeze my eyes shut and slip my arm over the back of the couch, behind her, without touching her. Her body slides closer to me, inch by inch, her toes slipping under my legs. Ten little nubs of dry ice—so fucking cold.

"Come here." I open my arms. "Get warm."

She curls into my side, and I pull her closer, placing her feet between my legs to warm them up faster. She shivers as I rub her back and arms and lean my cheek against her crown. I wish I had a blanket to bundle up around her, tuck under her feet, her chin. A little princess burrito.

"Was everything we did okay?" I ask. We didn't discuss anything like I wanted, not in a way that eases my conscience.

Zarina chews on her lip for a moment, taking time to answer. "I think so."

"I welcome a different answer any time," I murmur.

"Hmm." She snuggles closer, shoving her hands between her legs. I want to draw her fully into my lap, let my heat seep into her.

Instead, I settle for rubbing patterns over her goose bumps. "Anything you really liked?"

She snorts. "Would you like a ranking?"

I grin above her head. "Sure."

She holds up her fingers, starting with one. "Fucking my face is highest, bondage is a close second, and lowest is 'cheeky slut.'"

"Why's it lowest?"

She sniffs. "Because we're not British, and I'm a brat."

"Yes, you are." I bury my mirth in her hair, knowing that if she sees it, I'll likely earn a glare. "The overstimulation?"

Zarina gives a thumbs up. "Top tier."

"But below the face-fucking?" I clarify.

"Correct." She replaces her hands between her legs.

I trace my hand down her arm, over her wrist, fingertips brushing across her thigh where they disappear. "Are you sore?"

She snorts. "It was barely tight."

I chew on that, calling to mind the few moments I thought she might push harder, might brat more in the hopes of a reaction. And each time, I wished she would have. I lift her chin to meet my eye. Hers are bright, as if the sun is lighting them up from the inside. "Would you like it tighter?"

"I think I would."

I cock my head. "And the spanks?"

A shiver echoes over her body, and I don't think it's the temperature. "Harder next time."

Interesting. I drop my hand to her knee. "How do you feel about orgasm denial?"

"I could be interested." She scoots closer, head resting against the sofa cushions.

"And toys?"

She grins, eyes closed. "The more the merrier."

Her expression screams content, sated, and I want to bottle it up and keep it tucked away for later. I settle for gathering her as close as possible without dislodging her hands and feet. "Would you ever want to fuck while people watched?"

"Maybe." Her head falls onto my shoulder, my lips in her hair. "I'd fuck myself while you watched. You like to watch, don't you?"

How'd she know? "I do."

"You're not the only one who pays attention," she says, smug.

"Cute."

"What else do you like?" Zarina asks.

The question is so simple and innocuous, but it sits heavy on my chest. I'm always leading the conversation, providing answers without being asked the question. Because no one ever asks. They expect me to lead, and I want to, I do. But I also want sex to be a conversation as much as it is a pleasurable act.

I press my lips to her crown and hum. "I like to be in control, see the walls topple brick by brick because of what I'm doing or saying. I like leaving marks. And I really like to hear brats like you beg me to touch them."

"I can tell."

I smile into her hair and pinch her thigh.

She smacks my ribs. "We should fuck more," Zarina says. "Might keep me from strangling you the next time you piss me off."

I laugh. "I doubt it would help, but I'm willing to try."

"Noble of you."

"Thanks."

Quiet settles around us, soft as a blanket and just as unassuming. I rub her arm and leg, trying to keep her as warm as I can, and Zarina settles further into the couch. Into me. My mind circles back to the glaring reality that I just fucked Zarina Gallo in my queer, kinky club.

And goddamn, I want to do it again. And again. And again.

And I can. She lives in my house, under my rule. My Gallo princess to wreck and ruin until both our games are played out and I get what I want—a seat at the table.

"Tamayo?" Zarina's voice is a whisper, as if she doesn't want to disturb the quiet moment.

"Hm?"

"Why do you want to be a don?" she asks.

I almost laugh. Can she read minds? Instead, I take a moment, figure out a way to answer that's just enough of the truth. My knee twinges, unhappy with tonight's activities. Another reminder of the goals I've spent years pursuing. I lay broken and bleeding in an alley a decade ago because of Gallo orders. Never again. If I have to buy up every piece of land in mine and the Southern districts to oust the Gallo Family and insert myself, I will.

And I'll fuck their perfect princess while I do it.

I rest my chin on Zarina's head, speaking as quietly as she did. "Me and my family, we're excluded and exploited. We want more, better."

"That doesn't answer my question." Zarina pushes out from under my chin, leaning back to meet my face. "Why do *you* want to be a don? Not your family, not Darius, you."

Because I want to protect my people, myself, from ever feeling like I did in that alley.

But I don't say that. I stare at Zarina, her brown eyes flicking between mine as if she can read my thoughts in them. She doesn't know my origin story, the betrayal of her family against me. And why would she? She was a kid when it happened, thirteen years old and living in the lap of luxury with a golden spoon in her mouth.

But me? I didn't have parents to care for me, not after they found out I was gay. All I had was Darius and the Gallo crew I worked with. And then they treated me worse than my family—

hurled homophobic slurs at me as they beat me. I didn't get the option to live in ignorance.

I hitch a breath to answer, but a knock cracks against the door. Zarina grumbles, and I press a kiss to her hair before I disentangle from her and stride across the room to open the door.

Angie stands outside, holding a large, fluffy blanket draped over her arms. Pat's behind her, craning their neck to get a look past me. The club music grates against my ears as I step back to allow Angie entrance—and Pat the chance to see Zarina drinking water on the couch.

Angie shoves the blanket into my chest, and I catch it with a grunt, letting the door fall closed on Pat glaring at me with barely contained threat. I ignore them and Angie, beelining for Zarina and tucking the blanket around her.

"Do you need anything else?" I murmur.

She cuddles into the warmth. "Food."

I pull my phone out of my back pocket to shoot a text to Darius to order pizza. Before I can press send, Angie tosses down a bag of shrimp chips onto the sofa beside Zarina, who claps in excitement.

"My favorite!"

I shoot Angie a bemused look.

She shrugs, black-painted lips twitching with the hint of a smile. "The one outside asked for those and the blanket."

So many interesting things tonight. Angie doesn't talk to outsiders, let alone almost smile about them. I settle down beside Zarina as she munches on the chips and wish I could drag her back into my orbit again. But I refrain. "And the reason you brought everything yourself?"

Angie's gaze flicks to Zarina and back to me, brow arched as if to ask, *You sure you want me to say in front of her?*

Zarina snorts around a shrimp chip. "Go have your little covert meeting. I'm fine."

I ignore her, pulling her feet onto my lap and rubbing them over the blanket. "I'm assuming this is about our guest?"

"Plural," Angie says.

Plural? "Then Zarina already knows."

"I do?" she asks, mouth full.

"Logan took the bait." Angie tosses a flash drive at me, and I snatch it out of the air one-handed.

"That was hot," Zarina mumbles.

Angie rolls her eyes.

I tamp down on a grin, shaking my head. "And our people?"

Angie doesn't spare Zarina a glance, as if she's not here. "They're fine. Wendy says this better have paid off the rest of their top surgery."

"It does." I pocket the flash drive.

"Did he hurt them?" Zarina asks, worry lines on her forehead.

Angie shakes her head, eyes bright with mischief. "They fucked him."

"Make sure they get aftercare and the week off if they want it—except testing day." No one gets out of STI testing day.

"Already done," Angie says.

I cock my head. "Who's the other guest?"

She glances at Zarina again, but this time it's more calculated and annoyed than cautious. "Marcus Accardi is outside, demanding to see Miss Gallo."

Fucking idiot. He and Alonso have exercised every avenue they can to keep their names separate from mine, from the Den of Inequity, and all the underhanded bullshit they're doing. And he shows up here anyway? Making a scene? Men and their tiny, indefensible egos.

"The line is mostly inside," Angie continues. "Darius and Gemma are holding them at the door."

Zarina wipes her hands free of crumbs and studies Angie then me with a shrewd look. "Has the DA left yet?"

"He's recovering in his suite," Angie says.

Zarina turns to me, nudging my leg with her foot. "Walk him out."

"What?" Angie and I ask in unison.

Zarina sighs, exasperated. "Walk him out of the club as a courtesy. Make sure he had a good time, that he gets to his car safely, and that he passes right by Marcus. And then completely ignore the asshole."

I consider it, pursing my lips. "That will only rile him up."

"Exactly." Zarina's smirk is nothing short of malicious.

"I would prefer not to provoke him," I say.

"Marcus is already provoked—you've got his weasel and his snake in custody. He didn't show up here for me, not really. He came for you." She tosses the chips on the table, bag half-gone, and licks her fingers clean. "Walk Logan out, shake his hand, and invite him back anytime. It's double assurance—you have the footage, now make sure the Accardis know for certain that the district attorney is in your pocket and his actions are targeted."

The scope of her proposal sinks in. "Remove Logan's chance to double-cross."

Her smirk widens into a full-tooth grin. "Exactly."

I yank my phone out again to call Logan's driver, hand never leaving Zarina's feet. Until I hang up. She pulls her legs in, and I lean over to press one last kiss to her temple then her cheek. "Get dressed, princess."

"Why?" she asks.

"Angie, can you walk her out the back while I deal with Marcus?" I rise, striding to one of the closets along the back wall and pulling out a new shirt.

"Tamayo," Angie's voice is full of disagreement.

"I'm not having her exit through the front, Angela," I snap.

"I don't like this," she gripes.

I button up my shirt and tuck it into my trousers. "I know."

"There's a back exit?" Zarina asks, still bundled in her blanket on the couch.

"Sort of. Angie will show you the way. Pat, too."

Angie huffs and grinds her teeth, the action more sinister with her black lipstick and heavy eyeliner.

Zarina looks her up and down with a hitch of annoyance in her brow. "Will Angie also lecture me the whole way?"

I bend over the back of the couch and find her lips for a goodbye peck. "Likely."

"Fun," she grumbles.

I kiss her again. "Be good."

"No promises," she sing-songs.

I mock sigh. "I'll meet you at home."

Without another glance back, I open the door and jerk my head to signal Pat inside. They rush past me as I descend the stairs into the chaos of the club. The kink demonstration is finished, and the crowd has moved onto the dance floor, over the couches, into the private rooms. Those dancing are barely doing so, their hands and lips doing far more than feeling the music. Someone's tied to the spanking bench, a skirt scrunched up around their waist as their partner strikes their ass redder than a ripe apple.

I stride past it all, nodding when a soldier falls in behind me —a sarcastic woman named Carl. We ascend a second set of stairs that leads up to VIP suites and dungeons for rent. I rap my knuckles over a door and wait a few moments before it swings inward.

"Tamayo!" Logan greets me, fully dressed and arms wide in welcome. "What service your place has!"

"We aim to please." I affect deference, dipping my chin slightly and shaking his hand. "Your car is ready for you."

He claps me on the back, stepping out of the room. "And you've come to see me off?"

"Of course."

"A true host!" He pulls the door shut and falls in-step beside me. "I'll have to visit more often."

"We'd love to have you," I lie through my teeth as Carl and Logan's security follow us downstairs. "I assume you were well-entertained?"

"Yes, of course, of course." He double-checks his buttons are correctly aligned, his cuffs fastened. "I wish I could've stayed longer."

"Perhaps next time." I lead him out of the front door, his car waiting at the curb, and we slow to a stop beside it. Out of the corner of my eye, I spot Marcus angrily arguing with Darius and Gemma—a capo who weaponizes claw-like nails and makeup better than any gun—at the entry door, and I have to focus intensely on not laughing at him. Carl's already aware, shooting Gemma a frown as I hand Logan a specific business card—one for the capo that manages the sex workers—and shake his hand again, the exchange seamless. "Thank you again, Logan."

He doesn't notice Marcus behind me, despite the fact he's now charging over here. "It's a pleasure doing business with you, Tamayo."

"We'll see you again soon." I clap him on the back.

"You might not be able to get rid of me!" He winks, laughing at his own joke as if it's the funniest thing in the world.

I force a chuckle and a smile and pettily hope the next few moments discourage him from ever returning. I gesture to his driver, waiting with the car door open, at the same moment Marcus calls Logan's name.

Perfect.

I frown, like I don't know who could possibly recognize Logan here, in this setting, and then the moment I turn, my face shifts into anger while my chest fills with warm satisfaction. Marcus's expression is livid and also surprised. He might have had his suspicions, but he definitely didn't think Logan would actually be in bed with me, Andrea Tamayo, a lowly gangster.

Logan visibly pales as his mouth stretches into a fake, half-terrified smile. "Mr. Accardi!"

I almost snort. Almost. The man's never shown anyone else the same overwrought respect of addressing them so formally. My hands slip into my pockets, and my shoulders affect a casual slouch. I'm still wearing my mask of anger with a hint of disgust.

"Logan? What are you doing here?" Marcus stops a few feet away, his people behind him.

Darius takes his place behind my right shoulder, Gemma at my left, Carl behind her. And we watch.

"Visiting a sponsor!" Logan chuckles nervously. "You know me, always looking to expand my votership."

Marcus's gaze penetrates deeper without any further explanation. "Father wants to have you round for dinner to discuss business."

"Yes, yes, I got his message." Logan hedges, hand on the door and feet shuffling away from us both. "It's been a terribly busy day."

Marcus looks directly at me. "I can see that."

"Tell him I'll give him a call in the morning?" Logan takes one step into the car.

"Sure, Logan. He'll be interested to hear that I saw you *here*, of all places."

Logan clears his throat. "Ah, well. It's quite late, Mr. Accardi."

"Especially for a man of your age." Marcus takes Logan's hand and helps him into his car, leaning down into his space. "Take care of yourself. Heart disease is the leading cause of death in older men, especially those who have such high-stress positions as you."

"Thank you for your concern." Logan pats Marcus's hand still in his. "I'll be sure to rest well."

"See you soon." Marcus straightens and shuts the car door.

Logan's security waits until Marcus backs away from the car before sliding into the front passenger seat, and then the car drives away. All under Marcus's watchful eye.

And then he turns to me.

"What are you doing here?" I ask.

His lip curls in disgust, like he can't believe he's deigning to speak to me directly. "Where's Zarina?"

"Not here." I search the crowd, his driveling posse of fuckboy mobsters, and frown in faux confusion. "Where's Dan?"

He grinds his teeth, and god, I wish I could smile at that. "You know, I pity you."

I almost snort.

"You bit off more than you can chew—with me, with her. You think you can tame a girl like Zarina Gallo? She needs a firm hand. I would've given her that, but now…" He shakes his head like he pities us. Too bad he doesn't know I had her well-in-hand only minutes ago. "Now I only have an iron fist ready to crush you both."

"All I smell is fear, Accardi." I finally allow myself to grin, slow and malevolent. Only a little man with a little ego seeks to control others, to use violence to get his way. "You're rank with it."

His eye twitches. "Zarina will be mine, sooner or later."

"Zarina belongs to herself alone."

Marcus laughs. "See you at the party, Tamayo."

"I assume you'll dress as Tweedledum?" I snipe.

He lunges at me, but his soldiers yank him back by the arms as Darius and Gemma step ahead of me. Too bad, honestly. I'd much rather he start a fight so I can end his blip of an existence. Marcus tries to shove his people off him, but they don't let up, chanting, "Not here. Not yet."

Marcus finally yanks free and squares up to me, nose as close as he can get with Darius's hand on his chest. "You're just a cockroach," he spits. "A pest allowed to live by the grace of the Cardinal Families. We can eradicate you at the snap of a finger, Andrea Tamayo. Remember that."

"I prefer termite." I lean in, closing the gap between us and holding his glare with my own. "You all have sat still in your mansions, ignoring the people beneath them, for too long. Do you know what happens when you don't treat a termite problem quickly?"

Marcus doesn't answer. And he isn't meant to.

"The foundation collapses, Marcus." I straighten and brush off my shirt, as if being so close to him has sullied me. "You've left the foundation unattended for decades, cozy in your towers. I can't wait to watch it all crumble to dust."

Darius shoves him back into the waiting arms of his men.

"Get home safe, Marcus," I call as I turn my back on him. One of the highest insults I could give. "Daddy wouldn't want you out too late."

ZARINA

The lights burn too bright, buzzing over my sensitive skin. I hug the blanket tighter to me. Angie clomps down the hallway in her platform boots, Pat at her hip like some white-blonde puppy with their tongue out and eyes hopeful. If I had focus to spare, I'd snort.

But I'm too busy memorizing the path we're taking.

Because this is a maze—literally—hidden under the Den of Inequity. White walls and concrete floors and no markings to be seen as Angie turns us around and back again. I draw the path on my thigh and repeat the turns over and over in my head.

"How long have you managed the Den?" Pat asks.

Angie shoots them A Look and doesn't answer.

"I'd like to come as a pedestrian someday," Pat chatters. I know they're half-distracting her, but the other half might be flirting, and I want to tease the shit out of them for it. "Do y'all ever do any non-binary or trans nights?"

"It's on our socials." Angie finally utters words.

"I'll check it out." They hold open a door that doesn't look like a door. "I never would have guessed this was under the club."

"That's the point," Angie grumbles.

Pat hurries to walk beside her again. "Who all knows about it?"

"Me, Darius, Tamayo. And now you two." Angie stops, purses her matte-black lips and considers us one at a time. Her gaze is heavy as a judge's gavel when it pounds a verdict. "This family is all most of us have. We take care of each other better than blood ever could. Without the Tamayo Family, half of us would be dead."

"Would you?" Pat asks.

"Yes."

The proud Gallo inside of me wants to hiss and scratch this woman for her perception of me, for the accusation of a future betrayal, but I know that's not the way to convince her. Or anyone. And worse—a small piece of me wants to know how Tamayo inspires such loyalty. I don't think I've witnessed a single Gallo capo speak of my family with such raw belief.

I meet her judging glare. "You won't believe me, but I'd be dead without this family, too."

She scoffs, arms crossing her chest. "You're the Gallo princess."

"Promised to man who would kill me if he could." And still might.

"With the power of a Cardinal Family behind you." Her lip hitches in a sneer. "If you knew how to wield it."

"You mean steal it." Despite what Angie thinks, I can't simply walk into my family home and start commanding capos. They answer to my father—and my mother by proxy. I don't command their loyalty any more than an amusing niece they all put up with and assume will grow out of my rebellious phase.

Even if my parents ran the Gallo Family so far into the dirt that they now have to sell their daughter or be buried alive. Even then, they stay loyal to my father. Even then, I'm just his naïve, lesbian daughter, who can't be trusted because she has boobs and likes pussy.

"You have more power than you understand, Miss Gallo." Angie shakes her head.

"And a lot less than you believe, Angela," I murmur.

She steps forward, grabbing a hidden latch in the wall beside her, and opens a door to the back alley behind the club. "If you betray her, our family, you betray yourself."

I shrug off the blanket, balling it up and pressing it into her chest with too much force as I stride out the door. "Thanks for the blanket and snacks."

"See you soon!" Pat calls, waving with a wide grin as they rush to open the car door for me.

Angie rolls her eyes, letting the door fall shut without another word.

I slide across the bench seat. "You have drool on your chin."

"I don't." Pat drops onto the seat beside me and yanks the door shut. "But if I did? Understandable. I'd let that woman slap me and call me bad names."

I fake gag. "Gross. She's kind of a bitch."

"Exactly." Pat waggles their brows, and I smack their arm.

The car pulls out of the alley and onto the street. My feet ache, strapped into these heels for far too long, and my scalp is tender. My wrists, too. Both of which cause a shiver to ripple down my back, reminding me of Andrea Tamayo fucking me.

Pat nudges me, and I frown. They hand their phone over, a note typed on the screen: *Birdwatcher?*

I chew my lip and remember my promise to myself before I asked Tamayo to kiss me: *Giving in won't affect our deal or my goal. I can take what I need from her and still do what must be done.* And that's exactly what I must do. Because this is a game of blood and money, and I refuse to be collateral damage. Andrea Tamayo may have fucked me into next week, but I can't miss a chance to save my family.

To save myself.

I grab the phone out of Pat's hand and type out an answer: *It's an option.*

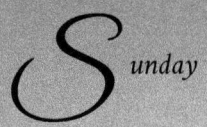
*S*unday

[Tamayo 14:22] Eat dinner with me

[Princess 16:03] can't, busy

[Tamayo 16:21] Doing what, exactly?

[Princess 17:44] planning

* * *

WEDNESDAY

[Tamayo 21:18] You haven't come out of your room in two days

[Princess 21:22] are you keeping tabs on me?

[Tamayo 21:22] More or less

[Princess 21:26] cute

* * *

MONDAY

[Princess 08:43] did you knock on my door before sunrise?

[Tamayo 09:01] It was 7 am

[Tamayo 09:01] I had breakfast for you

[Princess 09:03] i don't eat breakfast, let alone at the ass crack of dawn

* * *

THURSDAY

[Tamayo 11:49] If you don't eat lunch with me, you don't eat

[Princess 11:52] lol okay prince adam

[Tamayo 11:53] I'm serious

[Tamayo 11:58] Who's Prince Adam?

[Princess 12:01]

[Tamayo 12:33] …Prince Adam made several points.

TAMAYO

*W*hoever came up with the idea of fucking someone out of your system was a fool.

The more I get of Zarina, the more I struggle to hold myself back. Her taste is on my tongue, her smell on my fingers, her moans in my ear. I can't get the sight of her kneeling before me, ready and yearning, out of my head. And I haven't touched her since the Den. I need a fucking mouth guard with all the teeth grinding.

The lack of Zarina in my daily life since last weekend isn't the only reason my jaw aches. The list is too long to recount, but at this exact moment, each note from the quartet she hired for this party sets me further on edge. It's like she asked them to play only discordant horror scores. I readjust the ridiculous cape she picked out for my costume and force myself to relax.

"At least you don't look like a clown." Darius pulls his cuffs down again, his all-white suit meant to emulate the white rabbit. A pocket watch chain hangs from his waistcoat, and a monocle—real and usable—sits pinned to his breast pocket, its chain stretching to his lapels.

The door to our parlor opens, and Pat peeks around the frame.

"Next time, we source our own outfits," I grumble.

Darius blanches. "Next time?"

"Left to your own devices, you two would've arrived in all black and said you were ravens." Zarina sweeps into the room, her gown's gossamer skirts wide and brushing the floor. The bodice is a translucent corset, with red and black color blocks and small hearts embroidered throughout, and upon her head rests a delicate tiara with rubies and black opals.

"My Queen of Hearts." I offer her a bow.

She curtsies in return. "My knave."

I roll my shoulders like I can shrug off the cape snugly clasped to my suit. "Is that who I am?"

"Yes." She replaces my hair that fell out of place, bringing her face close enough that I could duck my chin and plant a peck on her nose. But I don't. Her lips are painted bright red, her eyes smokey blacks, with white hearts at the crest of her cheekbones. She settles back on her heels with her hands clasped in front of her. "And you look quite handsome."

I scoff. "I feel like a dandy."

"A dandy?" She chuckles. "Are we in a Shakespearean play?"

"We might as well be Romeo and Juliet," I say.

"Marcus Accardi is far more dangerous than Paris."

"I never said it was a perfect comparison."

Zarina plays with a bracelet at her wrist—tiny black diamonds in the shapes of hearts, spades, clubs, and diamonds. She twists it round and round until she plants her palm over it like she's trying to stop herself fidgeting. "Pat, Darius, please wait outside."

Pat pushes off the wall to open the door, holding it open for Darius.

He sighs, heading for the hall. "What're you dressed as?"

They glance down at their suit, the velvet patterned like snakeskin in a rich, bottle green. "Bill the Lizard."

"Why is yours better than mine?" Darius whines—actually whines. I almost yank out my phone to hit record and ask him to do it again.

Pat pats him on the back. "Zarina knows you don't like her."

"Petty," he gripes.

They let the door go. "That she is."

"I can hear you both," Zarina snaps.

"We know!" they call in unison as the door finally shuts.

I share an amused look with Zarina, her teeth biting her bottom lip to keep from laughing. "I think Pat's been a bad influence on him," I say.

She gasps in fake affront. "Excuse me, Pat is an angel. It's Darius who's influenced them."

"They're more stubborn than you. How could anyone possibly influence them?"

The smallest laugh falls out of her mouth, tinny and hollow even to my ears. I want to reach out, take her hands in mine, offer comfort in some way, but I don't. Just last week, I touched every part of her, drank her in, watched her fall apart. But today, I don't know whether I can touch her. Or if I'll ever have the chance again.

She sucks in a bracing breath.

"Princess?"

"We're scheduled to be announced in a few minutes." She smooths down her dress. "Are you ready?"

"I'm fine." I want to ask, *Are you?*

She nods too much. "You remember what to do?"

"Yes, princess. I read the brief." It was the only interaction we had all week other than random text messages, all initiated by me. It might give anyone else a complex. Not me, though. Disappointment and frustration have definitely not been mixing in my gut like a cruel cocktail, poisoning me for days.

She pulls her phone out of the folds of her dress and checks the time. Her fingers quiver just barely. "And no questions?"

Fuck this. I close the short distance between us and pluck her phone from her, tossing it on the armchair beside us, and take hold of her hand with mine. Breath catches in her throat as she cranes her neck to meet my gaze. "My only question is: Why have you been hiding all week?"

She swallows, gold-threaded eyes flicking between mine. "There was a lot to do."

"So you weren't avoiding me?" I slip a finger under her chin, rest my thumb below her lips.

Her tongue swipes a hair's breadth away from the edge of my nail. "You distract me."

I lean in until my nose brushes hers. "Perhaps you could use the distraction."

She grips my wrist, lifting my thumb to her lips and pressing a small kiss against it. "After this stupid fucking party."

"Deal." I press my own kiss to the back of her hand before offering her my elbow. "Shall we?"

She swipes her phone off the chair, shoving it into a pocket hidden in the skirt of her dress, and takes my arm. We stand still for a moment, Zarina inhaling a steeling breath as I cup her fingers. She stands straight, face set in stern arrogance. An expression I recognize for what it is—a mask.

She squeezes my bicep. "Don't fuck up."

"I'll do my best, princess." I knock on the door for Darius to open it.

TAMAYO

*T*he sound of a single cello heralds our entrance into the main hall.

Red roses cover the ceiling, trailing down at varying lengths and creating alcoves where there are none. Everything is presented unexpectedly—the food table looks like it's melting, the orchestra sitting in forced perspective to appear too large, a giant clock ticking on one wall with its numbers all wrong. It's disconcerting and all the more incredible for it.

I lead Zarina into a small circle created by the crowd, polite applause welcoming us. The four Cardinal patriarchs stand at their symbolic positions: In the north stands David Capone, wearing a maroon, velvet jacket with black lapels and his silk scarf folded into the shape of a heart. In the south, Riccardo Gallo glares, a real mustache perched on his lip, his suit the same shade as a walrus. In the east, Jimmy Falcone, a patchwork top hot sitting askew on his head, his suit made to match. And last but definitely least, Alonso Accardi in the west, the shoulders of his collar flaring dramatically away from his neck and gilded in silver embroidery, a glove with the appearance of a bio-mechanical skeleton on one hand.

I sweep Zarina in a wide arc and end with her pressed against me. The music pauses as we stand in the center, my hand at the small of her back and her neck gracefully arched. At the first note, we sweep into a simple waltz, a presentation of the impending union of two families. David steps forward and twirls his wife into the dance. And then Jimmy and his wife join a moment later. The leaders of each Cardinal Family step into the circle, symbolizing support and acceptance of the impending marriage.

Riccardo and Alessandra sweep onto the floor next. She's draped in silver gossamer and black pearls, her high collar shaped like a clamshell. A sliver of relief releases down my spine. It was never guaranteed that the Gallos would partake in tradition, not with the Accardis standing in the west, glaring daggers at the four couples on the dance floor.

Until Marcus steps forward.

He doesn't dance, rather standing stiff in all black with a heart-shaped patch over his left eye, a fur-lined cape draped across his shoulders. The orchestra plucks and thrums and the other dons ignore him, but the message is clear—the Accardis in the west do not approve of this union. With the majority rule, though, it doesn't matter. And so Marcus's glare follows Zarina and I wherever we dance, an immovable boulder against crashing waves of tulle and silk.

The song ends, and we bow to each Cardinal don.

"Welcome!" Zarina speaks to the room as a whole. "We are so grateful to celebrate our upcoming union with each of you, and even more grateful to have the blessing of our friends and families."

Alonso snorts outright.

"Tonight is made more special not only by your attendance, but by your generous donations to our favorite charity," I call. This is the only part of this farce I'm happy about. Well, that and seeing Marcus's anger all night. "Queer youth, especially those experiencing gender dysphoria, experience homelessness and housing instability more than many other groups. Alphabet House works to provide safe haven and counseling for young queer people in our community. All gifts and profits tonight will be given in donation to help Alphabet House build better housing and make much needed updates to their community center. Thank you!"

A few faces frown in the crowd, but they all clap. I accept flutes of champagne for Zarina and myself, thanking the server as they spin away into the crowd.

"Drink! Be merry!" Zarina raises her glass. "Careful not to tumble too far down the rabbit hole." She winks.

"Salut!" I cry.

"Salut!" The crowd raises their glasses and drinks.

The orchestra starts back up at the same moment David Capone strides forward to shake my hand, which was firmly around Zarina's waist.

I reluctantly release her to greet him. "Hello, David. Thank you for your support."

"Of course, of course." He claps my shoulder.

"You make a dashing King of Hearts," Zarina compliments him, offering her own hand.

"Thank you, dear. I must dance with my Queen of Hearts sometime this evening." He kisses her knuckles, and his wife laughs.

Zarina's lips twitch downward, but she twists it into a smile quickly. "I would be honored."

His wife presses a hand to his lapel with a fond smile. "I can't believe you got him to dress in something other than a black tux, Zarina. Impressive!"

She grins devilishly. "I can cajole when necessary."

"Andrea, how's business?" David cuts across his wife, who was about to speak and whom he has yet to introduce by name.

"Last week was difficult, but it's turning around." I sip my champagne and slip my arm around Zarina's waist again.

"Good, good." He waves his hand like he's waving away the niceties. "I'd like to meet with you soon, discuss some property you've recently acquired in Gachico."

"Excuse me, what property?" I hide my annoyance behind a mask of confusion. There should be no way David Capone knows about that deal. The shell company isn't under my name, and I haven't set foot in the area since last year.

"The one—"

"David, darling, stop the shop talk." His wife takes his elbow and tugs him away from Zarina and me, glancing back at the small crowd forming behind them. "We're here to celebrate, not conduct business."

"Excuse me, dear." He clears his throat and pats her hand. "Later, Andrea."

"Of course." I tilt my chin as they teeter away, playing the gracious host. In reality, all I want to do is rip off this costume and horde a plate of hors d'oeuvres to myself.

"Don't look like such a bored toddler," Zarina chastises under her breath.

"Make me," I snap. Ugh, I sound like her.

"Chin up, Tamayo." The next person in line winks, and a huge grin spreads across my face as warmth floods my chest.

"Rita." I breathe her name, and with it, tension releases from my muscles. "I'm so happy you're here."

"I couldn't miss this." She wraps both arms around me, and I return the embrace, despite Zarina's grip on my elbow. "Introduce me to your fiancée, you heathen."

I laugh, pulling back with my hand still on her shoulder. Rita's wearing a stunning light-blue gown with pearls embroidered into the seams. The colors are soft against her dark-brown skin, her twists tied back from her face with a bow perfectly placed in her hair. I've never seen her so done up, shining so brightly. She absolutely glows.

"Zarina, may I introduce you to the woman who changed my life"—Rita smacks my chest with a scoff—"and continues changing others's lives—Rita Pollard, Alphabet House's director and tonight's guest of honor."

Zarina reaches to shake her hand, but Rita ignores it in favor of a hug. "Oh." The word is squeezed out of her as she pats Rita's back. "Thank you so much for coming."

Rita offers Zarina one of her warmest smiles. "It's so lovely to meet you."

"And you. The dress is gorgeous on you—thank you so much for letting me style you."

I shoot Zarina a surprised frown.

She keeps her smile demure, but her eyes narrow in offense. "I'm not a monster. I'd never throw her to the wolves, even if she refused my help."

"Both of you can't keep your nose in your own business." Rita fidgets in her dress, like she's unsure where to place her hands when she's wearing something so fancy.

"I consider that a compliment," I tease.

She clucks her tongue. "Thank you for inviting me."

Zarina waves her off. "Of course, you were invited, you're the guest of honor. And thank god. I refuse to let this event be anything other than a queer celebration."

Rita takes her hand and squeezes, voice genuine. "And that's exactly what you've done. Even if the guests are anything but."

"Thank you." Zarina blushes with the compliment.

I wrap an arm around her shoulders and land a peck on her temple. "She's right, princess. You did amazing."

She squints up at me. "Even if you hate the costumes?"

"Even then." And I mean it. Because despite not wanting a theme and not seeing Zarina all week, she pulled off an event steeped in queerness and attended by the most toxically straight group of people in Louredo. And they absolutely don't know it, which makes it all the sweeter.

"Speaking of the guests…" Rita trails off, brow raised. "Don't play me for a fool, Tamayo."

"Never would." I lean closer, speaking so only she and Zarina can hear me. "Take their money and don't look at it too hard."

"Fine," Rita sighs. "Can you have someone make sure Jaime and Mais are taken home before there's any trouble?"

"Gemma's already on it." I aim my chin at the trio, Jaime and Mais posing wildly in the photo booth while Gemma giggles and encourages their antics. Rita shakes her head, muttering to herself. I think I catch the word embarrassment. "She'll take 'em home in an hour."

"I'd love to meet them." Zarina cranes her neck, trying to find them in the crowd but failing. "Jaime and Mais and the other kids."

Rita beams. "They'd love that, if only so they can tease Tamayo relentlessly. Bring her next time you visit, hm?"

"How often is that?" Zarina asks.

I don't know if I want Zarina to know too much about Rita and Alphabet House. Especially not what it means to me. "Not oft—"

"A couple times a month," Rita cuts me off.

Zarina covers her mouth as she snort-laughs. "Wow, tried to play it cool and failed."

"That's kind of her whole thing." Rita grins, obviously teasing.

"Zarina, dear!" Alessandra effectively crashes through our small circle to embrace her daughter. It's been more than a decade since I stood this close to her, and then, she was looming over me, painted in reflected neon lights coloring her face red. I shake the memory and focus on Riccardo behind her, standing like an unattended toddler waiting for their parent. Alessandra kisses Zarina's cheek, stepping back to look her up and down. "Where did you get this dress? It's stunning. Did Portia pull it together for you?"

Zarina's smile is plastered on her face like a painting. "No, Mother, it's a new designer."

Alessandra's hand trails down Zarina's arm to wrap around her bicep, her claw-like nails threatening to dig into her daughter's skin. "You must share their information."

"I doubt you'll employ them," Zarina mumbles.

"And Andrea." Alessandra turns, ignoring Zarina and boxing Rita out of the conversation. She cuts an icy scowl at me. "You look quite acceptable."

I snort. "A glowing compliment, thank you."

She twirls back to her daughter, using her body and wide skirts to separate them from the rest of us. "Zarina, dear, when will you return home?" she asks, as if the loss of her daughter is causing her great pain. "It's unbecoming for a woman to live with her fiancée before the wedding."

"We're a modern couple, Mother." Zarina continues to speak through her forced smile. "It's not like we haven't fucked already."

"Zarina!" Riccardo snaps from behind his wife.

She clears her throat. "I'll make you both a deal. You be honest with me, and I'll come home."

"Zarina, dear, we've always been honest with you. We miss you at home," Alessandra says through gritted teeth, her long, manicured nails digging into the space between Zarina's muscles. I step around Zarina's skirts to stand at her shoulder and erase the distance Alessandra put between us. She cocks her head, condescension dripping off her like the pearls sewn into her dress. "Besides, it's not like you'll have a real wedding, hm? It won't take place in a church, ordained by a priest, will it?"

Rita freezes. And it's not like a deer caught in the headlights of an oncoming car. No, it's the quiet arrest of the woods before lightning strikes. And though Alessandra doesn't know it, she's a copper wire at the top of a skyscraper.

"Then our living in sin hardly matters, does it?" Zarina surmises, her voice dripping with sweet poison.

"Alessandra, don't hog the bride-to-be." Riccardo steps forward to hug his daughter and cut the tension. Alessandra is forced to release Zarina and step aside. I take the opportunity to signal Rita to escape, and she does without hesitation, though she throws a heated glare at Alessandra on her way.

Riccardo embraces his daughter. "Congratulations, Zarina."

Zarina's muscles stiffen, and her jaw clenches. "Thank you, Father."

He steps back and threads his arm around his wife, like he's holding her back from invading Zarina's space again. "Have you set a date?"

"Christmas," Zarina answers.

That's news to me. I barely hold back a reaction, masking my surprise with a wide smile and a brush of my hand over the small of Zarina's back. I wish I could whisper in her ear without her parents hearing, because *what the fuck*. When was that decided? And then it occurs to me—that's the end of our three-month timeline.

When this sham of an engagement will be over.

Riccardo coughs. "So soon?"

"Why wait?" Zarina challenges, still speaking with candy-coated condescension.

"Indeed!" Jimmy slides into our small circle, clapping Riccardo on the shoulder. Jimmy's patchwork hat sits somehow more askew than before, and yet still clings to his head. He raises his half-empty glass of champagne. "I expect your wedding to be as unique as your engagement."

Zarina offers a sly smile. "Oh, it'll be the event of the season."

"I have no doubt." Jimmy downs the rest of his drink.

"Tamayo, Zarina!" Logan Anderson's voice clangs against my ears. He's dressed in all black, pauldrons formed of metallic feathers decorating his shoulders—a raven. He shakes my hand, grabbing it despite my failure to offer it, and then he kisses Zarina's, lingering too long on her knuckles for her comfort. Or mine. I barely stop myself from breaking his hold before he releases her. She slips her hand behind my back, wiping it across the fabric surreptitiously. I bite back a laugh at that.

Logan inclines his head to Riccardo and Alessandra. "Congratulations, Gallos! I am impressed by your daughter's wit and talent, though her beauty surpasses both to be sure."

Zarina grimace-smiles and drains the rest of her champagne, immediately trading it for another glass off a passing tray.

Alessandra frowns at Logan. "What's your name?"

I choke on a snort.

Logan's face falls and reveals the offended ego of a man who thought himself more important than he is. "Logan Anderson, Louredo district attorney."

Alessandra hums, regarding the man as if he's a beetle crawling over her most expensive shoes. "And how do you know my daughter?"

"I introduced them, of course." Jimmy steps in. He's traded his champagne for a glass of scotch. "Maybe next time Ricci comes to Casa Nostra, you can attend with him as Zarina did."

Riccardo's face pales. "Zarina?"

"You went to Casa Nostra?" Alessandra asks, voice more of a whisper.

"It was most entertaining," Jimmy says, as if he's speaking about this moment rather than Zarina's appearance at the infamous gentleman's club.

"She fit right in," Logan says. By the looks on Zarina's parents' faces, such a sentiment meant a number of things to them and absolutely none of them were acceptable for their well-bred mafia princess.

"My daughter at Casa Nostra?" Alessandra's hand wraps around Zarina's upper arm again, and this time, her nails dig directly into the skin. "What business could you possibly have there, dear?"

Zarina bears the claws threatening to break her skin without flinching, like this is a common occurrence. Normal pain. And that says far more than anything else could. "You know I've always been keen to learn the family business."

"Yet you attended without your family."

Zarina plucks a third glass of champagne from a passing tray, the movement forcing her mother to release her arm. "After years of refusals, I seized the chance I received."

She means the chance she created. I take a generous gulp of my drink, feeling the ghost of Zarina's knife scraping over my neck at the memory. I would have much rather left her at home that night. At least I get to watch her parents have a polite meltdown at the revelation of her attendance and my suspected involvement in the corruption of their perfect princess.

Jimmy squeezes Riccardo's shoulder in mock comfort, the Gallo patriarch leaning away in distaste. "She comported herself quite well, Ricci, no need to be worried."

"To be expected of such a fine young lady," Logan compliments.

Alessandra shoots him a withering glare. "The expectation of fine young *ladies* in Casa Nostra leaves much to be desired."

"Perhaps if their name is anything less than Gallo," Zarina snaps through a smile.

"Tamayo!" Jaime and Mais tumble into the circle, and I catch them before they accidentally tackle one of the most dangerous people in Louredo. Gemma's hot on their heels, grimacing an apology behind their backs. I just shake my head, amused and honestly happy to have an excuse to step out of the stifling ring of Cardinal Families.

Jaime's bright-blue hair is shaped into a mullet, and their costume matches—a glittering suit of azure with a fake hookah-pipe hanging from their lapel to represent the Caterpillar. In my other hand, Mais is wrapped in a ball gown made of tulle with red rose petals floating between the layers. His long, black hair sits atop his head, somehow shaped into a rose. I hazard a guess that Zarina provided both outfits, like with Rita.

"This party is so cool!" Jaime hugs me tight, unaware of the powerful people shooting disapproving looks around us. "Thanks for inviting us."

"Jaime," Mais admonishes. His tawny brown skin burnishes in the low light meant to simulate candlelight. Unlike his friend, he's very aware of the judgment they're receiving. "You're being rude."

"It's okay, Mais." I pull Jaime backward, further away from the Gallos and Falcones and Logan. Zarina takes the opportunity to follow me, hand at Mais's back. I hold Jaime at arm's length with a wide grin. "Let me get a look at you both."

Zarina stretches her hand to Mais, who graciously accepts it with a blush. "I am so happy you're here."

"Thank you, Miss Gallo." Mais's voice is soft.

She smiles wider. "Call me Zarina."

"Okay." The corners of his mouth twitch up into a tiny smile. "Thank you for the dress."

"It was made for you—literally," she says.

Mais's eyes widen, and his hands fall to pick at his skirt. "What?"

Zarina leans close to him, like she's telling him a secret. "Rita relayed your ideas to the designer, and she designed this. For you."

"What?" He can't seem to say anything different.

Zarina laughs, delighted. "She said you have a promising eye —the designer, that is."

Mais blushes fiercely, the apples of his cheeks darkening. "Who is she?"

Zarina cranes her neck, gaze flicking over the crowd. "She used to be a drag queen, and now—"

"Oh my god, you know Sally Vator?!"

"She's a dear friend." She laughs. "She designed mine and Jaime's, too."

Mais grabs Zarina's arm and hangs on, eyes wide with admiration. "You're so much cooler than Tamayo."

"Hey!" I grab my chest like he stabbed me in the heart.

He doesn't deign to even look at me, shaking his head. "It's true. You would never throw a party like this, let alone a party."

"That's the bar for cool?" I scoff.

Mais looks me up and down. "Among other things."

Zarina giggles, and my hand curls tighter over my heart, the muscle spasming under my ribcage.

"Not even married yet and you're already outshone." Jaime pokes my side.

I let my shoulders hang, dramatics on full display. "My years of toil and friendship mean nothing to you all, hm?"

"You're the moon next to Zarina's sun, T." Mais raises his chin, at his most haughty—the surest tell he's about to land a perfect repartee. "She is the light, and you a reflection of it."

Zarina hides her mouth behind her hand, eyes crinkled and shoulders shaking. I want to yank her wrist down and let her giggles spill from her lips, honeyed delight so sweet it'd rot her teeth. And mine. Because I would bottle it up, drink it down on days the weight of my choices, successes, and failures, threatens to bury me.

Instead, I shoot her a playful glare. "Don't encourage him."

"Whoa, that was deep, Mais." Jaime slow claps. "Did you watch *Pride and Prejudice* yesterday?"

"No…" Mais grins. "It was *Shakespeare in Love*."

Jaime bends over laughing, the sound bouncing off the floor and up to the ceiling.

"You're banned from the TV room," I jest.

"Aw, poor baby." Zarina pats my cheek in mock comfort. "Being the moon must be so cold and lonely."

I rest my forehead against hers, our eyes so close I can see the gold threading through her irises. "Thankfully, I have my own personal sun to warm me."

Zarina lifts onto her toes and captures my lips. It's so surprising, I almost rear back and shatter the illusion of *us*. Of two women in love, about to marry and spend our lives building an empire together. But I catch myself in time, leaning in rather than away, my arm reaching around her waist to splay my fingers over the bare skin of her back.

Outside our bubble of warmth and stolen kisses, Jaime fake gags and Mais smacks them. "Shut up, you fucking yeti."

They gasp. "Just because I'm tall and white—"

"And loud," Mais finishes.

"I hate the snow, though," they whine.

Zarina pulls back, gaze finding mine with something like bemusement in the furrow of her brow. Her thumb finds the skin below my lip and wipes away traces of her lipstick, which is unmarred on her own lips. I blink, the tingle of our kiss prickling through my jaw, my gums.

Why did that feel different?

Zarina clears her throat, turning out of my embrace toward the kids. "Mais"—her voice is tighter than before—"Sally Vator is here. Would you like to meet her?"

Mais's eyes widen, and he pats his hair. "Really? Oh my god, um, I don't know. Do I look okay?"

Zarina offers him her hand and an endeared smile. "I think she'd love to see her design on the person who inspired it."

Mais's eyes glisten for a moment before he inhales a steely

breath and rolls his shoulders back. Seventeen years old and already more poised and true to himself than ninety percent of the people in this room. I can't help but glow, watching Mais rest his hand upon Zarina's, as if they are both royalty gliding unbothered through a pit of vipers.

"Go with them." I nudge Jaime, who jumps to rush after them with a buoyant wave. Gemma hurries behind, shaking her head, Pat beside her. I watch them go with a soft smile, my heart warming in my chest.

ZARINA

I admit it—I've been avoiding Tamayo all week.

I was busy. Making Wonderland come to life, sourcing outfits that were on-theme for a dozen people, trying to fit in researching my family's financial straits. It took up most of my time. And I used it as an excuse. I wanted to see Tamayo, wanted to ask her to touch me again, to fuck me again, but maybe I shouldn't.

So I didn't.

But now we're here. The party is in full swing, and while some of the compliments are polite, the majority are glowing. I don't have to think about performing for the public unless I choose to after tonight. My last obligation.

And there Tamayo is, wearing that suit that hugs her ass, the cape hanging just so from her tall shoulders, smiling fondly at kids and letting them take the mickey out of her. She's hot. Annoyingly, stupidly, damningly *hot*. The thought makes my mind sink to dangerous places, to alcoves too dark to see wandering hands. Like the one behind the open bar, with all the flowers hanging in front of it.

"Zarina, dear, are you okay?" Sally Vator slips her hand

around my back and pinches the skin above my dress, which she designed. Her jumpsuit—another design of hers—is teal trimmed in gold brocade with a buckle shaped like a handle along at her waist. A small note hangs from the belt that says *Eat Me* in the most tasteful calligraphy. She offers Mais and Jaime an appeasing smile, speaking to me through her teeth. "You look...constipated."

I know she absolutely does not think I look constipated. I look like a cat in heat.

I clear my throat. "I'm fine, just warm."

"Hm, I find it quite cold, actually." Sally squints at me, over at Tamayo, back at me. She's fully made up in her drag persona, makeup bright and dramatic, pink wig jacked up to Jesus. A gem amongst rocks. "Wait—did you?"

I scrunch my nose and drink the last of my champagne. The bubbles sit in my gut, glomming together to become one, big, uncomfortable super-bubble.

"Oh my god. I need to know *everything*." She pauses and glances to Mais and Jaime, who are whispering to each other and probably not paying attention to us. Still, she raises her full glass of tequila soda to talk behind it. "Spill, bitch."

"Not here." I crane my neck for a passing server. I need something other than champagne or I might fill up with air and float away.

Sally clucks her tongue, disappointed. "At least tell me it was good."

I raise a finger to a server, and they nod, making their way through the crowd toward us. The kids are still not paying attention as I meet Sally's expectant gaze and hold it. "Better than good."

A knowing grin slinks across her face. "I'd expect nothing less of a kinky sadist like her."

"Sally," I playfully scold her.

"So, why are you staring longingly? Why aren't you getting

—" She stops herself, glancing to Jaime and Mais. "Having a private party?"

I order a drink with the server—vodka Collins, because Tamayo got me hooked on it—and avoid answering Sally's question. She knows more than she should already, which is almost everything. Over the past few years, I've spent too many nights lying on her couch while she sews or sketches or drinks with me, sharing deep thoughts about ourselves, our queerness, our gender expression. We talked about things that I could only trust with Pat before I met Sally. She's always been one of the few people in my life who was so authentic, it demanded authenticity in return. Something I have always been happy to give to her.

When I came to her for our engagement party, it took all of three probing questions for me to spill part of the truth—my parents tried to force me to marry a man, so I got engaged to a woman. Tamayo. But Sally doesn't know about the mafia politics, about the violence Marcus threatens with his very existence, about my family's precarious position on the edge of extinction. And I don't want her to know.

"You're engaged." Sally nudges me with her hip. "Eat the cake."

I nudge her back. "Trust me, I did."

"So, why not again?"

I pull in a deep breath. Why not again? Because I didn't strike a deal to fuck around. I did it to buy time enough to figure out why my parents wanted to sell me to the Accardi prince in the first place. And all the information I've gotten is thanks to the Birdwatcher more than myself. Fucking waste of a mafia princess, I am.

"There's a really nice spot behind the bar." Sally's voice drips with sensual suggestion. "If I orchestrate a distraction, you could...eat a snack."

I shake my head, accepting my drink from the server and

thanking them. I speak out of the corner of my mouth. "You're such a slut."

She winks, the movement exaggerated by her makeup. "I've got a plan—"

"A plan for what?" Jaime asks, all cute naïveté and boisterous excitement. Like a puppy.

Sally leans forward like she's telling a secret, her voice a stage whisper. "Zarina wants to surprise her betrothed with a gift."

"That's so sweet!" Jaime claps.

Mais nods along. "We want to help!"

I shoot daggers at her. That is not what I want. Not now, not later. In fact, I don't know what I would do if I had five minutes alone with Tamayo.

Images of my skirt thrown up, out of the way; of my lipstick smeared across my cheek; of Tamayo's breath hot on my ear as she says the dirtiest truths in that low growl she has flash through my mind.

Okay, yeah, I absolutely know what I'd do, and it makes anticipation and guilt blow the already-too-big bubble in my gut even larger.

Sally completely ignores me and my inner battle as she speaks to the kids. "We need a distraction, dears. To help them sneak away for their private moment."

"When?" Jaime's brows are furrowed, like this is of the utmost seriousness and they intend to do their absolute best to create the most effective distraction. Which I can imagine includes them making an unruly fool of themself.

Sally arches a brow at me, basically asking how much longer I can wait before I'm railed in a back room. Like I'm so thirsty I can't wait until we get home tonight. I glance over Sally's shoulder to Tamayo speaking with Darius, the two of them facing opposite directions. Her jaw is tight as she sips an old fashioned, and why the fuck does that send a trickle of heat directly to my core?

"Five minutes," I say. Damnit, I am that thirsty.

"What should we do?" Mais asks.

Sally rubs his shoulder with a smile, already endeared by him and his adoration for her. He was a gooey, mumbling mess when I brought him over to meet her. Behind the three of them, Alonso Accardi pushes through the crowd, making a beeline for me. His high collar makes him look like Dracula, and his disgusted face like he just drank poisoned blood.

"Gemma—" I turn to Tamayo's capo as I straighten and steel myself for the impending confrontation. "I think the hour is up."

Gemma follows my gaze and throws me a nod of understanding. "Jaime, Mais—how do you feel about Taco Bell?"

"It's my religion." Jaime clasps their chest.

"Let's spend Tamayo's money, eh?" Gemma waggles her brows.

Mais's eyes bounce between me and Gemma, reading far too well that something is amiss. He searches the room, finally finding Alonso headed our way, and mirroring the man's disgust on his own face. Mais threads his hand around Jaime's arm and pushes them to follow Gemma as they both call goodbye.

"What about the—" Sally starts.

I shoot her a laden look. "Maybe later."

"Miss Gallo." Alonso stops too close, not an inch of him offering a greeting in the shape of an inclined chin or handshake or warm smile. His spine is rigid, his shoulders high, his jaw grinding, and he doesn't spare a glance for anyone besides me.

Sally looks him up and down with a harsh, judgmental eye. "Find a new tailor, dear, your pants could fit an elephant."

Alonso tries to appear unflappable, but his mouth tightens into a thin line.

She smirks, leaning in to kiss my cheek. "Find me later."

I squeeze her shoulder. "I will." I turn to face Alonso, returning his same energy, holding myself straight and still without a single twitch of greeting. "Mr. Accardi."

"What do you think you're doing?" he growls.

I guess we're skipping formalities and jumping straight into fuckery.

"This entire party is a fucking masquerade." His voice is quiet enough to stay out of the ears of passersby but still harsh. "There's no way the Families will accept this."

I affect boredom. "It's already happening, Alonso."

"Not if you don't want to leave your family in ruin."

My mask stays in place. I search the room like anyone else would be more welcome and more interesting than this man before me. But inside, my whole being stills with focus. I know this basic truth—my family is in trouble—but I have no idea of the details. Does Alonso?

Unfortunately, spelling it out for me is not his goal.

"You threw your fit, had your tantrum." His collar casts shadows over his jowls, twisting his face into a sinister portrait of distaste. "Want to be treated as heir to the South and not just a spoiled princess? Do your duty. Save your family and marry my son."

I cock my head. "How does that save my family rather than ruin it?"

Alonso adjusts his jacket, and the movement makes the collar catch on his chin. Sally was right—his suit is too big. "You want to be treated as a queen, yet you know nothing of the state of your kingdom."

I peer at him, eyes traveling up and down his frame in my best impersonation of Sally's most razing glare. Alonso Accardi has no idea what I know and don't know. He assumes, like most men, that I'm a spoiled girl given everything she's ever wanted. Ironic, really.

Only men assume women do nothing and get everything.

"And you"—I don't lower my voice, don't pull the punch—"hope to be an emperor, yet know nothing of what it means to rule."

"I only need to know what it means to conquer," he sneers.

"Alonso!" Mother calls across the crowd like she's greeting an old friend rather than clawing her nails over a metaphorical blackboard. "How lovely to see you two chatting." Her hand grips Alonso's arm the same way it always does mine. The ghost of its pressure digs under my skin, the memory of her nails pressing half-moon marks into my muscles.

Alonso offers Mother the tiniest twitch of a nod in greeting. Bastard. "Alessandra, you look lovely tonight."

"Thank you." Mother affects a blush that is absolutely put-on. "Your son said the same."

Here we go.

"He has impeccable taste." Alonso pats Mother's hand like she isn't trying to gouge out a pound of flesh from his arm.

She beams up at him, her profile the perfect picture of a doting parent. "I absolutely agree—he chose Zarina, after all."

I will not be forced to endure more passive aggressive guilt-tripping, verbal sparring, nor continued praise of a boy who processes his bad feelings with violence and aggression. "Mother"—I turn away from Alonso, acting as if he's not there—"I've been hoping to get your opinion on possible wedding venues."

Alonso's face flushes red so fast I feel like I performed a magic trick.

Mother keeps her mask up, but after twenty-six years spent reading the infinitesimal twitches of her face, the tightness of her shoulders, the timbres of her voice hiding the truth of herself, I can see her frustration as clear as the brown of her eyes. To Alonso, she looks affable. To me, she looks murderous.

"Don't be rude, Zarina," she scolds with a fake smile that

promises ill intent. "Your guests deserve attention. We can discuss details at a later date."

But I'm already done. I don't live in her house, where she can make good on her silently promised consequences. She doesn't have unfettered access to my body, my space, anymore. And I refuse to continue entertaining their conversation about my future as if I'm not here. I plaster the fakest polite smile over my lips. "Then perhaps I could instead pick your brain as to why Mr. Accardi said marrying Tamayo would lead to the Gallo Family's ruin?"

Mother freezes. Alonso glares. And I blink in faux polite inquiry, as if I'm talking about the state of Mother's lawn rather than our impending doom at the hands of my parents and the man standing between us.

She snatches my arm with far less decorum than when she grabbed Alonso's. "Please excuse us, Alonso. I hope to see you on the dance floor later."

He barely adjusts his voice to be more genial than rude. "You have a slot on my dance card."

"Lovely." Mother shoves me to walk ahead of her until we exit the ballroom into a side hall, where I rip my arm out of her grip. I wave Pat off. They step back through the door to presumably wait on the other side. The hallway is empty, and I want Mother to think we have a semblance of privacy in the hopes she'll finally tell me what the fuck is going on.

"I must know your nail technician. Your claws are sharper than I remember." I rub my arm where she scratched four angry, red marks across my skin.

"Can't you ever keep your tongue?" She checks the hall, like we might not be alone. As if Mother doesn't always know exactly where to drag me for a verbal lashing in the middle of a party. "Don't you know what's at stake here? What we are losing each day you don't marry Marcus?"

"No! I don't!" I snap. "Because you won't tell me. That's the whole fucking point!"

She considers me, body full of disappointment, lip hitched in repulsion. "You're meant to trust us, to do your best by the family."

I did. For years. I did my best to show them—Mother, Father, the family—that I can do more than look pretty and play seductress. I flirted with boys and let them drop secrets into my lap, automatically trusting me because I had boobs and a vagina. And that's all that I was ever allowed to do. To be desirable rather than powerful.

At least with Tamayo, I'm both.

I don't let Mother's disappointment deflate me. "I'm worth more than a half-assed bargaining chip in a deal with the most evil brute in Louredo."

"We are not worth—" Her mouth clamps shut like she said something she shouldn't.

I stare at her. We are not worth what? Not worth more than this deal? It's the only thing that makes sense. And even then, she said *we*. I furrow my brow. "What do you mean, 'we'?"

Mother glances around like we might be overheard in this empty hallway, where I can barely hear the party on the other side of the door.

"Mother." I lick my lips. "What do you mean, 'we'?"

"Not here, Zarina," she hisses.

"You brought it up."

"*Not here*," she insists.

But this is the closest we've come to the heart of the issue. The thing her and Father refuse to utter a word about like I don't deserve to know why they're selling me off like cattle. Here, there, wherever it is, I refuse to drop the subject. "Does this have to do with the Gachico properties?"

Mother freezes. "How do you know about those?"

"So it does," I surmise.

She tries to grab my arm again, but I smack it away. Her fist clenches instead. "Zarina, how do you know about those?"

"I've had access to the ledgers for a while." I don't care that she knows.

She chokes, hand on her throat. "Oh no."

"We can recoup our losses there, though. I don't understand how it's enough to—"

"Shut up," Mother snaps. Her fingers tense, as if she's keeping herself from slapping her palm over my mouth. "We cannot discuss this here."

"What else is going on?" Because it's not just a bad investment. It can't be.

"For the love of god, Zarina, *not here.*"

"Then where!?" I throw up my hands.

Behind Mother, Marcus rounds the corner at the end of the hall. My arm drops, and every instinct inside me screams *danger.* I search the long corridor, paying attention for the first time. It's lined in doors, none of them marked as a restroom, which means no one will be coming here from the party.

Knowledge settles into my bones, heavy as lead. Mother brought me here for him. And I followed without a second thought. Naïve trust. Stupidity. Wishful thinking. Whatever it was, it doesn't matter now. Marcus is here, standing behind Mother with an empty hallway closing in all around us.

A smug grin stretches his lips. "Hello, ladies."

ZARINA

"*Marcus, dear.*" Mother turns to greet him with open arms, welcoming the interruption like it's expected. "You're simply dashing this evening."

"Thank you." He presses a kiss to her cheek, holding my gaze the whole time. "I couldn't help but dress to match my fiancée."

"You two make quite the pair." Mother looks between us like we're the apple of her eye, and I hold back a snort.

"Who's your fiancée?" I fake ignorance. "I haven't seen any bridge trolls in attendance tonight."

"Zarina Giovanna," Mother chastises.

Marcus shakes his head, faux fondness on his face but a malicious glint in his eye. "I very much enjoy our verbal sparring. I think I'll enjoy it when we're married even more."

Mother pats my arm. "I must return to your father, you know how he gets when he drinks champagne."

I grab hold of her wrist with the same strength and grip she always uses on me, my nails digging in between the tendons. She cannot leave me here alone. With him. "I'll come with. There's a sur—"

"I was hoping to speak with you," Marcus says, and despite

the innocence of his words, goose bumps prickle over my nape. The emptiness of the hallway becomes tangible in the way it compresses the air around me. I can hardly breathe.

"You already have." I try to push Mother toward the door, me with her.

But she pats my hand, forcibly removing it from her wrist. "Zarina, don't be rude to your guests."

"Now he's a guest?" I snap.

She steps out of reach. "Don't be too long, hm? There are the toasts to give."

Mother slips through the door, the noise of the party clattering against my ears. It echoes discordantly off the walls, into the carpet. I don't spy Pat through the crack of the door, can't depend on them to protect me. I let my hand fall to my skirt and sink surreptitiously into my pocket, through the hole I cut at the bottom, to grasp the handle of the knife sheathed at my thigh.

The door shuts again, and Marcus's friendly demeanor drops immediately. "Alone at last."

"Speak your piece," I say. Even though I know this will be more than a conversation.

His gaze ravages me as effectively as his hands could, promises of violence and malice dancing behind his eyes. For him, this is fun, a bit of foreplay before the main event. If I could vomit on command, I would.

He finally speaks. "You clean up well for a bridge troll."

"Flattery won't earn you safe passage," I quip.

"Would you prefer force?"

"Payment, actually." I affect relaxation, like I actually believe this is a simple tête-à-tête and won't turn into attempted assault or worse.

"How much?" Marcus relaxes, too, like he thinks me as daft as I pretend to be.

"More than you could afford."

"Money isn't a problem for an Accardi." The implication that it would be a problem for a Gallo hangs heavy between us.

"I wouldn't take payment in money." I clear the knife of its sheath. "But flesh would be commensurate."

Marcus grins, and it almost feels genuine. Like he's having fun trading barbs. His face isn't lined in aggression, playing the part of the alpha male with access to too many guns and not enough empathy. For once, he looks like a person rather than a caricature. He's almost handsome. It's more disconcerting than if he were to break out in choreographed song and dance.

I take a chance, hoping for an honest answer. "Why do you want to marry me, Marcus?"

His defenses don't draw up immediately, and I think, for the first time, we're speaking to each other rather than the masks we present to the world. "The same reason you don't want to."

"Which is?"

"The black hole inside of me demands it."

I frown. "Demands you marry me?"

"No, power."

My brows shoot up in surprise. How could Marcus see himself in me? We're nothing alike. *Nothing.*

But a whisper rises inside me, directly out of darkness lined in gnashing teeth that is never satisfied, that voices my worst impulses. I try to deny, to argue logically against it. I would never use people or violence the way Marcus does. I would never force someone to marry me for the power it would bring me.

Except I would. I did.

Am I not using Tamayo as a veritable human shield? Am I not willing to endanger her entire family to keep myself safe? If things go wrong, if I cannot escape Marcus Accardi's hand in marriage, I would murder him and start a war. I would convince Tamayo to marry me first. I would do *anything* it took to secure myself a future untethered to the man before me, *anything* to attain power that does not depend on being tied to anyone else. Let alone a man.

Marcus sees that in me. Someone as hungry for power as himself. But we are different. He's willing to act without conscience, never forced to function within the societal chains of feminine expectation. Empowered and sheltered and privileged, Marcus is the unchecked version of my own monster.

I don't care what he sees. I won't be his pawn. "Find another princess."

"But none are quite as deserving to be queen." He chuckles, and that sliver of authenticity disappears, tucked behind his black eyes and condescending tone.

This conversation is pointless. I pick up my skirt. "I must get back."

"And I must feed the beast."

My fists are clenched, one around the tulle of my dress, the other around the leather handle of my knife. Marcus holds my gaze, and I hold his, two mountain lions waiting to pounce. I breathe in a steady inhale. Marcus squares his shoulders. The black hole inside me is chomping at the bit, ready to be fed. I suppose his is, too.

The moment I exhale is the moment I draw my knife.

Too slowly.

Marcus snatches my wrist as it clears my pocket, his other hand grabbing my throat. His signature move at this point.

I smile despite his hold and wish I had blood in my teeth to show him just how much danger he's in. "I told you I'd do worse the next time you touched me."

He leans in, mouth so close to my cheek I can feel the heat of it. "What can a trapped kitten do against a lion?"

A lot, actually. I slam my knee into his groin at the same time I drop the knife to my open, waiting hand. Marcus is too busy feeling the pain pulsing from his vulnerable family jewels to notice the switch. My smile widens as I catch the handle and rear back to finally gut Marcus like the pig he is.

A secondary door in the hallway bursts open.

Marcus's cousin, Dan the Snake, who was recently bailed out of jail, saunters into the hall. His face is smooth as a baby's ass, hiding the rotten core inside.

And then three other doors open, a dozen armed men marching out of them.

Marcus blocks my stab, twisting my wrist until I'm forced to drop the knife. It falls to the carpet with a muffled thud, yet he doesn't stop twisting. "No pound of flesh tonight."

"I'll find my moment," I mutter.

He smirks, like he's looking forward to it. "I'll be waiting."

"What's the plan, then?" I snap.

Marcus rubs his thumb over my wrist in a soft caress, as if he's not bending it so viciously that it's on the verge of snapping. "We have a priest waiting at Saint Christopher's. Your parents will meet us there."

Understanding floods over me. Mother did more than leave me alone with Marcus to talk despite my attempts to escape with her. She dragged me *here*, into this hallway without foot traffic, without restrooms, only doors leading to empty rooms. Except for the one with a glaring, red exit sign above it.

The betrayal shouldn't hurt. This is expected, truly. They've done nothing to show me they have a singular concern for my well-being or happiness since they ambushed me with news of the deal they brokered with the Accardis. The one that sold me off like a medieval princess meant to bring peace to her kingdom.

Still. It hurts. A deep and aching pain that won't soften anytime soon.

I bury it deep enough that Marcus won't see, deep enough that the gnashing teeth grab hold of it and swallow it down whole. Like all the other betrayals, it will remember. "The Council won't stand for this."

Marcus kicks my knife down the hall behind me. "They won't have a choice, not with the full power of the South and West against them."

I shake my head. "My parents are idiots."

"Yes." He yanks on my wrist, shooting pain up to my elbow.

I follow after him, unwilling to be dragged like a wayward child. "The Gallos will cease to exist altogether after this."

"Most likely," he agrees.

We walk toward his men, who rush forward to meet us. I wish I was a hurricane. I wish I could toss them against the wall, rip their guns out of their hands, drown them in a tempest.

Marcus keeps my wrist in his harsh grip. "They negotiated your survival, at least."

"How kind." If I were a hurricane, the tears threatening to fall would be rain lashing against their skin. Not a sign of help-less rage. Not a *weakness*.

Marcus snorts. "You mean foolish."

I do. Nothing will go according to whatever contract they signed. And they should know that. "I assume you've already made plans to remove them from the equation."

"After our first child."

The thought of Marcus touching me in any way that would result in pregnancy causes nausea to churn in my gut. "I will abort every cursed cell that takes root."

"Hard to achieve when you can't leave the house, hm?" He jerks my hand up to his mouth by his hold on my wrist and brushes a kiss over the meat of my palm.

I gag. "I hate you."

"Save the passion for our wedding night, dear."

The exit door opens ahead of us, Marcus's horde of men lining the hall and cutting off any hope of an escape route. Guns ahead, guns behind, guns beside. The only way out is through that door. Each barrel counted dwindles the small possibility I have that, maybe, I can find a way out of this.

As the distance closes between us and kidnapping, the hopeless reality of that likelihood sinks in. I am alone and unarmed and weak. I want to be a hurricane of force, but I am not. And Marcus's painful grip on my wrist, the barrel of each gun pointed at me as we march down the hall, reinforces that fact.

I am a sheep. And I am being led to slaughter.

TO BE CONTINUED...

SNAKES AND SAPPHIRES

BOOK TWO COMING FALL 2025!

TAMAYO

This is meant to be my engagement party, but it feels more like performance art. The discordant music, the Alice in Wonderland costumes, the piles of tea cups, pots, flowers, playing cards artfully scattered around the room create a surrealism outside of reality. And yet the players are as real and tangible as the cape hanging heavy from my shoulders. The undertone of violence always a moment away from slipping onto center stage.

Not unexpected considering this party is celebrating my (fake) engagement to Zarina Gallo, mafia princess of the Southern Districts, and the only people remotely happy about the news are Zarina and myself.

My best friend and second, Darius steps up beside me, blocking anyone attempting to approach for business or disingenuous congratulations. Zarina and I are not here on genuine terms, anyway. But the whole party can't know that.

He hands me an old fashioned and mutters, lips barely moving. "Did you see the Birdwatcher?"

I take a sip of the proffered drink, gaze following Jimmy Falcone, don of the Eastern Districts, and shake my head. I've only ever heard of the city's most notorious secret keeper, only ever seen their face in photos or on the outskirts of galas. I haven't needed their business before and hoped to heaven they'd never take an interest in mine. "They're here?"

Darius hums. "Purple-striped suit at your six. Think they're meant to be the Cheshire Cat."

I don't turn to look. That'd be too obvious. Instead, I simply rest a hand on Darius's shoulder and continue speaking quietly —"Alone?"

He looks at me, not at them. "Currently speaking with someone dressed as a petunia."

"Keep tabs." I pat his shoulder, letting my hand fall to rest in my pants pocket.

When a man breaks through the crowd.

His suit is bright pink with glittering purple pinstripes and dyed blond hair styled to sweep off his forehead. Ostentatious and gaudy. Before I see his face, I know exactly who it is coming to wreck my perfectly fine mood.

Mateo Russo.

"Tamayo!" He raises a glass of champagne, almost sloshing it over his knuckles. I take in his sharp jaw, his full lips, and his tall-twink-frame and feel storm clouds gathering over my head. My eyes twitch with the need to glare.

Tension coalesces in Darius's body as the voice of his ex-boyfriend and first love, burrows into his ears. He turns, slow and measured, to face Mateo.

"Congratulations!" Mateo gulps down his entire glass. A drop spills out the side of his mouth and drips down his chin, falling to his neck. He overturns the flute like finishing his drink in honor of my engagement is meant as a public service. "Never thought I'd see the day."

Ass. I keep my face pleasant, my voice low—"Perhaps you mean the day you could approach me without threat of a broken nose."

"Andy," Darius grumbles.

I want to roll my eyes at him, but I decide to continue pinning Mateo with my fakest, most simpering smile.

"Oh, I fully expect violence from a gangster, no matter who wears her ring." Mateo laughs too loud and too long at his own bad joke. I still can't believe Darius dated this guy, let alone can't get over him. "I meant the day you attended a themed party and dressed on-theme. How gay of you."

"What do you want, Mat?" I ask, purposefully shortening his name to annoy him.

"North, south, east, west. Round and round the compass rose with nowhere to go," he laments. He places his empty glass on a passing tray full of hors d'oeuvres, clearly not meant to take dirty dishes.

"Your personal circumstances aren't my concern." I don't care that Mateo Russo is the last living member of the fallen Russo family. I don't care that he was orphaned at age three when the Accardis wiped his family off the map. I don't care that David Capone took him in as a favor to his late father. I don't have one fucking iota of a fuck left to give about the man in front of me because he ripped Darius's heart out of his chest and stomped on it.

And for better or worse, I'm a loyal bitch.

Mateo grits his teeth, swiping his bleached blond hair off his forehead in a practiced move. "History is doomed to repeat itself, Andy. Don't be the fool who never saw it coming."

That specific grouping of words raises my hackles. I squint at him. "Saw what coming?"

He steps forward, glances at Darius and quickly back to me. But I don't miss the millisecond of painful regret that swims through his gaze. He throws his arm around my shoulder, like he can't hold himself up, his mouth inches from my ear and his voice drops too low for anyone to overhear.

"The sun sets in the West, no matter where you stand." He

squeezes my shoulder, fingers digging into my collarbone, like he's willing me to understand. "There's only a few minutes before the sun sets *tonight.*"

I frown. Mateo isn't lecturing me on the science of the Earth's orbit around the sun. The Accardis rule the West. And currently, it's well-past sunset, night blanketing the sky in dappled starlight long before Zarina and I stepped foot on the dance floor. No, this isn't about the sun at all. Not literally. Which leaves only one interpretation for Mateo's warning.

Darius steps around us, ignoring his ex-boyfriend as his eyes flicker over the crowd. "Where's Zarina?"

Realization settles deep in my gut: The Accardis are making a move. Now.

ACKNOWLEDGMENTS

Any creative project takes a village to create and a book is no different.

Thank you to my parents, Lanell and DeWayne, for always supporting and believing in me and my ability to achieve my dreams, especially when I couldn't. My sisters, Cassi and Mikayla, for humbling me every damn day (as sisters should) and remaining steadfast and gracious and always present. I am so grateful for the ways our relationships have grown and changed over the course of our lives. I feel so lucky to be so loved by you both.

To Kristin Dwyer, Mallory Hayes, Alexa Lach, and Gretchen Schreiber—you all are the harbor in the storm that my writing journey has been. It's been a decade on this ship and, while each of us has charted our own course, we remain constant in each other's lives. I would be lost without each of you, my Northern Stars.

To my dear friends, Lydia Greene, Olivia Raccuglia, and Carlie Belle Snell, I hope you see yourselves in the friendships between these characters because they are inspired by each of you. Ours are the friendships I have sought after most of my life and I feel so lucky and grateful to know each of you. I love you all dearly.

Garrett Beekner—even when you were busier than a bee, you found time to capture my author photos. Thank you so much. Alex Huffman—I still can't believe how much you've helped and supported me throughout my writing journey and this book, specifically. Thank you dearly. I can't wait to return your many favors. Michaela Richmond—thank you for letting me mine your event planning expertise and for helping me celebrate the publication of my debut novel. Taylor Scoma—thank you for inspiring art in real life, for planning a celebration of queer art and joy that exceeded my wildest imaginings, and supporting me and my dreams so fervently.

My fellow indie authors, Stephanie Paine and Jamye Smith, thank you for taking a chance on an unpublished writer who shared a similar dream to yours. Your experience and willingness to advise have been invaluable and so appreciated.

My fellow writers in the Perma-Zoom—you don't know it, but you all helped me through a very difficult transition and I am so grateful for your presence in my day-to-day when things were too hard to face alone.

Andrea Halland for editing a monster of a manuscript so well. Sandra Maldo for designing an incredible cover.

Finally, to my queer community, near and far: This book would not exist without each and every one of you. Even more so, I would not exist as I am without each and every one of you. So many moments of serendipity had to occur to arrive here, at the launch of my dream with a village of people around me, ready to help raise up this vision of queer love for queer people. We are messy. We are real. We deserve more than tragic pasts and too perfect love stories. I love you. I see you. I cherish you.

Thank you.

ABOUT THE AUTHOR

Lexie A. Lynn grew up in Iowa and traded those cornfields for the historical cobblestones of Europe, for the colorful temples of South Korea, for the moody pines of the Pacific Northwest, where she currently resides. Now, she thrives in queer community and attends as many BTS concerts as she can afford. And no matter how many roots she puts down, she'll never stop chasing new adventures in foreign countries.

www.ingramcontent.com/pod-product-compliance
Ingram Content Group UK Ltd.
Pitfield, Milton Keynes, MK11 3LW, UK
UKHW020724211025
8500UKWH00025B/474